Hazen J Burton

The Smith Will Case

the Probate Court at Boston

Hazen J Burton

The Smith Will Case
the Probate Court at Boston

ISBN/EAN: 9783337815899

Printed in Europe, USA, Canada, Australia, Japan

Cover: Foto ©Andreas Hilbeck / pixelio.de

More available books at **www.hansebooks.com**

THE SMITH WILL CASE.

IN THE PROBATE COURT AT BOSTON, MASS., BEFORE HON. JOHN W. McKIM, JUDGE OF PROBATE.

Petition of Hazen J. Burton, Jr. *et al.* for Revocation of Probate of Will of Ebenezer Smith, which Will was Admitted to Probate by Decree of Probate Court, November 17, 1864, and, on Appeal, by Decree of the Supreme Judicial Court, October 5, 1865.

Trial December 4, 10, 11, 17, 18 and 31, 1878, and January 1, 7, 8, 14, 21, 22, 23 and 24, 1879.

Petition dismissed by the Court, January 31, 1879.

ARGUMENTS FOR RESPONDENTS,

AND

OPENING ARGUMENT FOR PETITIONERS,

Phonographically reported by Walter Rogers, 15 Pemberton Sq., Boston.

HON. BENJ. F. BUTLER,   } *Counsel of Record*
ALFRED D. CHANDLER, Esq., } *for Petitioners.*

JOHN A. LORING, Esq., *Counsel for Isaac T. Smith.*

WM. H. DRURY, Esq., *Counsel for Dr. Wm. H. Thorndike.*

HALLOWELL, ME.
MASTERS & LIVERMORE, LAW PRINTERS.
1879.

CONTENTS.

ERRATA.

Page 69, at end of 2d line from top, for *was* read *saw.*

Page 79, 10th line from foot, for *examination* read *extermination.*

Page 83, 15th line from top, for *respect* read *regret.*

Page 89, 25th line from top, for *do* read *undo.*

INTRODUCTORY NOTE.

————•————

THE original petition in this case, the substance of which is sufficiently stated in the last argument herein printed, was filed in the Probate Court, May 6, 1878, by Gen. B. F. Butler, who was then counsel for the petitioners; and it asked for the revocation of the probate, both of the Will of Ebenezer Smith, who died October 12, 1864, and of the Will of his widow, Eliza Smith, who died May 22, 1875. So much of the petition as related to the Will of Eliza Smith, was dismissed by the Probate Court in July, 1878, after a hearing which occupied one day's session of the Court, on motion of the counsel of Mrs. Sarah W. Thorndike, the principal legatee and devisee in that Will. That part of the petition which related to the Will of Ebenezer Smith was set down, to be heard and tried September 3, 1878; at which time the Executors of that Will, Mr. Isaac T. Smith of New York City and Dr. William H. Thorndike of Boston, moved that the petitioners, before being allowed to proceed further, be required to refund to the Executors the sum of $5,000, which sum the petitioners received May 18, 1866, under a compromise of that Will, instead of $1,000, which was given to them in the Will. This motion of the Executors was sustained by the Court. After this action of the Court, Gen. Butler, who had appeared up to this time, did not again appear in the case. The money was not re-funded; whereupon the Executors withdrew their motion and waived the decree of the Court, and consented to a trial of the case, as if the motion and decree had not been made. New counsel was engaged by the petitioners, who, after an ineffectual effort on their part to procure the dismissal of the original petition without prejudice, were allowed by the Court to amend their petition as far as it related to the Will of Ebenezer Smith, by substituting the amended petition of September 23, 1878, which is herein printed. The trial of the case was begun December 4, 1878, and it continued through December 10, 11, 17, 18 and 31, 1878, and January 1, 7, 8, 14, 21, 22, 23 and 24, 1879. The petition was dismissed by the Court January 31, 1879. All the arguments, except the closing argument for the petitioners, were phono-graphically reported by Mr. Walter Rogers of Boston, and all which were so reported are herein printed, except the opening argument for Mr. Isaac T. Smith.

BOSTON, MASS., February 1, 1879.

THE SMITH WILL CASE.

IN THE PROBATE COURT AT BOSTON, MASS., BEFORE HON. JOHN W. McKIM, JUDGE OF PROBATE. ·

Petition of Hazen J. Burton, Jr. *et al.* for Revocation of Probate of Will
of Ebenezer Smith, which Will was Admitted to Probate by
Decree of Probate Court, November 17, 1864, and, on
Appeal, by Decree of the Supreme Judicial
Court, October 5, 1865.

Trial December 4, 10, 11, 17, 18 and 31, 1878, and January 1, 7, 8, 14,
21, 22, 23 and 24, 1879.

Petition dismissed by the Court, January 31, 1879.

ARGUMENTS FOR RESPONDENTS,

AND

OPENING ARGUMENT FOR PETITIONERS,

Phonographically reported by Walter Rogers, 15 Pemberton Sq., Boston.

HON. BENJ. F. BUTLER, } *Counsel of Record*
ALFRED D. CHANDLER, Esq., } *for Petitioners.*

JOHN A. LORING, Esq., *Counsel for Isaac T. Smith.*

Wm. H. DRURY, Esq., *Counsel for Dr. Wm. H. Thorndike.*

HALLOWELL, ME.
Masters & Livermore, Law Printers.
1879.

CONTENTS.

———————◆———————

———————◆———————

ERRATA.

Page 69, at end of 2d line from top, for *was* read *saw.*

Page 79, 10th line from foot, for *examination* read *extermination.*

Page 83, 15th line from top, for *respect* read *regret.*

Page 89, 25th line from top, for *do* read *undo.*

INTRODUCTORY NOTE.

THE original petition in this case, the substance of which is sufficiently stated in the last argument herein printed, was filed in the Probate Court, May 6, 1878, by Gen. B. F. Butler, who was then counsel for the petitioners; and it asked for the revocation of the probate, both of the Will of Ebenezer Smith, who died October 12, 1864, and of the Will of his widow, Eliza Smith, who died May 22, 1875. So much of the petition as related to the Will of Eliza Smith, was dismissed by the Probate Court in July, 1878, after a hearing which occupied one day's session of the Court, on motion of the counsel of Mrs. Sarah W. Thorndike, the principal legatee and devisee in that Will. That part of the petition which related to the Will of Ebenezer Smith was set down, to be heard and tried September 3, 1878; at which time the Executors of that Will, Mr. Isaac T. Smith of New York City and Dr. William H. Thorndike of Boston, moved that the petitioners, before being allowed to proceed further, be required to refund to the Executors the sum of $5,000, which sum the petitioners received May 18, 1866, under a compromise of that Will, instead of $1,000, which was given to them in the Will. This motion of the Executors was sustained by the Court. After this action of the Court, Gen. Butler, who had appeared up to this time, did not again appear in the case. The money was not refunded; whereupon the Executors withdrew their motion and waived the decree of the Court, and consented to a trial of the case, as if the motion and decree had not been made. New counsel was engaged by the petitioners, who, after an ineffectual effort on their part to procure the dismissal of the original petition without prejudice, were allowed by the Court to amend their petition as far as it related to the Will of Ebenezer Smith, by substituting the amended petition of September 23, 1878, which is herein printed. The trial of the case was begun December 4, 1878, and it continued through December 10, 11, 17, 18 and 31, 1878, and January 1, 7, 8, 14, 21, 22, 23 and 24, 1879. The petition was dismissed by the Court January 31, 1879. All the arguments, except the closing argument for the petitioners, were phonographically reported by Mr. Walter Rogers of Boston, and all which were so reported are herein printed, except the opening argument for Mr. Isaac T. Smith.

BOSTON, MASS., February 1, 1879.

The Petition of September 23, 1878.

COMMONWEALTH OF MASSACHUSETTS.

SUFFOLK, ss.

To the Honorable the Judge of the Probate Court, in and for the County of Suffolk:

Hazen J. Burton, Jr., of Brookline, and George S. Burton, of Boston, in the said Commonwealth, heirs-at-law of Ebenezer Smith, late of said Boston, deceased, respectfully allege that on or about the seventeenth day of November, 1864, a certain instrument in writing was admitted to probate by the probate judge of the county of Suffolk, as and for the last will and testament of the said Ebenezer Smith, and letters testamentary thereon were afterwards issued by the said judge of probate to Isaac T. Smith, Dr. William H. Thorndike and William Minot, Jr., executors named in the said supposed will, and that Ebenezer Smith, Jr., (now deceased), James [Hazen J.] Burton, Jr., George [George S.] Burton, Eliza Smith (now deceased), Isaac T. Smith, Eliza W. Smith, and Sarah W. Thorndike (now deceased), were named as legatees in the said will, and all reside in the said Commonwealth, except the said Isaac T. Smith, a resident of New York City.

The said Hazen J. Burton, Jr., and the said George S. Burton, petitioners as aforesaid, further allege :—

First. That the said Ebenezer Smith did not sign the said instrument.

Second. That the said Ebenezer Smith did not by his express direction authorize his name to be signed to the said instrument.

Third. That the said Ebenezer Smith did not make known to the witnesses thereto, either by word or by act, that the signature to the said instrument was his signature, or that it was written for him by his express direction.

Fourth. That the said Ebenezer Smith, did not declare in the presence of the witnesses thereto that the said instrument was his will.

Fifth. That the said Ebenezer Smith did not request the witnesses to the said instrument to attest it.

Sixth. That the said Ebenezer Smith never knew and understood the contents of the said instrument.

Seventh. That at the time of the execution of the said instrument the said Ebenezer Smith was not of sound and disposing mind and memory, but was wholly incapable of making a valid will, from the impairment of his faculties by reason of old age, of sickness, and other causes.

Eighth. That the said instrument and the supposed signature thereto of the said Ebenezer Smith were obtained and procured by collusion, by fraud, by undue influence, and by force.

Ninth. That the proof hitherto presented to the honorable judge of this Court, in the probate of the said supposed will, was uncertain and not competent to establish the due execution thereof, and the competency of the said Ebenezer Smith.

Tenth. That the probate of the said supposed will was obtained fraudulently and *mala fide*, by making false suggestions and by surreptitious and clandestine conduct in concealing from the honorable judge of this Court evidence material to the case, which, if now disclosed, will justify the revocation of the probate of the said instrument and of the letters testamentary thereon obtained.

The petitioners further allege that, always acting in conscience and good faith, they have used every reasonable diligence to discover proof of the aforesaid allegations; that the truth was long and studiously and successfully concealed from them; and their first knowledge of the irregularities herein alleged was not had by them till September, 1876, ever since which time they have diligently and thoroughly worked to ascertain the facts, and have promptly and persistently pressed their claim in the courts.

Wherefore your petitioners pray that the decree of this honorable Court admitting to probate the will of the said Ebenezer Smith, unlawfully obtained, as herein alleged, may be revoked and annulled, and that all subsequent probate decrees based thereon may be revoked and annulled, and that your petitioners may have such further or other relief in the premises as the nature of this case may require and as to your Honor shall seem meet.

May it please your Honor to grant unto your petitioners, the said Hazen J. Burton, Jr., and the said George S. Burton, a citation to be issued to the said Isaac T. Smith, Eliza W. Smith, Dr. William H. Thorndike, and to all other persons interested, requiring them to appear before this honorable Court, at a time and place to be therein fixed, to show cause, if any they have, why the probate of the said supposed will of the said Ebenezer Smith should not be revoked, and why the prayer of this petition should not be fully granted; and further to stand to, perform and abide such further order, direction and decree therein as to this honorable Court shall seem meet.

Dated at Boston, Sept. 23, 1878.

HAZEN J. BURTON, Jr.
GEORGE S. BURTON.

A. D. CHANDLER, *Attorney.*

Commonwealth of Massachusetts.

SUFFOLK, ss.

On this twenty-third day of September, A. D. 1878, personally appeared the above named, Hazen J. Burton, Jr., and George S. Burton, and made oath that they verily believe the allegations contained in the above petition are true.

Before me

RICHARD STONE, Jr.
Justice of the Peace.

Opening Argument of Alfred D. Chandler, Esq.,

Counsel for the Petitioners.

DECEMBER 4, 1878.

May it please your Honor : — At his decease, on the 12th of October, 1864, Ebenezer Smith was possessed of a fortune. The executors, I find, of his supposed will have accounted for nearly half a million dollars, and that, too, after disposing of property at forced sales. Who this Ebenezer Smith was, how he amassed this fortune. and how these petitioners, his two grandsons, have been defrauded of their rightful share, can soon be told. The facts, when revealed, will show the course of a life advancing from poverty to wealth ; they will show, on the one side, an honorable struggle to preserve and to transmit that wealth wisely, and on the other side, threats, intimidation, fraud, force, and at last forgery. in grasping that wealth from a man nearly eighty years of age, enfeebled and unconscious. Mr. Smith, I am told, was born in Cheshire County, New Hampshire, and at an early age in his life made his way to Boston, mostly on foot. So far as I can learn, his only resources were his health, his good sense, and his willingness to work. In a short time he developed into a shrewd, capable, long-headed business man. He was successful. His first venture was in a little store on Haymarket Square, in this city ; soon he bought that store ; continuing in trade he was enabled to buy an estate adjoining, and not long after an estate near to that ; till at last by these successive purchases he became one of the largest owners of real estate in that quarter of the city ; his property reaching through to the river, occupying a part of the present site of the Boston and Maine Railroad depot, and extending along the old Middlesex Canal.

Mr. Smith was married comparatively early ; he was the father of three sons and of six daughters, out of all of whom there were living at the time of his death but three — Isaac T., of New York City, President of the Metropolitan Savings Bank. Eliza W., now living in Natick in this State, and Sarah W., who was the wife of Dr. Wm. H. Thorndike, of this city. Though his family was large. yet from his success and increasing income he was enabled to provide suitably and even liberally for them. Nay, more, — and here your Honor will observe a pertinent trait in that man's character, — Mr. Smith was of a large, and generous disposition ; his acquisitions were not alone for his own personal benefit : he seemed to have been a man who was incapable of accumulating for the selfish love of accumulation itself; while he guarded his wealth as a wise man should, yet his was a liberal, a whole-souled nature. He was a patron of art and of music. He was a member of the Handel and Haydn

Society. Upon the advent of Jenny Lind, I am told he was a large buyer of tickets, for the mere encouragement of song. He was a loyal citizen and generous in his patriotism, being one of those toward whom the managers of campaign would confidently turn for the needed aid. I am told that Mr. Smith was one of a number who once contributed $1,000 each for the relief of Daniel Webster. But apart from all his more public benefactions, the extent of his private charities may never be known, for he was always silently giving, silently relieving the aged, and the poor. I have dwelt for a moment upon this, that your Honor's attention may be especially directed to the fact that Ebenezer Smith was one of the last among men to exhibit a spirit of meanness or of injustice toward any of his race, *a fortiori* to any of his own flesh and blood.

His sons were all given a liberal education, having, I believe, all of them, the advantage of a collegiate course. Whatever moral defects any of his children may have shown later in life, that father did all that an affectionate father could for their proper training and education. His daughters were given every advantage equally with his sons. Out of all the six daughters but one is now living, Eliza W., of Natick, and she is to be a principal witness in this case, for the petitioners. That your Honor may judge of the position and character she has held and maintained, I need but allude to the fact that she was for many years a successful and well known instructress of young ladies. Her success in Washington in this respect was very gratifying. Her seminary at West Medford, had a wide reputation ; and I find among the list of names upon the visiting committee of that seminary such names as these : — Rt. Rev. Manton Eastburn, D.D., President Walker of Harvard University, President Sears of Brown University, Judge Bigelow, Rufus Choate, Charles Sumner, and Professor Longfellow ; and among the references are the names of Edward Everett, Robert C. Winthrop, Abbott Lawrence, Samuel Houston of Texas, and others from Canada, Cuba, South America, and Smyrna. I speak of this because Mrs. Eliza W. Smith is to be an important witness in this case, and it is fitting that your Honor should have a proper conception of the position that this lady has held. Of that daughter who died a quarter of a century ago, and who was the mother of these petitioners, I may well make mention also. She was one of Ebenezer Smith's favorite children, and beloved by all. His fondness for her and for her two only sons was constantly shown. That daughter, Harriet, was married to Mr. Hazen J. Burton in 1846. Mr. Burton was then in the full tide of success. He had already acquired a large property. He considered himself as independent, and his fortune was increasing. Because of his independence and of his brilliant prospects, it was arranged between himself and his father-in-law, Mr. Smith, that the latter should make no formal settlement at that time in favor of his daughter, for it was unnecessary, Mr. Burton's circumstances being at that time quite equal to those of Mr. Smith ; but at the same time it was understood, and distinctly affirmed by Mr. Smith, and reiterated again and again later on, that in the event of misfortune, he would amply provide for Mrs. Burton and the children.

During the married life of his daughter Harriet, Mr. Smith was a constant visitor at the house of his son-in-law, Mr. Burton. His visits were often daily; and it was immaterial whether Mr. Burton was living at his house on Essex street, in this city, or at his country residence in the Highlands, or elsewhere; wherever they were Mr. Smith continued his visits.

Mrs. Burton died of consumption in 1853, seven years after her marriage. But the close, the cordial relations between Mr. Smith and the Burtons still continued. When Mr. Burton at last met with misfortune, losing his property, Mr. Smith even took him and his whole family into his own household out at Winchester, where they all lived together in harmony and friendship. During this time his conversations with Mr. Burton were often of a confidential kind. He had the utmost confidence in him and entrusted him quite as much as any man with his inmost thoughts. His affection, his love for these two grandsons, was continually shown in acts and words. He wished to be consulted on all that pertained to their present and future welfare. He gave his advice upon their training and education, and his advice was followed. For instance, it was an important step in the career of these boys' lives whether they should be given the advantage of a collegiate education, or be put at once into a mercantile career. Mr. Smith was in favor of the latter, partly because of the disappointment he had met in sending some of his own sons to college. In this Mr. Smith's wishes were yielded to. and the boys were, at *his* suggestion, taken into the business in which their father, Mr. Burton, was then engaged. Thus it was that this most important step in their lives was determined by their grandfather. As Mr. Smith advanced in years and passed the allotted period, he still continued to exhibit this affection and fondness for the two sons of his deceased daughter Harriet, always mentioning them by name, and invariably sending them his kindest love when he met their father on the street; and up to the very end, when racked and agonized by the family dissensions of which I am yet to speak, he said to Mr. Burton, one day upon the street, after expressing his fear that he would never see the boys again : " Remember me kindly to them, and tell them poor old grandfather thinks of them."

I have dwelt upon this, that your Honor may in a measure appreciate the partiality and good-will which this fond grandfather had for these two grandsons. I wish to impress this upon the Court, because it will show that the will which we now dispute is *of itself* conclusive proof that it does not express the views of the justice, the benevolence, and the affections, which that fond grandfather had for these grandchildren. That will is so repugnant to, so unmistakably in conflict with, the lifelong sentiments entertained by Mr. Smith, in that it cuts off these pet grandsons with a paltry $500 out of about $500.000, that we might confidently rest our case upon the proof of this alone, but for the duty we owe the Court and all concerned to lay bare the great wrong and great fraud of which some of these parties have been guilty.

So far as I have discovered, the first cause of estrangement between Mr. Smith and any of his family arose at the time of a great auction sale on Haymarket Square, about the year 1840. The character and value of the property which Mr. Smith then put upon the market was such that buyers were attracted from all parts. He had elaborate and valuable plans made and distributed. The sale was conducted by the most popular auctioneer of the day, and, I understand, was at its height, when Mrs. Smith sent word that she would not release her dower. The effect of this was to check all further proceedings. The concourse of buyers and spectators was broken up perforce, and Mr. Smith was subjected to a mortification in public for which he seemed never to have forgiven his wife. This jar (it was a serious one) tended to alienate the affection between the two, and from this and other causes, by degrees Mr. Smith became suspicious of his wife, there grew up a feeling of distrust between them which went so far, I understand, that after that they never occupied the same room again together. Mr. Smith then began to be suspicious of some of his children. In time he practically withdrew from their society, excepting that of his daughter Eliza and that of his deceased daughter Harriet, toward whom he always showed his friendship and respect and with whom he was always intimate, for they were indisputably his favorite children. To such an extent was this alienation from his family carried, that he had built in the basement of his house on Beacon Hill, in this city, a brick chamber or cell, wherein he kept himself secluded, allowing no intrusion, and rarely often even admitting any one. For a long time he was unwilling to take his meals in his own house when he could well avoid doing so. And it is even affirmed, that, so suspicious had he become, he was unwilling to drink till his cup was rinsed in his presence ; nor would he eat there till after others had eaten. These peculiarities, however, were never shown either at the house of his daughter Eliza, or at the Burtons, for in them he had confidence and in them alone.

Owning so much real estate, he often wished to make transfers; and to facilitate this, on account of the difficulty with his wife, he conveyed the larger part of his property to be held in trust, (and this is important), with power in the trustees to sell as he might direct, thus simplifying the difficulty he had in getting his wife's signature.

As his son Isaac grew to man's estate he more than once urged his father for money, and he often endeavored to impress upon his father the advisability of imitating the English rule of primogeniture, so that the bulk of the estate might fall to him, who was then the eldest living son. Finding that his father refused to fall in with his schemes, Isaac went so far as to threaten to put his father under guardianship, a subject he actually had the family discuss, including Mrs. Smith, and which the old gentleman stoutly resented, affirming to his daughter Eliza that such a movement would kill him. A man who had worked his own way into the world, managing his own great estate, still competent, Isaac threatened to put under guardianship, that he might then get control of him.

It was during these events that, in conversation with Mr. Burton, Mr. Smith expressed himself in regard to the disposition of his property, observing to Mr. Burton that the laws of Massachusetts were, in his opinion, very just in disposing of the property of an intestate, and that if he made a will it would not vary materially in its bequests from what the law would do without a will. It was the fear of his so acting, probably, that led his son Isaac, and other members of the family, to importune Mr. Smith on this matter. To what extent Mr. Smith was beset by these importunities, of how bold and desperate a nature they were, and how keenly he felt them, is shown in a startling way by these few lines addressed to Mr. Burton as late as April 11, 1862 : —

DEAR SIR. — Inclosed is Helen's bank-book. She has written to me for it to get the interest. It would give me pleasure to call at the house, but I am not able. *I must fight or be robbed of the last pound of flesh and last dollar.*

Best regards to all.   E. S.

APRIL 11, '62. Box P. O., Boston.

In the above note, Mr. Smith alludes to "Helen's bank-book." Helen was a daughter of Mr. Burton by a former marriage, and, though she was not related by blood to Mr. Smith, yet he had voluntarily and silently — as was his wont—deposited $500 in the savings bank for her as far back as 1853. He also deposited $500 in the same way for her sister Laura. At the time these deposits were made for the Burton boys' half-sisters, Mr. Smith reiterated what he had so often formerly expressed, "Never fear for the boys. I will look out for the boys. Give yourself no concern about them."

Mr. Burton had been well aware of the rupture in Mr. Smith's household; but, as the above note proves, he was himself in the confidence of Mr. Smith.

There seems to have been a determination on the part of other members to so manœuvre as to cut off the Burtons from their lawful inheritance. As Mr. Smith grew more feeble, and so was more easily influenced, he was kept a closer prisoner; the threats of guardianship were continued; and matters at last went so far that Mr. Burton and his boys were denied entrance to his house, even at his death-bed. Mr. Smith felt his imprisonment: so little confidence had he in some of those about him, that he sat in his sick-chair, even in his sleep, holding a cane across a little table close by, to prevent the removal, without his knowledge, of important papers he kept in the table drawer. Yet, in spite of these dying efforts, the papers in that drawer were taken away from him before his death, and were afterwards burnt up, when found to be at variance with the will which we now dispute. Thus it was that those toward whom Ebenezer Smith entertained suspicion, fear and distrust, now had him in their power; while those toward whom Ebenezer Smith had always bestowed whatever confidence, love, and affection he had to give, were cut off forever from his sight. Mark the result. The first will, of which I am now to speak, wrung from Mr. Smith while thus under surveillance, bears the date of August 13, 1864, two months prior to his death. By this will, after allowing a life-interest in one-third to his wife, one-half the entire remaining estate, including the reversion and remainder after the widow's decease, was given outright to his son Isaac. This would have proved to be equivalent to perhaps a quarter of a million dollars. So far the scheme worked well for Isaac. But in this business his sister Sarah was his match. In a short time, according to her sworn testimony in the Eliza Smith will case, tried in September, 1876, she procured from her father a codicil in her favor for a large amount, it seems.

which codicil, as she affirmed under oath, her mother dictated, and she herself wrote. Mrs. Smith had meanwhile secured from her husband a codicil giving her the fee in her one-third, instead of a life-interest. Thus Isaac was check-mated. Isaac's indignation on discovering that codicil procured by Sarah was great. He tried to destroy it. He wrote to his sister Eliza, begging her to destroy it. She refused to do it. But where that codicil is to-day I do not know.

And now Ebenezer Smith was about to die. Yet, in spite of this forced will, and these forced codicils, the conspirators were not content. They must have a new deal, and must be quick about it, or life would be extinct; for Mr. Smith lay in the last stages of dropsy, and to keep him up he was dosed with whiskey as a *dernier resort*. I would forbear to go into the details of this, but it is my imperative duty to do so.

On the 5th of October, 1864, seven days before his father's death, Isaac went to the office of James W. Rollins, Esq., then at No. 1 Devonshire street, Boston, and urged Mr. Rollins to draft a will for his father, at his [Isaac's] dictation. Mr. Rollins rightly preferred written instructions, from which he could draw so important a document with deliberation. But Isaac was imperative, and in his pressing haste, or from ignorance, even failed to give the correct names of these petitioners — the Burtons — to whom he was gracious enough to instruct Mr. Rollins to allow $500 apiece; while the brother and sister of Mr. Smith, to-gether with his nephews and nieces, up in New Hampshire, ten or twelve in all, Isaac coolly threw overboard altogether, not allowing them a penny, though they were all remembered in the former will. By this last will, the conspirators made what they considered a more equitable division for themselves of Mr. Smith's estate. The will drawn, and consented to by Isaac's con-federates, it had then to be executed.

On the morning of the 9th or 10th of October, so far as discovered, this will was executed, about noon, possibly a little later, of the 9th or 10th, two or three days before Mr. Smith's death, though the will itself bears date the 5th. Isaac himself entered his father's sick-chamber with this will. Mr. Ebenezer Smith was stretched out in an easy-chair; he was in a comatose, lethargic state, rap-idly approaching his end, his mind and body weakened by the fatal dropsy. His precise condition will be more fully given by the witnesses we are to call; it is sufficient now to say that Mr. Smith at that moment was wholly unable to comprehend or to transact any business, or to understand even the reading of a paper. Isaac advanced into the room, followed by his mother and his sister Sarah; his sister Eliza was also there. *The Burtons were not there*, nor was any one there acting for them. Yet the Burtons represented a quarter part of the whole estate, after deducting a third for the widow. Putting his hand upon his father's shoulder, Isaac tried to rouse him, telling him that he had his will for him to sign. The dying man was sufficiently conscious to murmur in sur-prise, " My will!" and then shaking his head, according to the testimony of some, said, " No." A moment or two later he had relapsed into a semi-con-scious state. Isaac then commenced to read the will to his father. But upon this the nurse, Mrs. Giles, — whose testimony I shall produce, — interposed, objecting that Mr. Smith was wholly unable to understand what was read. Some one then said, — the testimony points to Sarah as the one, — "We are losing time," or, "we must not lose time," or words to that effect. Immediately Isaac stepping round to his father's side, took his father's hand in his, and *wrote his father's name himself upon the will*. That spattered signature needs no expert to stamp it as a forgery. That dying man knew not what was done. He was still in his semi-conscious state. He never knew and understood the contents of that will, nor did he sign it. Within three days he died.

Witnesses were needed, and a messenger had been despatched meanwhile to call in the family grocer or butcher who lived hard by — a Mr. Foster — who came at the request. Mr. Foster seemed surprised at what he saw, but owing to his relations with the family — who were his customers — and the peculiar situation, supposing the whole family to be there, he did not interfere, but signed his name as a witness at the request of Isaac. The next witness was the nurse, Mrs. Giles, and the third witness was Margaret Patterson, then a young servant girl, both also signing at the request of Isaac. Mr. Foster, before leaving the room, endeavored to engage in conversation with Mr. Smith, but received no reply, no recognition whatever. Mr. Foster is now dead; but both the other witnesses to the will are living, and are to testify in favor of the petitioners. Thus it was that that will was signed and that forged will, never executed according to law, was admitted to probate by perjury, somewhere, and under it nearly $500,000 have been accounted for; one parcel of property alone, which the executors sold for $50,000, is now assessed for more than half a million.

But a few words more and this opening is concluded. The wrong done the Burtons by the other members of the family troubled Mrs. Smith, the widow. She was afterward more than once heard to say that the Burtons had been wronged, and that she would make it right. But the same evil agencies — cupidity and intrigue — which she had seen at work upon her husband, she found herself the victim of when her end was near. Her wish to make amends for the wrong done the Burtons was foiled by the very parties who had controlled her husband. But the shocking details of that I reserve for another suit. Allow me here to state that Mr. Smith, well knowing the characters of his family, tried hard to have his property distributed justly, and with this in view he put about nine-tenths, if not all, of his large estate in trust, to pass to such persons as he might appoint, and, on failure to appoint them, to pass to his heirs, no matter how many wills they wrung from him. That Mr. Smith had drawn up papers disposing of his property in accordance with these trusts, is known from the fact that he guarded such papers as long as his strength remained, and from the fact of his grief because Edward Bangs, Esq., of this city, the trustee named, was then in Europe at that time, and unable to receive the papers with instructions. Mr. Bangs returned from Europe a short time after Mr. Smith's death, but these papers were in the meantime burned up by some of the guilty parties. When Eliza told her mother that Dr. Thorndike had informed her that the papers had been burnt, the only reply was, " What a fool that man is to tell you that !"

And now, your Honor, these petitioners, the Messrs. Burton, are not here with the heinous design, as has been alleged, of blackmailing the defendants. Far from it. They can justly claim their full share of this estate. Whether they ever recover what is their due, or not, they insist upon asking this Honorable court to set aside that forged will, and, that done, they will cheerfully accept the consequences. Their self-respect and respect for their grandfather was sufficient to compel this course of conduct. These young gentlemen, whose characters are above reproach, immediately upon the discovery of these facts two years ago, commenced a thorough investigation, determined to bring these wrong-doers to account. That grandfather, who loved and cared for them, they now feel in duty bound to defend. That grandfather who died without a member of his family present (a stranger closed his eyes), now finds in these two grandsons, children of a beloved and loving daughter, the sole defenders of his honor, his name and his wishes; and we believe that if we can prove the facts alleged, as we think we can, there will not be found a Christian man or woman in the State informed on this, who will not but say, The Burtons are in the right.

And now, your Honor, I have covered substantially the salient points in this case. The facts that we have alleged are serious, but we have not done so without feeling that we had the proofs back of them to sustain them.

[The following argument was preceded by an opening argument in behalf of Mr. Isaac T. Smith, which is not here printed, in the course of which the particulars in regard to the making and execution of the Will were related.]

Opening Argument of Wm. H. Drury, Esq.,

Counsel for Dr. Wm. H. Thorndike.

JANUARY 1, 1879.

————◆————

May it please your Honor : — Probate was granted by this Court, November 17, 1864, in favor of the will of Ebenezer Smith dated October 5, 1864; and the only question of any real importance raised in this case is whether or not that probate was procured by fraud. But the opening argument of the able counsel for the petitioners is the old powder-boat petition over again, on which their case was first launched. Charges of conspiracy, forgery, perjury, robbery, poisoning, intimidation, force and every kind of fraud have been flippantly and presumptuously thrown about here and elsewhere, directed against people of high character and standing, without any regard to propriety, relevancy or ability to prove these charges. In his capacity for fiction and romance, and I may say for pyrotechnics, the present able counsel for the petitioners has surpassed even the illustrious counsel who began, and afterwards deserted their worthless cause.

Mr. Chandler : — Did he ? *Mr. Drury :* — The presumption is that he did. *Mr. Chandler :* — You can draw your own conclusions. *Mr. Drury :* — I know he went out of it. He is not in it here now, and has not been in it since a certain day. *Mr. Chandler :* — That is apparent. *Mr. Drury :* — He has succeeded in creating a public sensation, but it has been at the expense of giving this Court an opportunity to see his inability to sustain any of the statements he has made, by any evidence entitled to credit, and to learn the worthless and unreliable character of the four principal witnesses upon whom he has relied, whose testimony has any bearing whatever upon the case.

Now, if your Honor please, my desire is not so much to gratify the public through the newspapers, as to obtain the favorable judgment of this Court, and I shall content myself with soberly presenting our side of the case to your Honor, stating only what can be proved by credible evidence, and setting up only such defences as the law has given us.

We need not have gone to trial here. We could have avoided it, if we had chosen to avail ourselves of all our legal rights, but we preferred to go to trial now, before death and destruction have removed all the evidence, a great part of which has already been lost, by which these slanders can be completely refuted. And we welcome the opportunity which is now given us to show to the satisfaction of a court of justice, in which a lie has not such vitality as it has in public rumor, the baseless falsehood of the slanders which have been uttered. We have to carry ourselves back, sir, as well as we can, 14 years, and view matters from that standpoint; and the difficulties are apparent at once, because we know from our own inward experience, and from our experience in the course of this trial, that it is impossible to derive, from the memory of witnesses alone, the complete details of transactions of a time so remote.

The principal consideration which led to the establishment of the will of October 5, 1864, the will in question, was that in its general aspect it was found to be consistent with two prior wills and codicils, and that nobody adverse to it could gain anything, and especially the Burtons could gain nothing, by having it set aside. And the same considerations, after this long lapse of time, and after the estate has been settled, will have far greater weight now than it had then, not only in favor of the validity of the will, but also in favor of the stability of property and against the unsettling of that estate. I have therefore prepared a statement which I now present to the court, showing in a concise form and at a glance, the provisions of the different testamentary instruments of Ebenezer Smith, existing at his death, October 12, 1864. [*See Statement, pages* 18 & 19.]

The first will of which we have any positive knowledge, was the will of May 2, 1859. It was drawn in the office of William Minot, who is now dead, a lawyer of large experience in regard to all matters relating to wills, and a lawyer of high character. It was executed in the office of William Minot, the
• other witnesses to that will besides Mr. Minot being persons who were employed in his office. It was made when Ebenezer Smith was in the undoubted possession of his faculties, and was managing an extensive business. He gives the Burtons in that will $500 each; gives his wife the income for life of a third, and certain personal property absolutely; gives to Isaac one-third, Eliza W. one-third, and Sarah W. one-third, of the residue. At that time Eliza W. and Isaac were probably indebted to their father, because the will says that the debts due from them are to be deducted from their shares,—nothing said about the debts due from Sarah, because there were none. A few days afterwards, on May 16, 1859, he has occasion to consider his will again, and his son George Alexander having died, to show the regard which he had for his grandchildren, if he had any in that branch of the family, he gives them $5 each. In other respects he ratifies and confirms his will, leaving the Burtons $500 still. And the witnesses to that were William Minot, Eleazer S. Porter and Luther L. White, the same as the witnesses to the will. That codicil, also, was drawn in the office of William Minot. This was his will down to 1864.

Statement showing the provisions of the different Testamentary Instruments of Ebenezer Smith, existing at his death, Oct. 12, 1864.

Parties interested in the wills.	First Will and Codicil.		Second Will and two Codicils.			Third Will.
	WILL OF MAY 2, 1859.	CODICIL OF MAY 16, 1859.	WILL OF AUG. 13, 1864.	CODICIL OF SEPTEMBER 2, 1864.	CODICIL OF OCTOBER 1, 1864.	WILL OF OCT 5, 1864.
1. Sam'l and Sally Smith, bro. and sister.	$500 each.		$200 each.			
2. Esther, Catherine, Noah, John and Mary, children of bro. Samuel. Widow and children of nephew Eli Smith.	$150 each. $150.		$50 each, $75			
3. Asineth, Eliza, Elmira, and Sarah Ann, daughters of bro. Samuel.	$300 in trust for them and survivors of them.		$75 each.			
4. Phœbe Seaver, niece.	$200 and annuity of $100.					
5. Zachariah Seaver. Ebenezer Seaver. Charlotte Seaver.			$200 in trust. $100 $100 in trust.			
6. Eliza Smith, wife.	Furniture and other articles in house, except phonographic and phonetic library and diary. Also, income for life, or ⅓ of property left after payment of debts.		Same as in will of May 2, 1859.	In lieu of provision in will, gives her in fee, ⅓ of property left after payment of debts. Also, furniture and silver-ware, and his interest in property standing in her name.		All furniture and silver-plate, and his interest in property standing in her name. Also ⅓ of residue after payment of debts and legacies.
7. Ebenezer Smith, son, if living.	$100.		$100.			
8. Geo. Alex. Smith, son.	Testator's interest in house in Winchester, in which Geo. Alex. resides, for life, and annuity of $400.	Geo. Alex'r having died, gives his children, if any, $5 each.				$100
9. Hazen J. Burton, Jr., and Geo. S. Burton, grandsons.	$500 each at age of 21.		$500 each.			$500 each at age of 21.
10. Isaac T. Smith, son.	⅓ of residue and remainder in fee.		In fee ⅓ of residue, and ⅓ reversion of property given to wife for life.			⅓ of rest of property in fee.
11. Eliza W. Smith, (or Gen.) daughter.	⅓ of residue and remainder in trust.		In trust for her ⅓ of said residue and rever'n			⅓ of rest of property in fee.

	½ of residue and remainder in trust.	In trust for her ⅓ of said residue and reversion.	In lieu of provision in will, gives her in fee ¼ of his property left after deducting the portion set aside for his wife in codicil of Sept. 2, 1864.	¼ of rest of property in fee.
12	Sarah W. Thorndike, daughter.			
13	Isaac T. and Eliza W.		Debts due from them to be deducted from their shares.	
14	Executors and Trustees.	Wm. Minot, Jr., and Edward Bangs.	Wm. Minot, Jr., Edw. Bangs. Isaac T. Smith.	Wm. H. Thorndike, one of executors and trustees in place of Edw. Bangs.	Wm. Minot, Jr., Isaac T. Smith, and Wm. H. Thorndike, executors.
15	Witnesses.	Wm. Minot, Eleazer S. Porter, Luther L. White.	Wm. Minot, Eleazer S. Porter, Luther L. White, Moody Merrill.	Rollin H. Neale, Mary James Wight, Mrs. P. Roberts, Margaret Patterson.	Andrix A. Foster, James Wight, Mary P. Roberts, Anna G. Giles, Margaret Patterson.

Statement showing the effect of the Will of Oct. 5, 1864, as compared with the Will of Aug. 13, 1864, and its two Codicils. According to the accounts of the Executors of Ebenezer Smith, his whole estate, after deducting the Probate Court's allowance to his widow, the specific Bequest to her, and the Debts and charges of administration, amounted to $231,155 46.

	Amounts which would have been received under the Will of Aug. 23, 1864, and the two codicils thereto.	Amounts which would have been received under the Will of Oct. 5, 1864, without the compromise.	Difference in Gain or Loss.
Eliza Smith, Widow	$77,051 82	$76,718 48	$333 34 loss.
Sarah W. Thorndike, daughter	51,367 88	51,145 66	222 22 loss.
The Burtons, grandsons,	1,000 00	1,000 00	neither.
Other legacies	1,325 00	—	1,325 00 loss.
Isaac T. Smith, son	66,940 51	51,145 66	15,794 85 loss.
Eliza W. Smith (or Gen), daughter,	33,470 25	51,145 66	17,675 41 gain.
	$231,155 46	$231,155 46	

In July of that year he determined to make a new will, and he copied out in his own handwriting,—which has fortunately been preserved,—in his own handwriting I say, both the will of May 2, and the codicil of May 16. 1859; and in his own handwriting, which we have, and which we have already shown to the court, he prepared a draft of a new will, came up to the same William Minot, and that will of August 13, 1864, was prepared in the office of William Minot, and appears here in this court, in the handwriting of Moody Merrill, who was at that time in Mr. Minot's office, and who remembers the execution of it. And that will also was executed and witnessed in the office of William Minot, and varies from the will of 1859 only, substantially, with respect to Isaac, Eliza W. and Sarah. It gives to the Burtons, still, $500 each, to his son Ebenezer, if living, $100, diminishes the legacies to other relatives, and appoints Isaac one of the trustees and executors, together with William Minot. Jr., and Edward Bangs. In the following month he has occasion to consider his will again. The difficulties with his wife, towards the last of his life softened and he determines to revoke the provision made in his will for his wife, and gives her in fee one-third of his property left after the payment of his debts, also his furniture and silver ware and his interest in property standing in her name. And that codicil of September 2, 1864, is in the handwriting of that same old William Minot, and appears here in court, and is witnessed by the Rev. Rollin H. Neale, Mary P. Roberts and Margaret Patterson; and the latter has already testified to the circumstances under which she appended her name as a witness to that codicil. On the 1st of October, 1864, he again considers his will, and decides to give his daughter Sarah one-third of the residue, after setting aside the portion for his wife, and appoints her husband Dr. Wm. H. Thorndike, one of the executors and trustees, in place of Edward Bangs; and this is witnessed by three worthy people, James Wight. Mrs. James Wight and Mary P. Roberts. James Wight is fortunately alive,—his wife and his wife's sister having died last September and October,—and he has appeared upon the stand, and you have heard from him, an unprejudiced witness, the relation of the circumstances under which that codicil was signed and executed.

So far the testator has left the Burtons $500 each. And we now come to the will of October 5, 1864, which gives to his wife substantially the same as the prior will and codicils,—only he gives her a few hundred dollars less.

Mr. Chandler : Excuse me. Did you say in whose handwriting the codicil of October 1st was?

Mr. Drury : That was written by Paul Willard. He gives to his wife and to his daughter Sarah substantially the same that he gave them in the prior will and codicils, only he gives his wife about $333 less, and his daughter Sarah about $222 less; he gives to his son Ebenezer, if living. the same as he had previously given him : and, he gives the Burtons just the same—$500 each. The only change he makes of any great importance is in regard to Isaac and Eliza. Eliza, as the estate turned out, gets $17,675 41 more than the prior will and codicils gave her; Isaac gets $15,794 85 less; and certain legatees, relatives who were not heirs at law, lost by the last will $1325. Everybody except the Burtons and Eliza lost by the last will. It gives the Burtons just the same. Eliza is the only person who gains by it; and she gains at the expense of all others,—at the expense chiefly of her brother Isaac. And the testator appoints William Minot, Jr., Isaac T. Smith and William H. Thorndike, the same persons as provided in the prior will and codicils, as executors. This is witnessed by Andrix A. Foster, of whose character I shall speak hereafter, who is now dead, Anna G. Giles and Margaret Patterson, who have already testified. And this same statement also contains a comparison of the effect between the last will and the prior will and two codicils.

Now as we can show you, neither Isaac, nor the widow, nor Sarah, were eager to support this last will and have it set up;—it was an injury to them. When objection was made to it, they would have been glad to have withdrawn it and had it out of the way. The old lady preferred the prior will and codicils, and the only persons who did not prefer the prior will and codicils were Eliza and the Burtons;—they thought they could squeeze out something by throwing suspicion upon this last will, and availing themselves of some false story about it, which was then hatched up by Eliza W., who got that nurse, Mrs. Giles, into her hands soon after her father's death.

It was only by great effort on the part of Dr. Thorndike, that old Eliza Smith could be brought to making any compromise about the will. She knew she was right, and she was the last woman that could be turned away from what was right,—what she believed her legal rights were. None of these parties who have been accused were eager to set up the last will, because it would have been for their interest to have it set aside, and they went for it, and it was set up, because it was determined by this court, upon both wills being presented, that the will of October 5th was the last valid will and testament of Ebenezer Smith.

Mr. Chandler: Did you say Sarah's codicil was presented then?

Mr. Drury: The reason why Sarah's codicil was not presented, was, that the counsel for the executors decided that it would be better to put the prior will into the Probate Court at the same time, and carry it up to the Supreme Court at the same time, with the last will, and nobody could do that so conveniently as Edward Bangs. But Edward Bangs was cut out by the last codicil as executor, and he could not petition for letters testamentary to himself, if he put in the codicil of October 1st. So the lawyers decided that Bangs had better offer that will for probate with only the first codicil, and that after they should get up into the Supreme Court, they would present a petition there to be allowed to prove the second codicil; and I have the petition, signed by Edward D. Sohier and Paul Willard, which was prepared for that purpose, to be presented in the Supreme Court at the same time when the other testamentary papers should come to be considered; and that is the reason why the codicil of Sarah does not appear among the records in this court,—by the advice of counsel, to enable Edward Bangs to offer that prior will for probate.

If your Honor please, the gentleman who has just preceded me has stated some of the parties who are represented here, but there is one party whom he left out, whom we on this side represent. We represent Ebenezer Smith.

We stand here to sustain his right to dispose of his property as he saw fit. Nobody complains except these Burtons, and we show you that through the last years of his life the testator made at least, before this will, two valid dispositions of his property, and gave them $500 each, and if they were defrauded by anybody, it was by Ebenezer Smith, who had the right to give them what he saw fit to give them,—what the law gave him a right to do. Before that will of October 5th, there was substantially this same testimentary disposition in regard to his wife Eliza Smith, and I represent Eliza Smith and her right to receive the property which her husband gave her, and to transmit that property as she might see fit afterwards. Before that will of October 5th there was substantially this same disposition in regard to his daughter Sarah, and I represent her and her right to receive the property which her father gave her and to transmit that property to her husband, who is now my client, and to her children, one of whom is now of age and three of whom are minors, but who have not even received the respect of legal notice of these proceedings, although they are the persons principally interested in these proceedings.

Mr. Chandler: It has been published. *Mr. Drury:* And they are principally interested through their grandmother, Eliza Smith, who, in her will, gave to them the bulk of her property.

Isaac Smith is represented by my brother Loring; and he stands here to uphold the will which greatly injured him.

Eliza W., if she is represented by anybody, is represented by the counsel for the petitioners. This will benefited her, as the estate turned out, to the extent of over $17,000, and she appears here to break it.

Now, your Honor, I have dwelt upon these prior wills because they throw a great deal of light upon the last, and they negative the idea of fraud; and you can read the action of the testator's mind from 1859 down through the wills and codicils of 1864, and down to the last will, and we see there the exhibition of a constant purpose in regard to his son Ebenezer and his grandchildren the Burtons, a constant purpose to diminish the legacies to other relatives outside the immediate family, and a constant purpose to regard his wife, Isaac, Sarah and Eliza W. as the principal objects of his bounty,—and the only variation as to them is as to the proportions in which he gives to them. Here in the codicil of September 2 he is determined to be more just to his wife; here in the codicil of October 1 he brings his daughter to an equality; here in the will of October 5 he brings the three children to an equality and back to where they were in 1859. Now this is all inconsistent with fraud, and is consistent only with the genuineness of this last will—his most reasonable will; and I say from internal evidence, the testamentary history of the man, and on its face, this last will is the most reasonable will, taken as a whole, that he ever made. On its face, I say. I dont say it was really, because Eliza W. had already sucked out of her father a large share of his fortune, and if she had received what the will of August gave her, she would even then have received more than her just share of his estate. She was a spendthrift, a vain, extravagant woman, and it made no difference whether she received little or much, she was sure to squander it if she received it, and it would have been more just, perhaps, considering the circumstances, to have let the disposition remain as the will of August and its codicils left it; but there were no reasons why the testator's daughter Sarah, who never had called upon her father for money, who had never been assisted by him, should have been reduced below the third; and there was good reason why more than a third should go to his favorite son, who had been a credit to his name, and the only one who bore the name of Smith, who had been a pride to his father.

I speak now of that as the internal evidence. If your Honor looks at the last will, I call attention in the first place to the appearance of the signature to that will. It was the same fourteen years ago that it is to-day. Any lawyer would have noticed it at that time. It has not been changed since. Age has not affected the appearance of that signature, and it was just the same fourteen years ago as it is to-day, such as to excite anybody's inquiry, and it is an insult to any lawyer to suppose that it did not excite his inquiry, and that he did not investigate the circumstances which led to that peculiar appearance.

When this will came before this court fourteen years ago, the presumption is that the essential facts necessary to establish it as a valid will were proved,— the testator's knowledge of its contents, that he was of sound mind, that it was signed by him, or by his direction in his presence, attested in his presence by three witnesses, and legally declared to be his last will. Now it is not incumbent upon us to show that this was established at that time; but the burden is upon these petitioners to show that those facts were not established. And I candidly ask your Honor, looking over the evidence which has already gone in, if they have shown one particle of evidence yet bearing upon any one of those points;—one particle of evidence, in all the testimony of many days which has already gone in, upon the very points which it is incumbent upon them to show. Not one particle! And they must not only show an omission of testimony, but a fraudulent concealment, and there is no evidence bearing upon it. But, your Honor, we propose to go further than the law requires us to go, and we shall prove all that would be necessary to establish *de novo* the will of October 5th as the last will and testament of Ebenezer Smith, and a valid disposition of his property. And here, perhaps, is the best point for a consideration of the testimony of Mrs. Giles.

Her testimony is false. My brother thinks she is mistaken. I do not. I do not credit her with honesty myself. But whether she is honest or dishonest, her testimony is false. We can prove it to be so, conclusively,—*first*, as to the proceedings which took place at the Probate Court fourteen years ago; *second*, as to the date of the execution of the will; *third*, as to Ebenezer Smith's mental condition at the time of the execution of the will; and *fourth*, as to the proceedings which took place at the time of the execution of the will, and prior thereto, and subsequently thereto. Now, first, in regard to the probate proceedings in this court. That is important; and I have noticed that your Honor has regarded that as a vital point in this case. That witness, Mrs. Giles, undertook to remember positively the questions which were asked her, and the questions which were not asked her, fourteen years ago. She was so rash as to say she could remember that a certain list of questions, which I put to her, were not asked her, and that certain questions were asked her, fourteen years ago. Well, now we know, your Honor, that that is impossible, and a witness who will do that from pure memory, or pretend to say it from pure memory, utters what is false. Now, if your Honor please, it is very fortunate, very fortunate, that we have the minutes of the proceedings of the Probate Court. And it is very curious—the source from which those minutes came;—they came from an adversary,—from the hands of the enemy, in the handwriting of Thomas P. Smith, the son of Eliza W. Smith, who appeared here fourteen years ago in this court as an attorney in behalf of himself, and who afterwards took an appeal from the decree of this court;—and they show upon their face that they are the minutes of the Probate Court of November 17th, 1864; that Andrix A. Foster was examined; that a long series of cross-interrogatories— 15 cross-interrogatories—were propounded to him, and among those interrogatories were these: " Was Mr. Smith able to sign it?" " Did Isaac move his hand?" " Did he ask Isaac to help him?" " Did he attempt to write himself?" " Who put the pen in his hand?" " Did he move his hand towards the paper?" Those questions were asked to Andrix A. Foster,—cross-interrogatories.

Next came Margaret Patterson. The minutes show that she was sworn. She was asked if she saw him sign it, and who requested him to sign it; whether Ebenezer Smith said anything; whether he heard what Isaac said; how he signed it; "Did he talk with his children?" "Was it all said in his presence?" "What was his condition?" "Did he move his hand?" "Where were you?" "Did he speak to Eliza?" And here is a long list,—those minutes show that a long list of questions were put to Mrs. Giles. The very questions were put to her which she solemnly denied were put to her, and pretended to remember were not put to her, at that time: "Did you see Mr. Smith sign that?" "Were you requested to sign it as his will?" And the fact of her objecting to the reading of the will came out in reply to the Judge of Probate. "Did any one else express their satisfaction?" "Mrs. Thorndike and Mrs. Gen did." " Mrs. Smith," she testified, "and the family agreed upon the will with Ebenezer Smith." "Where did she sign it?" "Who took the paper from the board?" "Did you hear him make any declaration?" "What did Mrs. Gen say?" "I am here, father; all is harmonious." She then said— " I thought that he was so weak he could not understand a word of it." The minutes show it. "Are you of the same opinion now?" She said—"Yes." "Dr. Thorndike was attending him." "Where did you first see this paper?" (Question by the Judge). Then here is a list of questions by Mr. Woodbury: "When did Dr. Thorndike apply to you?" "Were you present during the whole time of completing?" " How long from the time of your objecting to the signing?" "After Dr. Lewis visited him that morning?" "Yes." "Who was assisting him then?" Then Mr. Hazelton, counsel of Arthur G. Smith: "What relation is Dr. Thorndike?" "Did he know you signed as witnesses?" "Did he say anything, or indicate that he knew you were signing as witnesses?"

"How long were you present," says the Judge, "the whole time from that of bringing in to the completion?" "Yes." Then Dwight Foster, at that time counsel for the Burtons, who, they swore, was not here, put this cross-interrogatory, the only interrogatory which appears to have been put by him: "After Mr. Isaac Smith had guided Mr. Smith's hand, did Mr. Smith ask what that was?" "I should not like to say positively if it was before or after, but I think Mr. Smith asked what that paper was, and Mr. Isaac or Mrs. Ebenezer says, 'It is your will.'"

So this pretence that all these matters have been discovered now for the first time is annihilated by the traces which were left fourteen years ago by the son of that very woman who has built up this monstrous charge against her mother, her brother and her sister. And in the course of my statement, I will show that we have other evidence as to the proceedings in the Probate Court, in the writing of Edward D. Sohier, a witness not of any doubtful character or reputation.

The date of the execution of the will of October 5th is very important as bearing upon the testator's mental condition, and this has been recognized by the counsel for the petitioners. It has been very important for him to establish that it was dated back and was executed on the 9th or 10th of October, when the man was almost dead. They have recognized the importance of that, and they have dwelt upon it. And fortunately we have seven independent sources of testimony bearing upon the date of the execution of that will. 1. The date of the will itself. 2. It was written on the 5th day of October, and Isaac remembers that he took it immediately from the office of Mr. Rollins, who wrote it, up to the house, and it was executed on the same day. 3. Mrs. Giles herself said fourteen years ago, and Mr. Sohier put it down,—"I went to Mr. Smith's the night before the will was signed." And she went there on the 4th; that fixes the date on the 5th. 4. Dr. Lewis called October 5th, and the minutes of the Probate Court show that Anna G. Giles testified that the will was executed that day. 5. Dr. Thorndike remembers the date with reference to the execution of the codicil of October 1st, which was Saturday, and he remembers that the execution of this will took place on the following Wednesday. 6. The Doctor remembers also when Isaac came. He came the next morning after that codicil of October 1st was signed, and he left on the night of the day on which the will was executed, Wednesday, October 5th, and was absent from Boston during all the rest of his father's life, and did not arrive here again until the morning of the 12th of October. And (7) finally, conclusively, the Bank records in New York show that Isaac was in New York from the 6th to the 11th inclusive. He could not have been here to see the will executed on any day later than October 5th. Can they break through that evidence as to the date of the execution of the will? With their failure to establish it on any other date than the 5th, their case is gone.

Now, the testimony of Mrs. Giles is false, and we will show it so, as to the mental condition of Ebenezer Smith at the time the will was executed,—for according to her own testimony, she gives the lie to herself. If it was executed on October 5th, his mind was very clear. She relates the conversation of Ebenezer Smith. His memory goes away back to the time when he was a boy; he tells how he came to Boston; he carries his mind away back to his boyhood—an old man at that time 78 years of age;—and a great deal of conversation as to those former days takes place up to the time of the consultation of the physicians, on October 8th, all of which gives the life to herself, if the will was executed on the 5th. And secondly, the statement which she made, and which Mr. Sohier took down, and which I shall again refer to and read, shows more mind than she gave him the credit of having when she testified fourteen years ago, and infinitely more mind than she now gives him the credit of having had at that time. And then, thirdly, upon that point of mental condition is Dr. Storer's testimony, that on the 8th of October he saw Ebenezer Smith, three days after the will was signed, and Mr. Smith talked about his younger days, when they were Odd Fellows together, and his mind, Dr. Storer said, appeared then as clear as it ever had been. The fourth is the testimony of Miss Patterson, one of the attesting witnesses, who has always been of the opinion that he was of sound mind and understood what he was doing. Fifth, the testimony of Andrix A. Foster, which Mr. Sohier remembers, and which he will, relate which was uttered here fourteen years ago, to the effect that Mr. Foster, realizing to the full extent the importance of the act which he was called upon to perform, took particular pains to satisfy himself that the man whose will he was called upon to sign and witness was of sound mind and memory, and he looked at him and asked him if he knew him, and held a conversation with him as to their younger days when they sang together. Edward D. Sohier remembers the testimony which Andrix A. Foster gave upon that point. It struck him at that time, and he regarded that man's testimony at that time as the important testimony as to the mental condition of the testator, and the validity of the will And furthermore, Dr. Thorndike, who was the regular attending physician of Ebenezer Smith during all his life, after he married one of the family, came to the house and into that room at just the time when Mr. Foster was talking to Mr. Smith, and heard the conversation which did take place there at the time, and he remembers it. Now, the testimony of the nurse is false, and I dwell upon her testimony, because it is the only testimony on that point which has been produced yet,—because the character of Eliza W. Smith, as she has shown herself on the stand, is such as not to entitle her to a moment's weight.

The testimony of that nurse as to the proceedings at the time of the execution is false; whether mistakenly or intentionally, it is false; it is not true. Fourteen years ago she made a different statement, which Mr. Sohier took down,—entirely different. At that time she said, " that she went to Mr. Smith's the night before the will was signed; that the next morning before dinner, Isaac, Mrs. Thorndike, Mrs. Gen and Mrs. Smith came in; Isaac said, ' father, we have brought your will;' he said, ' what will?' Isaac said, ' the one we have drawn up by way of compromise,' and began to read it; Mrs. Giles objected; then he asked each of them if they were satisfied; called for his wife first; she said she was; Isaac said he was; then he called for Eliza, and she said she was harmonious; then asked for Sarah, and she was; then they sent for Mr. Foster; then, as he was sitting in his chair, he called for his specs, with the will before him; his wife got them; then Mr. Foster came in, and we were asked to witness; Isaac guided his hand; we signed; then a conversation took place between Foster and Ebenezer Smith as to the Handel and Haydn Society." Mr. Edward D. Sohier took this statement down at that time.

Mr. Chandler: Did he say that Ebenezer Smith asked the witnesses to sign it? Does that appear there? *Mr. Drury:* I have given you what the whole thing was. *Mr. Chandler:* I have got it correctly, thank you.

Mr. Drury: This bears not only upon what the occurrences were at the execution of the will, but also upon Mr. Smith's mental condition at the time, and particularly upon the preposterous pretence that everything of any importance was not known fourteen years ago. And the Probate Court proceedings show, the minutes of the Probate Court proceedings show, that she made a different statement at that time as to what occurred at the time when the will was executed, from what she does now. Dr. Storer's testimony also falsifies the present testimony of Mrs. Giles, and so does Miss Patterson's testimony. And I have a statement which was drawn within a month after the old man died, which Mrs. Thorndike gave to her confidential adviser, Paul Willard, in regard to the circumstances under which the will was signed, and also purporting to contain a statement which the nurse Giles had made. It was not until after I had discovered that statement that I had positive and indisputable evidence that Mrs. Thorndike was present when the will was signed. Her memory was that she was not present. She declared to me that she was not present. She could not come to the point of saying that she was, although I considered that it would be very advantageous to her case if she had been present at the time of the execution of this will. It was not until after she died that I found the positive evidence that she was. She had so far forgotten it that she solemnly swore in the Supreme Court at the time of the Eliza Smith will case that she was not present. Here she has left a statement to her confidential adviser, before this matter was tried here, as to the circumstances under which it was executed, which corroborates the statement made by the nurse at that time as it appears in Mr. Sohier's handwriting, and it is corroborated, and will be corroborated by testimony of witnesses whom we shall call here.

Mr. Chandler: The date of that paper—the date of that statement? *Mr. Drury:* There is no date to it. I can fix the date by other evidence. This I found among the papers of Paul Willard, her counsel at that time, and this was the statement which she made to him at that time, and it was made when her mind was fresh, and there is more probability in favor of the correctness of that statement than there is of the correctness of any evidence which depends upon the mere memory of witnesses as to transactions which took place fourteen years ago.

But Mrs. Giles, we shall show you, was an uncertain witness fourteen years ago. Eliza W. got hold of her,—a shrewd, crafty womam of the world, who knew how to get round ignorant women like Mrs. Giles,—took her out to West Medford and moulded her mind to her own purposes, and talked this matter

28

over then, and she was an uncertain witness at that time. But she did not go to the length which she has gone now, fourteen years afterwards, after her memory has faded.

False the witness is, whether honest or not, in pretending to remember so much, and we know that it is impossible for a woman like her, an ignorant woman, a woman of very little understanding, to remember so much, when others remember so little. I asked the witness Mrs. Giles one question; it was not a matter of much importance, but it shows you what a reckless witness she was. I asked her if she would have remembered a thunder-storm, if it had occurred while she was there. "Oh, yes, of course." Now there actually was a violent thunder-storm on the morning of the 8th of October. I looked this up to refute the testimony which the nurse had given at the time of the taking of her deposition, fixing the time of Isaac's coming back there as on the 8th, and saying that Isaac said at breakfast, "what a clear night it was coming up the Sound," and to show it utterly improbable that he would have made that remark in regard to a night on which there was a violent thunder-storm. Well, she could not remember it, of course. Nobody could have remembered it. But it shows how she pretends to remember. Why, she could not go back one year, to the places at which she had lived, when I asked her those questions. Why, these witnesses, these able men whom we shall call here, remember hardly anything. Mr. Sohier remembers but very little. Dwight Foster, a man as clear headed as any man in this State, remembers almost nothing; he does not even remember being here at the time of the probate of the will. Dr. Thorndike cannot remember who were present at the time of the execution of the will, to save his life. He could not swear that Eliza W. Smith or his wife was present at that time, from independent recollection, bare memory. And to show how much at fault her testimony is, and how reckless she is also, she declares that there was a consultation at which Dr. Lewis was present. Now, neither Dr. Storer nor Dr. Thorndike ever held a consultation anywhere with Winslow Lewis during all their lives. The only consultation which took place was the consultation on the 8th, when Dr. Thorndike and Dr. Storer were present, and they were the only ones present, and Dr. Lewis was not there. That is all fiction. So much for Giles : and with the worthlessness of her testimony exhibited, the case for the petitioners will be swept away. She is a reckless witness : of poor understanding ; pretending to have a miraculous memory, a memory which we know no person under Heaven ever had, to remember so accurately the proceedings of fourteen years ago. We know from our own experience that it is impossible.

Now, your Honor, before stating the legal principles and the evidence bearing upon the charges which have been made, let me say that I will not so insult anybody's understanding or nature as to credit him with believing those charges, or with making them in good faith. Considering the enormity of the alleged offences ; the number of persons engaged in them,—5 persons, Eliza Smith (the widow), Isaac, Sarah, Eliza W., Dr. Thorndike ; considering the number of persons to whom they must have been known, eight persons in all, the three witnesses besides those five persons; considering the open manner in which these crimes were committed, if they were committed; and the amount of money which was involved, well calculated to bring out what was done in such an open manner; and considering the reputation and standing of some of the alleged offenders;—considering all these things, it is incredible that these offences were committed, or if committed, that they were not found out before; and a person must not only have unbounded credulity and lack of common sense, but he must be endowed with great depravity in his own nature, to believe that such offences were ever committed. And yet, to satisfy those who do not know the truth, I will proceed to state a few legal principles, and the evidence, which bear upon the charges which have been made.

The Burtons encounter at the outset certain stubborn presumptions of law which are thrown around the position which we occupy, which they must break through, but which they never can break through. And the first is, that presumption which the law throws around every person who is accused,—the presumption of innocence—a presumption which gains strength in accordance with the magnitude of the crime of which a person is accused—the presumption that such crimes as have been charged here were never committed. This is followed by another presumption of law, that everything was done in due form, a presumption which gains strength with age. As other things grow weak with age, this presumption grows stronger. As witnesses grow old, forget and die, as the memory of past transactions become faded and dim, this presumption becomes stronger than ever, and in time becomes conclusive. *Ex diuturnitate temporis omnia praesumuntur sollenniter esse acta.* After long lapse of time everything is presumed to have been done in due form. Then this is followed up by another presumption to which this maxim applies with as much force as it does to wills,—the presumption of the regularity of judicial proceedings,—that after a court has once passed upon a question, the decree of that court—the judgment of that court—was made upon evidence justifying that decree. The decree of this court admitting that will to probate appears here, dated November 17th, 1864, and signed by your predecessor, and the presumption is that that decree was made upon evidence before him which justified that decree, that the witnesses who testified here when their memories were fresh in regard to the transactions about which they testified, gave evidence which undoubtedly established in his mind, to his satisfaction, that it was the last will and testament of Ebenezer Smith. And then we find, if your Honor please, that an appeal was taken to the Supreme Judicial Court, and it is a matter of record in that court, that a jury found that that will was signed by Ebenezer Smith, or by some person in his presence by his express direction, that he was of sound and disposing mind and memory, that the will was attested by three competent witnesses in his presence, and that it was not procured by undue influence or fraud.

Mr. Chandler: You don't mean to say that there was a trial. *Mr. Drury:* I mean to say that it appears on the record of that court of which I have an attested copy among my papers, that those issues were tried and passed upon by a jury, and the verdict of the jury appears there in that court upon that question.

Mr. Chandler: You don't mean to say there was a trial. *Mr. Drury:* I have said exactly what the truth is, that the records show that three or four issues were submitted to a jury, and the records show the verdict of that jury signed by the foreman of that jury, and afterwards, what appears here also, that the court, the highest court of the Commonwealth, issued a decree establishing that will as the last will and testament of Ebenezer Smith. And the presumption is that that decree of that court was made upon a showing which justified that decree and no other. *Res judicata pro veritate accipitur.*

We also find, if your Honor please, that there was a compromise made among the parties, a family compromise, signed by the guardian *ad litem* and Dwight Foster, counsel of the Burtons,—able counsel, honorable counsel,—a family compromise, which the law specially favors, which our Supreme court has said is entitled to the highest consideration in a court of Equity, even. And there is the strongest presumption in favor of that compromise

Now against these presumptions the Burtons have nothing except that presumption which arises from presumptuousness and audacity.

Now, if your Honor please, what is the evidence in regard to a conspiracy? That is one of the charges, a conspiracy—a conspiracy. That is a charge made in the opening argument. It is a charge which has been made in various ways from beginning to end. It appears in that old powder-boat petition filed by General Butler, that it was a conspiracy to defraud these Burtons out of receiving their share from the estate of Ebenezer Smith, and it has been paraded in the newspapers and by the counsel here as a conspiracy of these persons. Now what evidence is there of conspiracy? What evidence has been given of a conspiracy? Suppose that those persons who are charged with a conspiracy had done nothing? Would these defrauded persons have fared any better? No. These conspirators, the three that are put forward as the principal conspirators, had every reason to be satisfied with the state of things before the time of this pretended conspiracy, a conspiracy which did not benefit them, and did not defraud these Burtons out of a dollar, and they know it, and always did know it. And I dismiss that charge without any further comment, as being too utterly contemptible to deserve consideration.

Forgery is another charge, which is the making of a false writing to the prejudice of some other person's right.

Mr. Chandler: Excuse me. Is that alleged in the petition? *Mr. Drury:* You have alleged it in your opening argument as "grasping by threats, intimidation, and finally by forgery," which you had published in the *Advertiser* and to the world, and which was paraded in large, leading letters.

Mr. Chandler: It is not in the petition, Mr. Drury. *Mr. Drury:* No. You went outside of your petition. You were even ashamed of your predecessor's old petition. You did not allege it, but you had the audacity to make the charge outside of your petition, and I propose to meet that charge. Forgery—a forged will;—that has been the burden of the whole song here, and that is what the world is thinking about. Why, the world has been prepared by the statements which have been made and published, to think, and is thinking whether this was not a forged will. What has been the object of this expert testimony? What was the object of the preparation of those lithographs which were in the newspapers this morning,—facsimiles of the different signatures of Ebenezer Smith? What is the object of all those—this expert testimony and this parading of signatures in the newspapers? Why, to raise an atmosphere, and make people believe that a will has been forged, a will disposing of $250,000, or, as they falsely state, $500,000—$250,000 really, which was all the man was worth. Now I have no wonder the counsel is ashamed of this, and says this charge does not appear in the petition. But that is what he has been trying to show, to gratify his malignant clients. Forgery, your Honor,— whose right, let me ask, was prejudiced? Whatever the mechanical contrivance by which that signature was affixed to that will, any lawyer of any common sense knows that there was not one element of forgery in it. Every lawyer knows that wills are executed every day of the year, and are admitted to probate every day in the year, the signatures of which are affixed by the same contrivance by which that signature was affixed, and every lawyer and every judge knows that it is right and legal, and the pretence of forgery is preposterous. Forgery in the presence of seven people, without any attempt at concealment! Forgery by that cumbersome process, by holding the pen in the hand of another man! How much easier to make a forgery by holding the pen in the hand of the man who commits the forgery! The idea of committing a forgery with the pen in the hand of somebody else! And there was no fraudulent purpose or intent in it, as the result shows, because the result was to cut down that man who committed that alleged forgery, $15,000 below what he had before by the prior will. Can you see any motive for forgery?

And it has been charged that there was a fraudulent procurement of the attestation, and perjury in procuring the probate of the will. Now we shall show your Honor,—and I don't think that point will be even denied,—that the witnesses knew that they were attesting what purported to be the last will and testament of Ebenezer Smith, and they saw how the signature was affixed to it, and how it was executed; and they heard everything that took place there; they saw the way it was signed; they were there and signed it themselves in the testator's presence, and they witnessed everything that was said and done. And an attesting witness—and I call your Honor's attention to what is very familiar to the law of probate, that an attesting witness who impeaches his own act is not entitled to credit. Lord Mansfield said that such a witness deserves the pillory; and the evidence of such a witness must be looked upon with suspicion. They attested it when all the proceedings were fresh, and when they saw what was done. We are now removed fourteen years, your Honor, from that time, and unfortunately the only substantial witness to that will is dead; but the evidence derived from a consideration of that man's character will have great weight upon the whole of this case. He was a man of unsullied reputation for truth, honesty, character and intelligence; a shrewd, practical business man; a religious man; he was either deacon or officiated as deacon in the church of Dr. Herrick; he was at that time a man somewhat advanced in life, who had known Ebenezer

Smith a great while; and I could bring a hundred good men of the city of Boston to come here and support that man's character. He was a man of too much intelligence to be imposed upon by a forged will. He had the sense to realize the act which he was called upon to perform, and took particular pains to satisfy himself of the sanity of the man; and he was not the kind of a man, and Isaac knew it, and everybody knew it, that a conspirator would call in, or a forger would call in, to witness a fraudulent transaction. I have investigated that man's reputation, and I find that there is not a blemish upon his character in any respect. And he was not the man to give perjured testimony in regard to the execution of that will. He testified in court as everybody admits. Now this consideration, your Honor, is of very great importance. Suppose that a will were produced upon which your Honor's name appeared as a witness, and fourteen years afterwards somebody should say that the signature to that will was a forgery, obtained by a conspiracy, and that that will was admitted to probate by perjury. Those claiming under that will would point to your Honor's character as a vindication complete against the charges. And so we now, your Honor, point to the character of Andrix A. Foster, and we say that if that signature, that attesting signature of Andrix A. Foster is his, it is conclusive proof that the signature of the testator was lawfully put there, however it was done, and it is conclusive of its due execution, and you are not going to believe this woman Giles if she says the contrary.

Well now as to the other charges. I am going to consider the other charges. I propose to meet this whole case submitted in the opening argument, and in the petition both. As to the charges of robbery, poison and intimidation, force and fraud, I dismiss those as being of the same piece of cloth as these other charges, made recklessly without any proof to sustain them, without any consideration of what they meant by making such baseless and preposterous charges.

Now it is pretended that the circumstances of the execution of the will were not known. It is absolute nonsense. It was their own fault if they did not know these circumstances. They had only to ask the witnesses to the will. Dwight Foster did ask Andrix A. Foster, the witness, and had a conversation with him, and Andrix A Foster was not a man to lie to Dwight Foster, and Dwight Foster then learned, because we know that he was a man of sufficient shrewdness to learn,—one of the ablest lawyers of the Commonwealth,—we know that he gained from that witness a relation of the circumstances attending the execution of that will, as far as that witness knew them. He had the opportunity,—and he says he undoubtedly did appear here, although he has forgotten it,—he had the opportunity to ask those witnesses as to those circumstances, and we find that he did ask, we find that he knew, we find that he was present and knew all about it and had opportunity to know it.

We never sought to conceal anything. The circumstances were known, and the counsel of the Burtons, after learning everything of the circumstances, was glad to effect a compromise, and get for the Burtons five times as much as Ebenezer Smith ever intended they should have of his porperty, and Dwight

Foster told them and their father and their guardian *ad litem* that they had no case, after he knew all the facts.

And every charge which has been made public here is swept away, will be swept away, by the testimony which we shall produce, and it will show that the will of Ebenezer Smith which is now disputed was his last and valid will and testament; and if so, he had a legal right to make it and dispose of his property as he saw fit under the law. How desperate and reckless and groundless are these charges, directed against respectable people, which have been so outrageously paraded, and confidently published to the world, even before a trial originally!

I call your Honor's attention now, lastly, to the evidence which is derived from a consideration of the character of the parties in this case. First, the Burtons; I don't know whether they are in sympathy with each other or not, the elder one at any rate is responsible, but they both appear as petitioners, and I take it for granted that the younger ratifies all that his brother has done, and is participant with him in everything. All I want to know about them is, whether or not they had anything to do with bringing that Burns boy up to the point of swearing that he witnessed that probate order, at the request of Dr. Thorndike, in the absence of Eliza Smith;—whether or not, I say, they had anything to do with bringing that boy up to that point, all I want to know is, that after they had procured undoubted proof that the boy's testimony was untrue, and that a great wrong and injury had been done to Dr. Thorndike, a man of respectable standing, a man of respectability, they did not take the trouble to inform him of it. That is all I want to know about them. And the records of this court show enough from the character of the affidavits which they piled into this court, and which they or somebody for them tried to have published, but which were so vile that no newspaper could be found to publish them, and which had, and they knew it, and everybody knew it, not any bearing whatever upon any part of the case. That is all I want to know about them. And seeing the way in which this case was prosecuted at the start, the way the publications were procured before it came to trial, I denounced it then, in the presence of Gen. Butler, as a case of blackmail, and I say here that it is in my belief the basest and meanest case of blackmail which was ever attempted to be palmed off upon a court of justice. Hazen J. Burton, Sr., is not a man of such character that he is above suspicion. What kind of sons are these? What kind of pride have they to bring their old father out of that hole into which he crawled thirty years ago, and parade the infamous character which he then bore, so that the public can know it again? Family pride, decency!

Well, another party is Eliza W. Smith. In the first place she was made one of the co-conspirators; she turned states-evidence; had all the appearance of a would-be accomplice. She was willing then to convict herself of crime and enormity, in order that she might convict her mother, her sister, her brother, and her brother-in-law of odious crimes. What she can gain by breaking this will up, I cannot conceive; but the probability is that if it were set aside, she would get something in some way out of the Burtons. Your Honor has obtained some insight into her character already. A woman who had so little regard for her mother that even at the funeral of her own husband, she requested the Rev. Dr. Neale who officiated there, not to mention her mother in his prayer! Her motive is greed of gain in some way. That is one of her motives, and perhaps another motive, as strong with her as any, is hatred. She was eager to pour out all her own blood if she could only see her sister's blood poured out first,—like women of ancient times. A woman, a sister, following up this attack which was made in the first place against her sister, against a woman! It was directed mainly against Mrs. Thorndike, when she was alive—this whole case, this whole attack by these nephews and this sister. A sister who, in order to injure her sister is ready to convict her own mother, and her own brother! She is a travesty upon the very names of sister and daughter, and by as much as those very names of sister and daughter are suggestive of tenderness and love, by so much are the remarkable conduct and character of that sister and daughter worthy of greater abhorrence. These are the parties who bring these charges.

Who are the parties against whom these charges are brought? One is Dr. William H. Thorndike, a man now standing in the front rank of his profession, and in the highest branch of his profession as a surgeon, who has been in practice here thirty years; a visiting surgeon at the city hospital since 1866, one of the six men among the surgeons of this city selected by the trustees of that institution as a visiting surgeon; a man widely known, of unblemished character. He is one of the parties. Fortunately we live in a community, your Honor, in which character goes for something. When a man has led an upright, honest life, and has acquired a high reputation in the estimation of his fellow-citizens, we give him credit accordingly, when monstrous charges are brought against him. He is a man whom nobody ever even attempted to smirch until it was done through the acknowledged falsehood of Samuel J. Burns, in the trial of the Eliza Smith will case, in 1876. If your Honor please, I think that I have a proper appreciation of the character of the eminent men in my own profession, and I will say to the able counsel for the petitioners, I will say to anybody, that, if at the end of his life he shall have acquired in his profession a reputation and character for truth, honesty, modesty, ability and success, equal to that which Dr. Thorndike has already acquired in his profession, he may consider his life a success, and may die contented and happy.

Another is the son of the testator, not so widely known in this community as the eminent surgeon of whom I have spoken, but if the confidence of his fellow-citizens, if positions of high honor and trust are any indication of a man's character in the estimation of his fellow-citizens in the community in which he lives, then that son is a gentleman of unquestionable character. For years he was a Commissioner of Emigration of the State of New York. Fourteen years ago that great State appointed him as a Presidential Elector, to help cast the vote of that State for Abraham Lincoln. He has risen from one position to another in the savings bank with which he has been for many years connected, until he is now its President, and under his management that institution has stood firm through these troublous times, despite the efforts which have been made to shake its stability and weaken the confidence of the people in institutions of that kind. He has always been a man of prominence wherever he has been, during his whole life.

And it cannot be denied that Eliza Smith, the widow of Ebenezer Smith, is implicated, or was implicated, in all these crimes, if they were ever committed. If she were living now, she would be alleged as one of the conspirators. She was at that time 77 years of age ; a woman of positive character, and largely interested in public, social and religious matters. It has been attempted to be brought against her, even, that she was a religious woman, that she was a Baptist. She was a religious woman, a member of the Woman's Club, and a member of Dr. Neale's church during all the time of his ministry of over forty years, and she lived to the ripe old age of 88 years, honored and respected.

And there is finally Sarah W. Thorndike, the wife of Dr. Thorndike, the mother of his children, and the faithful manager of his household. Her tastes were mostly social and domestic. She performed those duties which belong peculiarly to a wife ; consequently her position depended upon that of her husband, and the high character and position of her husband gave her a position which she had the character and ability to maintain with credit and success ; and no woman could have done it better. Her tastes and occupations being what they were, I cannot say that she was widely known, except as the Burtons, instigated by malice and hatred, by giving publicity to lies and the false statements of thieves and perjurers, gave her a notoriety which she did not deserve. No woman in this community is safe against attacks of that kind. Any woman's reputation may be injured in that way ; only, thank God, it is the misfortune of but few women in this world to have such men as they are for nephews. She was the youngest of the family of Ebenezer Smith, and as is often the case, she had the misfortune to be the favorite of her mother, whose chief comfort and support she was during all the trials and troubles with which that unfortunate family were afflicted. This was the source of all her woes· All her misfortunes had their origin in filial duty and affection. I wish that she might have lived to see herself again vindicated, as she will be, far less ably, but I trust no less conclusively, than she was formerly vindicated upon another occasion, when that very able and upright man Judge Hoar met, before a jury, the attack which was made upon the will of her mother. But she died while this case was pending. She is free from the care and anxiety which would naturally come from such outrageous conduct as her nephews have been guilty of, and I believe that she has gone to a better place than this, especially as their former illustrious counsel, in making in this place for the first time in his life of which I ever heard, a profession of religion, had the piety and gentlemanliness and kindness to wish that she might go to a worse place.

Now these are the parties on the one hand who bring this case, and on the other the parties against whom these charges are brought. Persons of mean character, or at least of suspicious character, with every presumption against them, presumptions which would be against them even if their character were the very best, bring these charges against people of the highest character and standing, who have every presumption in their favor, presumptions which would be in their favor, even if their characters were bad. They bring a case which would require the highest order of proof, establishing the crimes which they charge beyond a reasonable doubt, but they fall short of even the lowest order of proof. They bring such a case, your Honor, as was never sustained in this Commonwealth, which nobody else ever had the audacity even to attempt to sustain in this Commonwealth. With all the presumptions of law in favor of the rightfulness of what has been done, after all this long lapse of time of fourteen years, when the memory of transactions of a period so remote is dim, faded and defective, when even those who were engaged in this case formerly have forgotten what evidence was given, what amount of evidence would it take to convince your Honor that these parties were guilty of the charges which have been made against them, or would induce your Honor to unsettle an estate of a quarter of a million dollars so long after it has been settled?

That is all I shall now say in regard to the evidence in this case. We have not raised as yet any technical objection to trying this case here. We are now eager to have it tried, in order that the people may know what a groundless case has been brought. We have done more than the law required us, and considering the way in which the case has been prosecuted, I think we may fairly claim the right of a trial, under these circumstances, although it was not necessary to a determination of the case in our favor.

When the first petition was brought I moved to dismiss that part of it which related to the will of Eliza Smith, and it was dismissed. I was not so clear at that time that the same principles of law which applied to that case also apply to the case of the will of Ebenezer Smith; but I am satisfied as the case now stands under the amended petition,—I am confident, that the same principles do now apply which applied to that case, and I shall take, your Honor, perhaps twenty minutes longer to consider the legal points.

(*Recess till 2 o'clock.*)

May it please your Honor: When the court adjourned this forenoon, I had come to certain legal positions which I was about to present to the court as part of the defence upon which we rely. That is, that this court has not the lawful power to revoke the probate of Ebenezer Smith's will in this particular case. That will was in the first place admitted to probate by the decree of this court, and an appeal was taken from that decree. Now, it makes no difference really, whether the decree of this court was in favor of the will or against it, as far as this case is now concerned. The will does not rest upon the decree of this court, this minor court. It rests upon the decree of the Supreme Court of Probate, because this case went up there upon the same issues. The same issues were raised in the reasons for appeal upon which it went up to that court, that are raised in the amended petition. It makes no difference, I say, it would have made no difference, whether the decree of this court was for the will or against the will. In either case the effect of an appeal would have been the same. An appeal vacates the decree. That is the point. And that is familiar law, and it has also been decided by the Supreme Court of this Commonwealth, in the case of *Boynton* vs. *Dyer*, in the 18th of Pickering, page 4, and in the case of *Paine* vs. *Cowden*, in 17 Pickering, 42. But it is so familiar as law that it is hardly necessary to cite any cases in support of it. This matter was also decided in England, and I need only refer to the name of Sir John Nicholl as an authority, in the case of *Newell* vs. *Weeks*, 2d Phillimore, page 230. Sir John Nicholl in that case held that it was too late to ask for the revocation of the probate after a decree of the Appellate Court sustaining the will. Why, your Honor, if it were not so, if after the Supreme Court has passed its judgment upon the same issues, the petitioners can turn right round just as soon as the case gets back in this court and carry it up to that court again by appeal from the decision of this court,—why, a man could keep a case going back and forth between these two courts forever, and there would be no limit. Suppose this case goes up to the Supreme Court now, and they are overruled in that court, what is to prevent their beginning again just the same as they have begun here, and go right over the same ground again, unless your Honor at the outset dismisses their petition because it has been decided? Now I refer to the reasons of appeal filed in this court fourteen years ago by Andrew N. Burton, guardian *ad litem* of these same petitioners. There were three sets of reasons of appeal in this case upon which this case went up; one by the Burtons, another by Arthur G. Smith, and one by Thomas P. Smith. Compare the allegations in the present petition with the reasons of appeal on which this case went to the Supreme Court of Probate fourteen years ago. All through, your Honor will find that the same issues were raised in the reasons of appeal in regard to the validity of that will which are raised here in this petition. That part of the case has been decided which is comprehended by those reasons of appeal upon which the case went up. It has been decided by the Supreme Court of Probate, and in fact it is a matter of record, that certain issues were framed there for a jury covering these points that were raised. One of those issues was that the will was signed by Ebenezer Smith, or by some person in his presence, and by his express direction, and was properly witnessed; also that Ebenezer Smith was of sound mind, and also the issue of undue influence, and fraud. These issues were framed in that case, and were decided upon by a jury in favor of the will. And the whole case was passed upon by the Supreme Court of Probate, and that court having made its decree, the will stands upon the decree of that court, and this is not the place to attack a decree of the Supreme Court of Probate. The will does not stand upon a decree of this minor court, but upon that of the Supreme Court. What is the use of taking an appeal, and what does an appeal amount to, unless that appeal is conclusive upon this court? There would be no end to the discordance between this court and the Supreme Court, if a decree of that Supreme Court could be attacked here in this court. Why is it an Appellate Court? Why is it made so by statute, if the decree of that court is not conclusive and binding upon this court?

Furthermore, what is still more important in this case, is, that these petitioners are estopped from attempting to procure the revocation of the probate of this will, estopped by their acquiescence after they had learned the facts. They are estopped to assert the nullity of a will after accepting a bequest under that will, and retaining it after obtaining knowledge of the facts on which they seek to set the will aside, and after beginning litigation to procure the revocation of the probate of the will. *Mr. Chandler:* Have you any authority for that? *Mr. Drury:* Yes, sir. *Mr. Loring:* An excellent one.

Mr. Drury: A great deal of authority. I will state the case of *Hamblett* vs. *Hamblett*, 6 N. H. 333; *Bell* vs. *Armstrong*, 1 Addams 365; *Braham* vs. *Burchell*, 3 Addams 256; *Holt* vs. *Rice*, 54 N. H. 398, where a case went up on an appeal and a lawyer of Lowell was the guardian *ad litem*, and accepted a legacy after it had gone up to the Supreme Court, and accepted it under a mistake as to what the effect would be of accepting it. This confirmed the case of *Hamblett* vs. *Hamblett*, to which I have already referred your Honor. The same considerations apply in the case of *Hyde* vs. *Baldwin*, 17 Pickering 308; *Smith* vs. *Smith*, 14 Gray 532. In both these cases,—one was a case at law and the other was a case in equity—it was held that a person who had received a benefit under the will was estopped from denying its validity—that was held to apply both to law and equity. *Landis* vs. *Landis*, 1 Grant, Penn., 249. The law is that if a man does an act ratifying a deed or will by taking property under it he shall not afterwards dispute the validity of it. *Deslondes* vs. *New Orleans*, 14 La. Annual 552. "When heirs at law have once acquiesced in a will by accepting some bequests under it, neither they nor those claiming under it are at liberty to assert its nullity." They accepted the money given to them by that will, and they still hold on to the money; held on to it for two years after they pretended to have found out new facts—pretended they had found out only two years ago—that is only pretense as we shall see—and still hold on to it. That is an acquiescence in, and ratification of, the will and they are estopped by it. They have never even offered to give up that money which they have received, and it has been shown that they did receive it. They received it. It was paid to their guardian properly. Their guardian was properly appointed. They cannot put up the plea of infancy, and it was not paid to them until after they became of age. They had the money after they became of age. They received it then, and they still hold on to it and they never have offered to give it up.

They also not only are estopped because they received, and still retain, the benefit under the will, but they are also estopped because they received, and still retain, a larger benefit under that compromise which was made; and at the proper time, your Honor, I shall refer you to the authorities bearing upon the validity of that compromise.

So the two legal positions which we hold are that this Court is concluded by the decree of the Supreme Court of Probate, the decree of this court having been vacated by appeal therefrom, and the will standing upon the decree of the Supreme Court. Secondly, these petitioners are estopped by their acquiescence in the will and in the compromise they have made, accepting the benefit and holding on to it, and thereby at this very moment acquiescing in and ratifying that will and compromise. They have not placed themselves in a situation in which they can legally contest the will, or defeat the compromise, on any ground whatever.

Closing Argument of John A. Loring, Esq.,

Counsel for Isaac T. Smith.

JANUARY 21, 1879.

May it please your Honor : — In the words of another, " the time has now come when I feel that I shall truly stand in need of all your indulgence. It is not merely the novelty of this proceeding that perplexes me, for the mind gradually gets accustomed to the strangest things; nor is it the magnitude of the cause that oppresses me, for I am borne up and cheered by the conviction of the justice of my client's cause, which must by this time be shared by all who have heard the evidence given in. But it is the very force of this conviction, the feeling that it operates on the mind of the court, the feeling that it operates rightly, which now dismays me with the apprehension that my unworthy way of handling it may, for the first time, injure it. And while others have trembled for a guilty client, or been anxious in a doubtful cause, or been crippled with the consciousness of some hidden weakness, or chilled by the influence, or dismayed by the hostility of public opinion, I, knowing that here there is no guiltiness to conceal, nor anything save the resources of perjury to dread, am haunted with the apprehension that my feeble discharge of this duty may not be worthy of the cause I represent." But with the assurance, may it please the Court, — and I now speak my own words, — that the clear merit of my cause may more than suffice for the weakness of its advocate, I will lay before your Honor, as briefly as possible, the facts that are material to be considered.

Fourteen years ago, Ebenezer Smith, a man well known and honored in this city of Boston, died. He left a paper bearing his name, and purporting to be his last direction for the distribution of his property. His spattered signature now attacked was attested by three witnesses, who state as follows: " The above instrument was signed, sealed, published and declared, by the above-named Ebenezer Smith, as and for his last will and testament, in the presence of us, the undersigned, who, at the request of the said Ebenezer, and in his presence, and the presence of each other, have subscribed our names hereto."

(Signed)   " ANDRIX A. FOSTER,

ANNA G. GILES,

MARGARET PATTERSON."

This court, after hearing all the evidence in the presence of the able lawyers who then represented all the parties opposing the will,—I need not catalogue them, for they are fresh in the mind of the court, these contestants being the children of Eliza W. Smith, the Burton boys, and that is all,—decided that this paper was what it purported to be, the act and the last will of Ebenezer Smith. After the will had been finally established by this court, by the Supreme Court and by agreement of all the immediate heirs at law of the testator, the executors named in that will proceeded in their duty, in the duty they were bound to perform, to execute the trust imposed upon them. They sold the lands to those who bought them, relying on the validity of the probate of the will; they distributed the proceeds to creditors and legatees, who received their money and signed a due acquittance; and then, having settled up their trust, they were by the further action of this court discharged therefrom, and the estate of Ebenezer Smith became among the things that were.

Among those who had attacked this will at its inception were two boys, children of a daughter of Ebenezer Smith, who had died eleven years before him, and of her husband, Hazen J. Burton, Sr. These boys who had, since their mother's death, been alienated from their grandfather's family, had in all the wills made by Ebenezer Smith, from 1859 to 1864, being one will in 1859, one will in August, 1864, and two codicils, and one will on October 5, 1864, which was this will, received just $500, and they had stood by the wills of this testator from 1859 to 1864 the recipients of $500 in all the wills that he made, and of nothing more. The father of these two boys whose character I shall touch upon, gently perhaps, but sufficiently hereafter,—the father instituted proceedings to set aside that will of October 5, 1864. His counsel was Dwight Foster, a former judge of the Supreme Court, whom he retained before the will was offered for probate, who investigated the case, saw Andrix A. Foster one of the witnesses of the will, gave the matter all that attention that was necessary, applied to it all the diligence for which he is so famed, and all the skill and ability for which he is so well known. He and Charles Levi Woodbury together, and Hazelton & Ware,—these three firms, or these three lawyers, had the case of this will under their consideration, and they bent all their energies to seek how they might set it down, prevent its being set up, and the result of it all was that they came to the conclusion that the will of October 5, 1864, was the last will of Ebenezer Smith, and a compromise was made by which these young men, through their guardian, received $5,000. Here were five or six appellants; the case could have been kept in court some two or three years, and the real estate, which had then fallen almost down to its last point and was falling more, would realize less and less. A long litigation would have been ruinous—and the executors, well knowing the character of Burton, senior, adopted the idea of a compromise. A compromise was made, and the guardian of these boys, authorized by this court so to do, received the $5,000, signed an agreement by which he accepted that sum in full settlement of all the claims of these wards upon the estate of Ebenezer Smith. In addition to the counsel whom I have named, to wit: Dwight Foster, Charles Levi Woodbury, Hazelton & Ware, I will add Thomas P. Smith. I have named all but the last. I know him not, and as Judge Hoar reserved to himself that caution, when asked a question as to whether if two witnesses swore that his Honor the Judge of this Court was seen standing on his head out in Court Square, he would believe it, and replied, I believe, "for the veracity of one I will not vouch," so I will not vouch either for the veracity or the integrity of Thomas P. Smith. He added not enough to the power that came from these others whom I have named to bring a successful result, for, as we have seen, their efforts were not successful.

After the will had been established the estate was settled, and as a consequence, titles have been passed, houses have been built, and innocent men have spent their money, relying upon the judgment of this court as giving them title. And now, after these fourteen years have elapsed, and after these lands have passed into the hands of innocent purchasers, upon which, as in West Medford, they have spent a hundred thousand dollars in improvements, after these fourteen years enjoyment of the $5,000 which was paid their guardian upon the faith of their honest compromise, protected not now by infancy, having not infancy for an excuse, but with the knowledge, although without the honesty or the self-respect, which I shall have occasion to note hereafter, which they would have were they not tainted as they are by something that I will name hereafter, they again besiege your Honor's court with new charges against the will.

There is a certain lack of good faith in this proceeding, and as I recall the testimony in the early proceedings, this whole thing looks very much like the tail to a kite that was the chief toy or instrument of their amusement, or like the tender of a locomotive which they were to drive through the judgments of this court. Two years ago they attacked their grandmother's will; two years ago they commenced proceedings here which resulted in the will of that grandmother being set up, by which will these two same young men got just $500, as they had from their grandfather. Five hundred dollars was the mark set upon their heads from 1859 through the whole life of their grandfather, and the same mark or brand, whatever it may be called, was set upon them as their value, or at any rate as the measure of regard which they were held in by both their grandfather and their grandmother. They attacked their grandmother's will, they opposed its probate, the court set aside their opposition as vain, they appealed to the Supreme Court, and they had for their counsel no less a counsellor than A. A. Ranney, who, when he strikes, strikes from the shoulder, and when he hits it is felt. Judge Hoar, who has made himself familiar to this cause, and somewhat has occupied, and does occupy, quite a prominent position as one of the instruments by which we have unearthed these scandalmongers and perjurers, one of the strongest weapons that has been furnished us by which to expose their fraud and wickedness, — he and his son acting for the executor of the grandmother's will, resisted the attack upon that will.

It would seem as if the attack upon their old grandfather's will, which gave them but $500, with the little evidence which they had been able to discover against it, would have been sufficient to have deterred them from attacking the will of their grandmother, but it was not sufficient. And it was twelve years after the old man was buried, beyond the infelicities of his pestered existence, beyond the reach of creditors, beyond the reach of Eliza W. Smith's persistent efforts to grasp his money, that his widow died, and died in the arms of Mrs. Thorndike, and was not murdered by Mrs. Thorndike as the Burton boys foully suggested in the office of Judge Hoar, and she was buried, too. The dull tones of the funeral bell were the tocsin which summoned the tribe of Burtons to that attack; the vultures gathered for another unholy feast because they were not satisfied with their grandmother's will, that they should have but $500. And to get more the same cry was raised then that is now, of fraud, of undue influence, and I may add of murder, for this was a subject which they considered, and they even suggested that crime as having been committed by their aunt, Mrs. Thorndike, the wife of Dr. Thorndike, who is esteemed in this community among the first. By reason of their presenting in his presence two affidavits, one from a doctor, and the other from a nurse, that her medicine was drugged, Judge Hoar denounced them, and told them to leave, and they left. But these cries rang out, and these unholy hands were again laid, and this time on the fair record of a spotless life. Why, it was in that case that the Burns boy,—I believe that was his name, I have heard of it in this trial, and I remember it, although it was months ago,—it was in that attempt to defame Mrs. Thorndike that the Burns boy testified. He testified against her; he stands indicted to-day for his perjury. How many more witnesses there were in that case who were indicted for perjury I know not, for I was not then engaged, may it please your Honor, in the painful and disagreeable duty, and the revolting task of writing the biography of Eliza W. Smith and Hazen J. Burton, Sr. How many of them who have testified here deserve that dispensation I think your Honor and myself would agree.

Three weeks, or more, were occupied by the court, his Honor Judge Colt and a jury, and these same young men contested then, I doubt not with the same zeal, I know not whether with the same disposition, for I knew not then of all their eccentricities, to say the least. The result of that contest was that the grandmother's will was set up, and there seemed to be an end of the strife. The will was set up, sustained by the verdict of a jury, and final judgment was entered thereupon, and "all the clouds that lowered upon our house" seemed in the deep bosom of that judgment buried. But this was not to be. The spirit that inspired all this previous litigation survived so many defeats, and so we are here. Fourteen years, compromise signed and sealed, the opinion of wise counsel given them, the judgment of the Supreme Court and a verdict of a jury presented for their careful consideration, and what is the next step that is taken?

It would seem as if after so much labor, so much waiting, attended with always the same result, their litigious spirit would have lost its energy, it would seem as if they, by that time,—as if this Hazen J. Burton, Jr., would have "let by-gones be by-gones," as his good old grandmother used to tell him whenever he went to see her, and, as I argue, he was complaining to her of the $500 which his grandfather had given him, and no more. One would have supposed after all this that he would have let the by-gones be by-gones. But no.

About the month of May last, I should think it was, the owners of real estate, the lawyers and all others who had been wont to regard the decrees of this, and of the highest court of the State, to be final in all matters and questions submitted to their determination, as established facts, as sure safe-guards and protections if regarded and obeyed, were startled by the announcement that what fourteen years ago was decreed by this court to be the last will and testament of Ebenezer Smith, and also so decreed by the Supreme Court on appeal thereto, was not the will at all of the alleged testator, but was a fiction and a fraud. Startled at the facts announced, at the consequences claimed, at the wickedness alleged, and at the theory that, if these facts were proved, the decree of this court and decree of the Supreme Court of the Commonwealth were nullities, and of no effect, the public were informed that a will made and approved fourteen years ago by two courts, a will, under which nearly $500,000 worth of property had been held, divided and conveyed, gave no right to hold and no power to convey. The novelty of the announcement was not greater than the terror it excited, and well it might. We met curious and anxious conveyancers running hither and thither from the office of my brother Drury, and hither and thither to the office doubtless of Mr. Chandler, to know whether the titles which they had passed of the property in West Medford, and which was held by banks under mortgage, and to take which they had been induced by the certificates of these wise men, good counsellors and good conveyancers,— whether these titles were of any value, and whether all this proclamation which was then paraded in the papers had any force, or was merely something they knew not what. And this alarm was not diminished, may it please the Court, and I think you will realize that fact fully, by the fact that this doctrine was proclaimed in the papers by that remarkable lawyer and man, whose name was double leaded in the columns of the day as its champion and proclaimer. He was a bold man to take this ground, and to announce this purpose, and Benjamin F. Butler is that man. His courage, not to say audacity, led this charge, and your Honor well remembers the abundant epithets he heaped on my client, Mr. Smith, and the fierce denunciation he hurled at all who ventured to deny *his* so called *facts*, and his so called law. He endorsed the sworn statement of these two young men, once obscure and unknown, but now conspicuous and notorious, and gave emphasis to them by his powerful invective and his bold assurance. He cried fraud, coercion and compulsion, and the press of the day echoed his ravings. But his voice was soon hushed. After two hearings before your Honor, quietly but vigorously met, as he was by my friend, Mr. Drury, feebly supported by myself, that great man disappeared from this contest, if I can dignify it as such, and the place that once knew him has known him "no more forever."

I hold in my hand the original petition for the vacating of the probate of this will, well styled by my friend, Mr. Drury, the "old powder-boat petition." I have here this budget of affidavits in its support, and I shall have the honor to submit that they are as harmless as nursery rhymes, or as a disastrous political campaign. And not only did these petitioners assail the final judgment of this court upon the will of their grandfather, but they assailed the judgment of this court and of the Supreme Court upon their grandmother's will. And this crusade, this rough handling of final decrees, they undertook, not wearied at all by the unsuccessful effort of that pious but persistent father of theirs in 1864 and 1865 to prevent such a decree on the first, and of their own in 1876 to prevent the last. General Butler is not here, but his mantle with new decorations has fallen on other shoulders, and we have a new campaign inaugurated. The old double-barrel petition has exploded, and a new one of only one barrel is brought to bear. In the attack on the wills of Eben'r and Eliza,—and the Court remembers that the original petition joined those two together,—filed in 1878 in this Court, they charged that both these wills were false and forged, and everything else, and that the judgment of the Probate Court in regard to both of them was "all vanity and vexation of spirit."

Under the lead of their new commander, under the guidance of their new counsel and without the aid of the hero of many battles whom they had chosen to lead this desperate attack, without the aid of the man who is heralded as the friend of the oppressed and the poor, without the aid of him whom we find standing at the head of more desperate legal battles than any man of his day, or of many a day before him, — a man who could spend I don't know how many weeks trying to wrest a verdict from a New York jury in a claim against General Sheridan for I don't know how many millions of dollars, and do it and come out as fresh as the rosebud which he carries in his lappel, without a verdict for one cent, — without his wonderful ability under the guidance of the new counsel whom they have chosen, they bear down upon us. The attack on the wills of Ebenezer and Eliza, which was made by that original petition supported by all those affidavits,— the attack on those two wills was abandoned. My impression is, — I venture to suggest, that it was too much for the successor of him who was removed, and so the present commander of this "band of noble brothers," aunts and brothers-in-law, with his headquarters I should think somewhere on the Stonington Line between here and New York drops the attack on Eliza's will and brings all his force against Ebenezer's. One barrel of the original, and as I have called it, double-barreled petition, had exploded and they have rammed their whole charge into the other barrel and they fired their gun and the smoke has cleared away and the will still stands up to the present day, but the petitioners are here asking the same thing they have been asking for a large portion of their matured lives, and in vain. And we then, and thereafter, from the inauguration of the present counsel for the petitioners, have encountered an amended mode of warfare, less merciful, more malignant than that which was waged with such vigor and force by my friend General Butler, whose retiring from the cause and whose absence therefrom I have never ceased to regret from the time that he left those two young men and their cause never more to come again. I should have welcomed him back on the 4th of December when we began and I should have welcomed him each morning down to the 21st of January when we begin to see the begining of the end.

Your Honor remembers that while the cause was in the hands of General

Butler, the executors moved that these boys should pay back to the executors the $5,000 which they had received under the terms of a compromise made in good faith by the executors in regard to all these controversies, and that that motion was opposed with great energy and power by General Butler himself, and that the result of that was that the court granted the motion of the executors, and ordered these petitioners to pay back that $5,000, or they must stop enquiry as to this will. And so long as they held the $5,000 which they had received, paid to them in good faith upon the condition that they would stop all talk, and take that as more than they were entitled to, for the sake of getting rid of them, until they paid back their money, it was determined that their voices should no longer be heard in this court. The money was not repaid, and these petitioners appealed, and had the executors maintained the position which they then occupied, your Honor certainly would not have been occupied as you are at this period, because that cause could not have been decided by the Supreme Court to which they appealed that question for months after this, and there would have been another year's delay. What did the executors do? Well, they had heard this talk ever since the trial of the Eliza Smith will, they saw the undying spirit of fight, and I don't know what to call it,—litigious and quarrelsome temper of those boys, their determination to bring a suit against somebody, in the hopes that that somebody would pay them some money in order to get rid of them, whether they were entitled to it or not, and they said, " well, we will not interpose any technical objections ; they charge us, Isaac T. Smith and Dr. Thorndike, with forgery ; they charge us with fraud and coercion ; they charge us with,—well, enough crimes, if half had been committed, to make us outcasts from society ; let us hear what they have to say ; we shrink not from the investigation ; we desire it if they mean what they say." And so they waived,—these two gentlemen whose characters up to that time never had been assailed, never had been assailable—Dr. Thorndike here in this community having established for himself by his skill and his knowledge and experience, having gained for himself, I may say, the first position in one branch of his profession above all his peers, and Mr. Smith, who, up to that time had not been publicly attacked by anyone, — these gentlemen waived repayment of the $5,000. That eccentric sort of a defamer, Mr. O'Connor, if that is his name, who appeared here this morning, brought on here from New York, invented by Hazen J. Burton, Jr., discovered by him and put into action this morning ;—he exploded through the cross-examination of my brother Drury and Mr. George P. Smith ;—well, there was not enough remaining of that O'Connor as a witness to do anything with, excepting to mark the spot where he once stood. How much of his time he had spent in going round,— well, I don't believe there were business men enough in Boston who would allow him to speak to them, from his own story, or who would listen to a charge from him against Issac T. Smith. I will come to that by and by. But up to that time, sir, the character of Mr. Isaac T. Smith had stood where it stands now, and where he has placed it by his own integrity, his own industry, his own fidelity to his conscience and his God, and by which he will stand to

7

the end of his days. And yet they are assailed! General Butler has headed off a petition charging them with fraud, and the newspapers had circulated it, and they had been slandered so far as evil tongues could slander them. I don't mean the tongue of General Butler to be evil, but I mean the tongues of the Burton boys and their venerable old father. I mean, that their tongues had been slandering and slashing away the characters of two good men, one a citizen of Boston, and the other of New York, who said " we must meet it." We must meet these attacks upon our character, which were then, so far as evil tongues could slander them, befouled either by the actual guilt or by the wicked slander of these Burton men, if I can call them men, who have spent so much of their own time, and so much of the time of this county in this nefarious scheme, in the bold assaults of blackmailers, and we must sift the whole thing to the bottom, and see whether there is any merit in their case, or whether they are what they seem to be. The press of Boston was at every hearing polluting the atmosphere by detailed recitals of the foul things charged upon these gentlemen. The morning papers were made entertaining at the breakfast tables and at the evening cigar, by Isaac T. Smith's atrocities and Dr. Thorndike's abominations. And conscious of no wrong, assured of their own integrity and uprightness, they removed all technical obstacles to a full investigation, and so we are here, and we have had a busy time. With their new counsel commenced a new petition as an amendment to the old, and then ensued such a flood of interrogatories, depositions and motions that life was made a burden to my brother Drury and myself. Those sacred letters, " B. C. " were given a new significance, and Burton and Chandler were synonyms of harrassings, worryings, harryings, badgerings, annoyances and plagues. But clear consciences, good constitutions and a kind Providence have " lengthened out our lives," and brother Drury and myself have come to see " this joyous day ; " and it may be well called so, both by us and by your Honor, I think, for we begin to see the beginning of the end of, what we regard on our side, a most atrocious and uncalled for attack. We congratulate ourselves, and allow us to congratulate your Honor, that so near appears to be the probability that we shall have some other business to attend to than to ferret out the iniquities of the Burton family and Eliza W. Smith.

May it please your Honor, I listened with astonishment as the petitioners' counsel stood in this presence as a lawyer and sketched with a certain facility of rhetoric the story upon which he proposed to ask this court to set aside its own decree, entered fourteen years ago, and upon which titles to millions now rest, which some say must be shattered if the request of these petitioners is granted. This story was of the threats, intimidations, fraud, force and forgery by which Ebenezer Smith's large wealth was grasped from a semi-conscious, dying man ; of the brick cell, wherein the old man could be safe from the power of his own wife and children, not from the power of Isaac T. Smith, because he lived in New York ; then of his fear of poison, causing his cup to be first rinsed and his food to be first tasted by others before he would venture to partake,—and Hazen J. Burton, Sr., is the man who testifies to this,—of the doctrine of primogeniture which his eldest son sought to inculcate to his father. This, may it please the court, that I am reciting, is the opening speech or picture which was made by the present counsel for these petitioners, and which was sent broadcast through the land, and which was sent to the trustees of the Metropolitan Savings Bank by somebody, conceived by somebody, in order to blacken the character and the fair fame of my client Mr. Smith. These are his statements; we will see by and by whether they are his witnesses' statements. He spoke of the bold and desperate importunities which so beset the testator that in April, 1862, he writes to Hazen J. Burton, "I must fight or be robbed of the last pound of flesh and the last dollar." The bold and unjustifiable application of that phrase in that letter to the old man's suffering by reason of his children's misconduct, instead of relating to the sufferings which the mind of that successful manager was then enduring by reason of the downfall of value, is the boldest and the "baddest" attempt that ever I listened to in a court of justice where we seek to do justice to our antagonists, however severe we may hold them to the consequences of what they say. I shall show your Honor that that letter was not written having in mind any unkindness of his children toward him or being a freak of any unkindness on his part towards his children, for he loved his children and they loved him, and those children were not robbing him, but his creditors were. He speaks of the manœuverings to cut off the Burtons; of the closer imprisonment to which the old man was subjected as he grew feebler and so more easily influenced. He speaks of the distrust of those about him; that he guarded his treasures with a cane in his hand *even when asleep*. And these were the words of the gentleman who opened this case. He talked of papers destroyed by Dr. Thorndike, who burned them because they were in conflict with the will; and of the fear and distrust the old man had of those about him and in whose power he was, and of the affection and love he bore these petitioners who were cut off forever from his sight. The counsel then asks your Honor to mark the result of all these doings, namely, the will of August 13, 1864, by which the old man's widow gets one-third of his estate, his eldest son, Mr. Isaac T. Smith, one-half of the residue, and his two living daughters the other half between them; then certain legacies to relatives in New Hampshire, and the sum of $500 to each of these Burton boys. Then he says that even then the "conspirators" were not content, and to accomplish more for themselves the old man just about to die, in the last stages of dropsy, was drugged with whiskey as a last resort; and I remember distinctly that his own witness, by whom he sought to prove that these children and this mother were drugging and drowning the senses of their dying parent and husband, their own witness, who administered the whiskey, said that he put a glass of whiskey and water on the table at night and there would be most of it there the next morning, and that was all he took. Drugging with whiskey! Where is his proof? Did he state that on his own responsibility and think we should believe it because he said it? If he should make his statement again in the opening of a case, I should wait until he proved it, as I have in this case, before I should believe it. A vivid imagination possibly may have led him from that accurate investigation of his cause, because this drugging by whiskey is as grave a charge as the poisoning by Mrs. Thorndike of her blessed old mother, —stealing away from him by rum his wits in order that he would make a will which he never would make if he had his wits about him. We stand here where justice needs no disguises and where we establish fame and " defame," — when the truth so renders it necessary. And reaching this point of the drugging of this good old man by this widow and these daughters, the counsel, I presume shocked with the horrors he had painted,—I remember him perfectly, —with a sad and serious countenance, said, "I would forbear, but the story must be told," and he told it, and it is his story, but the story of no one else. He need not have told it. He had done better had he forborne, for his story was a fiction, for which he is responsible and which his witnesses do not prove.

One fact he does state, and I give him the benefit of that. I state the same as a fact. He says Isaac T. Smith did go to Rollins's office on October 5th, and October 5th has a mystic power. October 5, 1864, he says that Isaac T. Smith went to Rollins's office and asked him to draw a will for his father, that it was drawn to the satisfaction of the "conspirators and confederates," as he calls them, but cutting off the Burtons with only $500 each. And here is the climax of his story, — and I ask your Honor to be patient with me in my reference to what he said, because I think that statement made by counsel, who are recognized by their brethren as men upon whom we can look as guides to their clients through the perils of litigation, are important. I think there is a character given to the causes we represent by the mode in which we conduct them, and by the statements that we make in regard thereto. I speak not now of the duty which we owe to the community, nor to our clients. I speak of the effect of our own personal conduct upon the causes we represent, and therefore I dwell upon his opening remarks. Here at this very point, after stating that Mr. Smith went to Rollins's office, I find the climax of his story. Here is the era in his case which settles all its future. The petitioners' counsel says the will was executed about the 9th or 10th of October, a day or two after a consultation of physicians who pronounced Mr. Smith's case hopeless.

Mr Chandler: Excuse me, that is not so stated. *Mr. Loring:* He says this will was executed about the 9th or 10th. *Mr. Chandler:* Yes. But what precedes that? You will find I stated it very carefully. Suppose you read what I said in this connection of yours.

Mr. Loring: You said this will was executed on the 9th or 10th of October. *Mr. Chandler:* Those are not the words I used, sir. Here are the words: — "So far as discovered, the execution of this will took place about the 9th or 10th." "So far as discovered." I was very careful to put these words in.

Mr. Loring: Then so far as he had been able to discover he had found that that will was executed on these days. Now if he meant to say that with a mental reservation, giving him a chance to say that he hadn't discovered anything about it, but using that equivocal expression in order to cover up a conviction that it was not signed on these days, I will leave that for him to say. If he meant to say " so far as has been discovered," why couldn't he have gone on when he was carrying his expressions that extent and say " we have not discovered anything, we know it was signed on the 5th ?" He says within three days after that he died. Well, he died on the 12th. He said that without any " so far as has been discovered."

Mr. Chandler. Nine and three are twelve.

Mr. Loring. Well, I am astonished at the attempt by a playful reference to arithmetic to strip this criticism of its force. I say he stated that that will was executed on the 9th or 10th, and I refer to the very accurate,—and I doubt if there is an *i* not dotted or a *t* not crossed in that opening of his,—that romance of his that appeared in the Daily *Advertiser* of the next morning. I believe there is not an error to be found in that between that and his opening, and his own production, and I say in it he said that the will was executed on the 9th or 10th. He said the testator was then in a comatose, lethargic state, wholly incompetent to transact any business or to follow the reading of a paper, that this will was produced and he was told it was there for him to sign. This counsel for the petitioners then informed this court that the testator knew enough to murmur and knew no more. He knew enough to murmer " my will" and to feebly utter " no," and then, that he relapsed into a semi-conscious state. And then, says this counsel, " Isaac T. Smith took his father's hand in his and wrote his father's name himself upon the will." And then he exclaims " that the spattered signature (and that is the spattered signature, which your Honor remembers) needs no expert to stamp it as a forgery." Well, my experience and my acquaintance lead me to make this simple remark, that a forger generally tries to imitate the hand of the original, and if Isaac T. Smith was a forger of that, he did not make the attempt that a forger invariably does. I will come to the forgery by and by. He says " the dying man knew not what was done." He says that man " never knew or understood it." He said " he never signed it and died in three days." He dont say " so far as he discovered" he died in three days, but he says he died in three days after he signed it. And this will was admitted to probate, says the learned counsel, by perjury. And in his peroration he informs us that these petitioners are not here wtth the heinous design of blackmailing the respondents, that whether they ever recover anything or not they insist upon asking that this forged will be set aside, and that done they will cheerfully accept the consequences. That these two irreproachable young men immediately upon discovering two years ago this fraud, commenced a thorough investigation, determined to bring these wrong doers to account, compelled to this by their self respect and by the respect they had for their grandfather ; they feel it a duty to defend him ; that they are the sole defenders of his honor, his name and his wishes. And then he informs us what " every christian man and woman" will think of the Burtons if these facts are proved as he believes, (or he said he believed it,) and thus ends his tale.

I will inform him, and I think your Honor's decree will inform him, what will be thought of the Burtons not only by Christians, but by Turks, Hottentots and even " the Heathen Chinee" now, in that these so-called facts have been proved to be the boldest lies supported only by the perjury, and by attempted subornation of perjury, and by the efforts of the ringleader of this band of malignant villifiers and slanderers. Humanity shudders when filthy ghouls sneak into the sepulchre and steal away the body of the dead, but darker is the crime and blacker is the infamy when, fired by an unholy lust of gold, men seek to take away the reputation of the dead, whose silent lips cannot defend themselves. And all this clamor and these calumnies, his story having been told, were spread through the columns of the press, and the case has been made notorious and these foul slanders have been trumpeted abroad.

I remember one of the papers intimated that Mr. Isaac T. Smith probably would not be seen about the precients of this court room, he having been absent at the next hearing. I don't know who inspired that intimation, but Isaac T. Smith's presence this morning must have inspired the conviction that he was here and that he was not afraid to be here, and Mr. Chandler's cross-examination of him, which he claimed was going to do so much good, Mr. Smith was willing to meet and hear what he had to say. I remember, may it please your Honor, and I regard this as my own duty, that when application was made, or when the court was informed that counsel for the petitioners desired Mr. Isaac T. Smith to be here, the counsel stated to your Honor, and the statement was made public, that I promised at the former hearing that Isaac T. Smith would be here and I had not kept my promise. I denied his statement then. I said to him that what I did say was this, at the former hearing, that he asked me if Isaac T. Smith was going to be here and I said "I have every reason to think he will," and he accepted the amendment. The acceptance of an amendment does not wipe out the offence of the first bill. Where is the apology? Opportunity has been offered him to give it. He has let the opportunity pass and it will never be offered him again. When a man makes an attack in public, the same publicity should be given to his apology.

Mr. Chandler: Didn't I speak to you after that hearing, sir? *Mr. Loring:* You did, sir; and I will say what you said : that you perhaps did a little over-state that. And I said you should be careful how you deal with your professional brethren, that you had enough to do to deal with your parties. And you said you did perhaps a little over-state that. I didn't regard that as an apology. *Mr. Chandler:* No apology is needed, sir.

Mr. Loring: Perhaps, with gentlemen of the professional views and propriety of my brother, it does not. Perhaps others may differ.

The charges which the petitioners have made are so grave that no gentlemen would make them, no honest men would make them, no honorable lawyer, who realizes his duty as such, would present them without proof enough, at least, to raise a suspicion of their truth; and certainly the ninth allegation, to wit., that the evidence upon which your predecessor set up this will in 1864 was immaterial and incompetent, sounds more like the grumblings of a disappointed litigant than the intelligent attack of a well-bred lawyer.

As I have before remarked, the order of this court, made while this cause was in the hands of General Butler, whereby these petitioners were forbidden to proceed with their attempted proofs until they paid back the $5,000, was waived by these executors, to avoid the appearance of opposing technical defenses, behind which they might be thought by some to hide from a full disclosure of all the facts, and so a full opportunity has been given the petitioners to proceed. All this clamor and all these slanders have gone out to the world, trumpeted everywhere; and as a lie is good until it is denied and until it is proven to be a lie, we desired to hear their proofs, to meet and strangle this serpent of calumny, which would otherwise be hissing around us, even if it could not sting, and so the petitioners, keeping the $5,000 paid them on the faith of a compromise, were allowed to proceed, and they did proceed. And a mighty clamor was made by their counsel in his story of romance, which took the place of an opening, and which was to our ears, knowing its utter falsity, as sound and fury signifying nothing. That opening was such as never to my knowledge any advocate, however inexperienced, has ever dared to make upon such utter lack of proof. A wise man has said that "there is nothing so prolix as ignorance." But can even that poor excuse be made for statements like these I have referred to about the cell and the poison and the whiskey and the letter in which the old man says he must fight for his life, as showing that he was afraid of his children whom he loved and who loved him, a letter which would be presumed to have been written of strangers and not of his own kith and kin? These petitioners or this counsel certainly knew it was written by a kindly man because his description of old Ebenezer Smith's kindness was such that I envy him his rhetorical skill in presenting it. He must have known that that letter was written by a kindly man who loved his children and who was loved by them, and he ought to have known it was written years before his death and that it had nothing to do with his will, that it indicated no oppression and no evil influences and no coercion and no bad influence upon him on the part of his family. They ought to have known that he was struggling with all the strength God gave him to protect his property for his children, and yet this lawyer shuts his eyes to the facts and flings to the four winds of heaven a statement that this sentence was a charge against the dead man's wife and children. A reckless statement, unless proved, and in the absence of poof a statement which I should think one would hesitate to make, whether layman or lawyer, unless he could connect it with its consequences.

I leave his opening, referring to one more statement. To pursue all its peculiar sketchings and representations which have failed of proof would only weary the indignation, and I will not expose it to such a test. He has stated publicly that this will was a forgery. I do not mean to occupy the time of your Honor by arguing the absurdity of this charge, as matter of law, at this stage of my remarks. I only comment, and call your Honor's attention to the fact, that these petitioners themselves, personally having some fear of the State Prison before their eyes, or with possibly a reviving conscience, or possibly some unheard of consequence that would fall upon them, made no such charge in their petition. They never have sworn that that was a forgery, but they sat by and allowed their counsel to charge it in his opening. They sat by and he stood up, he charging the forgery, and holding up in triumph the spattered signature needing no argument in proof thereof. It does not appear anywhere in the petition. But after so called experts, two of them, had been called to support this theory, and when the newspapers had been filled with lithographic signatures, and when fraud and forgery had been trumpeted for weeks, charged for weeks on these respondents, the petitioners' counsel, either trying to shelter himself from the just accusation of my brother Drury, or for something else, coolly said here in court, that " there is no charge of forgery made." Well, if he withdraws it, that will save me some time, but I have seen no indication.

Now, after six long days occupied in putting in his proofs, he can do no more, save to talk. He has given us the evidence upon which he has based so tumultuous an opening, and I can only say, and all who have heard the stuff and nonsense, the prevarications and the perjuries which have wearied the dull hours of these long days, can only say, *Parturiunt montes nascetur ridiculus mus.* The mountains have labored, a silly mouse has been produced.

Why, may it please the Court, the newspapers of this city have been made marketable for the last three months by the revelations of family dissensions ; of Eliza W. Smith's success in exciting the amorous desires of a superannuated old public functionary ; of Hazen J. Burton, Sr's. manly mode of coming on to Boston to meet the charge of swindling which the grand jury of the county had brought against him in 1848, that manliness consisting in not escaping the clutches of John Wilson, the chief of detectives, who, meeting him in the wilds of Pennsylvania, politely accompanied him to Boston, and lodged him in Charles Street Jail, where in the same manly spirit this grey-haired old hypo- crite abode for weeks, while his fond father-in-law (the testator) stood aloof from him who had thus brought disgrace upon the family of which he had be- come a member through the blindness of woman's love.

These things, and more to which I shall refer as I proceed, are but specimens of the idle gossip and indecent history with which our ears have been regaled, and with which the time of this court has been occupied,—the time of your Honor, this tribunal, respected and revered as the guardian of the property of widows and orphans, whose time is occupied by the requirements of that branch and the other branch of the business of the court, but which has been mortgaged to the Burtons and to those hearings, and wasted in this cause. Self-respect and respect for their old dead grandfather forsooth ! though they don't get a dollar, that they are impelled by that respect to do all this ! Well did my friend, Mr. Drury, hurl his just maledictions at these two adventurers, and as he said, and as I say, these audacious blackmailers, when he spoke of their willingness to drag their old father, Hazen J. Burton, Sr., from the hole in which for thirty years he has been hiding his dishonored head,—willing thus to drag their names at the cart-tail of public obloquy. And this is their manifestation of self-respect.

These six days were spent in slandering the living and defaming the dead, and all for their own self-respect and their love for their grandfather !

Assuming, may it please the court, that what has been disclosed in regard to the making and execution of this will was unknown at the time of its probate in 1864, and that the respondents withheld it then, and that we are therefore called on to show that that judgment of the Judge of Probate was wise, and that the so-called will of October 5, 1864, was the last will of Ebsnezer Smith. and was duly executed, I now approach that point

This assumption, I shall have the honor to submit, is not forced on us, because I shall contend that the petitioners have shown no concealment or fraudulent withholding of evidence from the outset of this whole history. That there has been shown in this court some testimony which has never been presented in regard to this will is true. The only evidence which has been withheld or was never had before was the testimony appearing in favor of this story, and if discovered at the time, if known at the time, if it had been thought necessary at the time when Judge Ames had considered and enquired into it, this would have been produced. But it is Mr. Isaac T. Smith's testimony, and it is his testimony only, that is new in this case, — that is the only new evidence which now occurs to me of any importance, — and that is all in favor of the will.

I shall also pass the point that these petitioners having received $5,000 in 1865 under a compromise and holding it now, cannot deny the will or assail its validity.

I have then the honor to submit that the document of October 5, 1864, was the last will of Ebenezer Smith and that the judgment of this court should so be were it now for the first time offered. And following the order of the petitioners' allegations in their petition, I aver that we have proved —

1st. That Ebenezer Smith did sign the will, and this answers their 2nd allegation that he did not authorize any one to sign for him.

3d. That Ebenezer Smith did make known to the witnesses thereto that said signature was his.

4th. That Ebenezer Smith did declare to these witnesses that the instrument was his.

5th. That Ebenezer Smith did request the witnesses to attest it.

6th. That Ebenezer Smith did know the contents of the said instrument.

7th. That at the time of the execution of this instrument Ebenezer Smith was of sound and disposing mind and memory, and that he was entirely capable of making a valid will and that his mental faculties were not impaired at that time either from sickness, old age, or any cause.

8th. That the said instrument and the signature thereto were not obtained and procured by collusion, fraud, undue influence and force.

9th. I pass this allegation as an insult to your Honor's predecessor, Judge Ames, who allowed this will and never was guided to my knowledge by uncertain and incompetent evidence. That allegation is that that was set up upon uncertain and incompetent evidence, and I don't deem myself called upon to show what that evidence was, but I assume it to have been in his judgment sufficient to sustain his decree, and I leave the point confident that there is no other view that can be taken thereof.

10th. That the probate of this will was not obtained fraudulently, and *mala fide*, by no false suggestions, by no surreptitious and clandestine conduct, by no concealment from the court of evidence material to the case which if now dis-

8

closed will justify the revocation of the probate of said will and of the letters testamentary.

These petitioners charge the contrary of all these nine propositions in just nine allegations of the record. And what are these charges? The opening argument of Mr. Chandler states them vividly. Fraud, forgery, perjury and force are the chiefest.

Now, who are the accusers? Hazen J. Burton, Sr., once a Sabbath-school teacher, I don't know but a class haranguer, perhaps a preacher, who, in the midst of his sacred professions, fled from Boston in 1848 to escape an outraged community and law, to return to Charles Street jail and never to preach any more forever,—to prayer I would commend him. He comes here, it is true, acquitted of the crimes alleged against him in 1848, when he was indicted, acquitted by the spells of that arch magician, Rufus Choate. I think he is now plunging deeper into crime and he is deepening the darkness of his own corruption. These words are strong, but I use them, for I find proof to convict him, and use them as no rhetorical flourish. I have no facility of rhetoric, but facts when stated simply carry eloquence of themselves. The fire of his wickedness has broken out again in his old age, and, except by special intercession, we fear the grave will open for him to an eternity of remorse. Hazen J. Burton, Sr., I submit to the court, is the father of all these lies. He was indicted, may it please your Honor, in 1848, having for his creditors A. & A. Lawrence, James W. Page, Samuel Frothingham, Coolidge & Haskell, and my memory fails to mention the others,—I wish I had the list,—and he says he was indicted by them to blackmail Ebenezer Smith. He says that the first merchants of this city got him indicted in order to force unjustly and dishonestly and corruptly and to intimidate Ebenezer Smith and to induce him to pay old Burton's debts.

Well, these gentlemen some of them swore that Hazen J. Burton had swindled them out of thousands of dollars, and he says he was acquitted because old Mr. Coolidge, of Coolidge & Haskell, perjured himself. Old Mr. Sam. T. Coolidge, of the house of Coolidge & Haskell, well known in this city as an honest and honorable man, associated with such men as A. & A. Lawrence, James W. Page and Samuel Frothingham, men whose names and whose examples are cherished by all good men and are defamed by none but bad men, and then only when they think they can thereby escape the toils of their own wickedness. He lugs the names of these gentlemen and drops them in the dirt, names that have heretofore signified the Christian gentleman and the honest man. He says that there was perjury and he says there was blackmailing. Well, I have heard it charged in this case by my brother Drury, without any qualification, that this whole proceeding is an attempt to blackmail Isaac T. Smith and Dr. Thorndike, or to force them, for fear of enquiry and for fear of the filth that might be thrown upon them by these men, to pay money. Well, the first time that blackmail was mentioned in the evidence in this cause came from the lips of Mr. Hazen J. Burton, Sr. He says the indictment was procured by his creditors for the purpose of blackmailing, and that the indictment was attempted to be supported by old Mr. Coolidge's perjury. Well, familiarity with a subject renders it sometimes to some men suggestive of occupation, and possibly having had that evil scheme tried upon him in his early days, he thought possibly he would try it upon these men in his later days. He charged here in this court these gentlemen with committing high crimes, and he says they did it to force money from Ebenezer Smith. Well, the same thought may have been suggested to him, and may have lingered with him and so he does what he says his creditors did to him. He charged them with being blackmailers,—these men of upright character. Now it seems to me it does not lie in the mouth of Hazen J. Burton, senior, who, as I have said before, fled his country because his creditors at least thought he had cheated them, to say this. I remember distinctly now, I recall the effort that was necessary to extract from him that at that time some of his creditors did think he was a dishonest man. He said there always was a difference,—some debtors were honest and some were dishonest. It was a pretty hard undertaking for me to get him to acknowledge that he did get that idea between February, 1848, when he went to New Orleans, and some time in May, when John Wilson brought him back. He says he didn't bring him back, he came back quietly, but he landed in jail when he came here. John Wilson was the Chief of detectives in those days. I remember his grey old head and his steady eye. Everybody went for John Wilson when they were after a rogue, and when he went for a rogue he always caught him. This man came home with Mr. John Wilson, who treated him very politely, but when he got here he left him in jail.

Right there, may it please the Court, I want to refer to something which illustrates Mr. Burton's character. When counsel said that Mr. Ebenezer Smith was afraid of poison, and that he had his cup rinsed with hot water, and his food tasted by others before he would eat it, I said this case begins to need attention, and I gave it attention. What did Hazen J. Burton, senior, say, may it please the Court, when he testified in answer to questions put by the gentleman who represents these petitioners? Why, that the old man never drank anything from a cup unless it was rinsed with hot water before he drank it, and you will find if you look at the short-hand reporter's notes that somebody said it was because he was afraid that his wife would poison him. Burton said himself he didn't quite believe it, but that was the story; that was the evidence which was put in here by Mr. Chandler to prove that old Mrs. Smith sought ways of getting rid of her husband. She put hot water into his coffee cup, and into his tea cup, and that was the way the poison was to be driven out. Well, may it please the Court, I would not pause a minute on this excepting that I do desire to recall the utter vanity and folly of such attempts to establish what never had an existence. Well, on the cross-examination, I asked Mr. Burton if it ever occurred to him that this hot water was put into his cup so that the old gentleman might have a hot cup of coffee instead of a disagreeble one; he said it had not. "Who had control of the water that went into the cup?" "Well, Mrs. Smith, she turned the hot water into the cup." "Did the old gentleman ever take any pains to find out whether the water was poisoned in that pot before it went into the cup?" "No." That ended that part of it. And so, too, we are told in the opening, and Mr Burton testified, that old Mr. Smith never tasted food until it was tasted by others! As atrocious, as false and groundless and abominable an attempt to prove that old Mrs. Smith sought to poison her her husband, — as atrocious and as wicked as the intimation of these men, who go round apparently with their pockets full of affidavits, in Judge Hoar's office, that Mrs. Thorndike murdered her mother. Why, what was the story about this eating, and about his having others taste his food before he would venture to taste it himself? I asked him, may it please the Court, if Mr. Smith didn't sit at the head of his table, and do his own carving. Well, it was a long while before he would admit that old Mr. Ebenezer Smith had anything on his table that required carving, it was chiefly hash or hasty pudding; that was the way he tried to escape from me there. He finally admitted that the old man did sit at his own table, and did do his own carving, and that he helped his family before he helped himself, and he took what remained, if there was enough, and if there was not he sent for more; that he took his own food from the same piece of beef, and put it on his plate and ate it, but he didn't pass it round and ask some member of the family to taste it to see if it was safe for him to eat his dinner. That is all there was of that. Well, I wonder at the patience of the Court, I wonder at the stability of counsel who have been able to endure this, — and that is a fair specimen of the attacks which have been made by this counsel with his witnesses, and these adventurers with their frauds.

Mr. Chandler: I didn't state in my opening what you say I did. *Mr. Loring:* Well, read it. *Mr. Chandler:* "In fact so suspicious had he become, *it is affirmed*,"—mark these three words—"that he refused to drink at home till his cup was rinsed in his presence, nor would he eat there till after others had tasted." And I put on this witness who *affirmed* it, and that is the whole story.

Mr. Loring: Now he has made his statement once. Then if he had let it alone, why didn't he have the courage to come out and say "*it is affirmed*" that it is a lie. It did prove his case to be an atrocity, and an abomination. It is a lie, and I drop it there "It is affirmed!" Well, I beg to know who is the affirmant? *Mr. Chandler:* The witnesses.

Mr. Loring: "It is affirmed" that he was so suspicious that he would not taste from his cup or eat from his table. May it please the Court, is it not the same as if he had said that he didn't dare to because he was fearful that something had been done to the food and the drink? If it is not, then I have wasted perhaps five minutes on that subject. *Mr. Chandler:* There is no doubt of that. *Mr. Loring:* No doubt I have. Not half has been told in regard to it, but in the words of my distinguished friend representing the petitioners "I will forbear."

I have taken a little diversion because I had Hazen J. Burton, senior, in my mind and I desired to illustrate his character as I went along, and I think I have selected two good specimens of his testimony which he gave. I don't know that he told anything that hurt anybody except himself. It strikes me he did not. He undertook to state the relations that existed between himself and the old gentleman, he undertook to say how loving and kind he was, he undertook to say that the old man told him when he married his daughter that he should not give him anything, but when the time of trouble came he should come to his rescue, and he said too that the affection which the old man bore for these children was quite marked clear down to 1864. Well, that does not support the position of these petitioners one iota, because I am perfectly willing to admit that old Mr. Ebenezer Smith did have a kindly regard for these two boys now grown men. What does that prove? Why, Hazen J. Burton, senior, said that that will of October, 1864, was entirely foreign to all the sentiments that the man had expressed, and was not like him a bit, and therefore it was not his will. How is it about the will of 1859, when the boys got $500? He had just enough affection for them to give them that sum then, so the fact that he did not give them any more in 1864 does not amount to anything. Why didn't that father who told Burton when he married his daughter Harriet that when the hour of need came, he would help him, stand by and help him and his children? Why did he leave that graceless father to lie in jail and give the sons of that father the paltry sum of $500 in his will? And I will tell you why. It is in the life of Burton. That is the answer to it. That good old man abhorred some things. He was fond of others. He was fond of music. One thing did not find sympathy in his large heart, which the counsel for the petitioners enlarged upon so pathetically,—and he exhibited the photograph of that man in order to impress us all with the kindness of his nature, the first time I ever have seen evidence of that kind introduced, and it was amusing. The door having been opened I have got a little picture which I am going to exhibit in a few minutes. I think there is one thing old Mr. Smith abhorred, and that is a man with the character of old Hazen J. Burton. There is no question, may it please the court, that Burton did lose caste and character here by reason of charges that were brought against him. Whether they were true or false is not material. It is true beyond a question that the relations which existed between Ebenezer Smith and Hazen J. Burton and these boys were peculiar, from 1848 down, during Mrs. Burton's life. Doubtless the old man loved that daughter as he did all his other children, but from her death and from the time when Hazen J. Burton was indicted, there certainly was but little intercourse between them. My own impression is, (it is not material to establish it,) that it was the fact that Hazen J. Burton was indicted and that he ran away and was brought back and tried, which was the cause. The atmosphere didn't suit the old gentleman's nostrils, and he was not fond of a person who had gone through with that. I think he regarded him as a person who was a disgrace to his family and as a man whom he didn't want to have anything to do with, and it may be, knowing the disgrace, he didn't propose to foster the children whose blood was tainted with that sort of corruption, though his own blood mingled with theirs. I rather think that to him the English of the Latin was God's truth, "*Fortuna non mutat genus*," What's bred in the bone won't out of the flesh. I think he felt that Hazen J. Burton was no credit to his family. At least, I think I am safe in saying that. I don't think I shall be called exaggerating when I say he didn't regard him as a credit. My impression is he thought he was a disgrace and a man who had, from the blindness of woman's love, connected himself with his family, and that he would have but little to do with him, and he would not give his children more than $500 each, and he did not. He didn't give them more, because he didn't see fit to give them more. It was his own money, and he had a right to do thus. In 1859 he gave them the same, and the fertile imagination of the present counsel for the petitioners has failed to extend to that period, and he leaves the will of 1859 untouched by any insinuations unaffected by any charges that the testator wasn't his own man then. But we can say he was as much his own man in 1864 as he was in 1859. So much for Hazen J. Burton. I say, may it please the Court, that in regard to him I need not spend a moment more upon any branch of this case. What he said didn't amount to anything; admitting all he said was true. But when you come to apply the test to his testimony, well, it is not testimony to be tested, it is no testimony at all, he don't know anything, Could I recall two or three more instances I would, but I leave my brother Drury to finish that little sketch. He may come across it as he closes his sketch, and if I have omitted it he will fill up the gap.

We come next, (I am now dealing with the parties to this suit) to Eliza W. Smith, a remarkable person, a peculiar person, who will stand more cross-examination than almost any woman I ever knew, once a gay and festive sort of a charmer, I should think, — clearly a diplomat armed with the fascinations which gave to the women of France such power over the great men of that great Kingdom. She got $60,000 out of Ebenezer Smith during his lifetime and there wasn't a single other child of that old man who could get a penny. I believe he did give one of the Burtons, when he was a little boy in swaddling clothes, some candy, and told that little boy not to go near his grandmother. Then the grandmother gave that same little boy in swaddling clothes some candy and told him not to go near his grandfather. And that was the testimony which is given here to show the affection of that grandfather for those boys, and that was the testimony which was given seriously here in court, and from that time, from the time of their candy days, they had had nothing to do with him. There was an attempt made, — part of the case was to show that these two young men had been beloved by this old gentleman. The story of that candy is the only fact that I recall as having shown an affection, and the young man notwithstanding these cautionings, would go right straight from the first one who gave him the candy and go to the other and get the candy, and he didn't care. I dislike to dwell on trifling things, but these trifling things were what they thought necessary to bring into this case.

She who could (Eliza W., this is one of her exploits, I shall not be long upon her) induce the Secretary of War to grant an honorable discharge to her son then a deserter from the U. S. army lurking among the mountains of Wyoming, procured his appointment as Consul or Vice Consul to France in reward for his cowardice. She is the woman who, loaded down and harassed by debts, sought refuge from the Scylla of their torments in the blandishments of a second husband all the way from France, only to escape from that entanglement which she describes as her Charybdis, from which she sought relief, by divorce. (I refer to a letter which she wrote.) This is Eliza W. Smith who leads off this long procession, and comes here to attack this will. She says that her father was unconscious, that he said "no" when he was asked to sign the will. I will not repeat the scene now. She, desiring to impress the court with the idea that she was a very excellent woman and had been all her life, and that she had aroused the tenderest emotions for herself in the heart of her mother, had said that she was beloved by that mother and that that mother loved her and that she was an especial favorite of her mother. She said that her mother would sit at the window waiting and looking for her, wondering why she didn't come, and that she never had trouble with her. And the result was, on cross-examination, she gave a graphic description, and it seemed to me to be exaggerated, it was quite touching, the love she had for her mother and the love the mother had for her. Yet just at the point where she reached the climax of her power of description, when the picture was drawn vividly and with her shapely skill, when I could see in my imagination, with the aid of her productive memory and inventive power, a domestic picture that was quite interesting, there was handed to me a letter, and I read it to her, and asked her to look at it,—this letter which I am going to read, if your Honor please, because with that I can drop her.

"BOSTON, Feb'y 21, 1861.

ELIZA: Your father handed me the letter he received from you to-day, and requested me to answer it."

(I should add, to make this of full effect, that her visits to her mother's house were frequent, and she was going to and fro all the time,—the latch string was always out.)

"I will by saying that it will not be convenient nor agreeable for us to receive you, nor any of your family into our house as visitors. We are a very happy little family by ourselves, and we do not mean to be intruded upon. Garry" (Eliza W.'s daughter) "is a stranger to me. I have never been acquainted with her, and I do not wish to make it now. Eben, when he was here in the summer, was a very good boy, but what he is now I do not know, since he has been under such an influence, where such disgraceful letters, to entire strangers, have emanated from, intended to disgrace myself and family; but, the wrath of man shall praise Him and the remainder He will restrain. ELIZA SMITH."

Well, that settled one question; that she would in 1878 swear one way, swear to a thing which in 1861 wasn't anything at all. She swore her mother loved her all the way through, and there is a letter from her mother telling her not to cross her threshold! That is all there is in that. Perhaps, may it please the Court, when this letter was written, that mother knew that this daughter had requested the Rev. Dr. Neale, in 1854, when Eliza W. Smith's husband died, not to mention her mother in his prayers to God at the funeral of that daughter's husband. She may have heard that Eliza W. Smith requested the clergyman while praying at the funeral of her own husband not to mention in his prayer, as is wont among good people, the mother who bore her, but I think it was not that simple incident alone which inspired that letter from that mother to her daughter. That letter showed that the life of that woman, or her treatment of her mother, or her conduct, had been such that she could not allow the contamination or the corruption or the pollution of her presence within her house, and yet, if your Honor please, her testimony would have given you to believe, and the testimony was offered to prove the fact,—it was offered to prove the relation between them,—that the mother and she were as mother and child. Take the fact that she and her mother were as mother and child, but as a mother whose heart had been either frozen by her daughter's follies or hardened by her daughter's crimes so that she had for that daughter neither love nor respect. "But the wrath of man shall praise Him and the remainder He will restrain." Well, that restrained Eliza from crossing that threshold, I fancy.

Again, sir, upon this question of the character of Eliza W. Smith, she swore that Arthur G. Smith, her son, carried away her chattels from Medford, that she complained to her father about it and he told her not to blame Arthur, because Isaac had done it all. That testimony was given in when the attempt was made by them to show that Ebenezer Smith, the father, distrusted his son Isaac T. Smith, didn't like him, and as one cause for the dislike, one circumstance showing why he distrusted him, she repeated what my brother Drury read this morning, and so comment is unnecessary upon what it was, excepting that she swore that these things were taken by Arthur from her house before her father's death in 1864. She swore that when they were taken she went to her father to complain of it and her father said to her, the things having been taken away and she complaining of Arthur, "don't blame Arthur, for Isaac has done it all." Why, may it please the court, the record of the court of New York, the judgment roll of that court shows that those things were not taken away until 1868, and that record shows that she swore that they were not taken until 1868, and she swears that in 1868 the things were taken away, and yet here, when it is necessary to prove that her father had no confidence in Isaac T. Smith, she swears that her father was alive in 1868 and that he told her a story that he could not have told because he had been in his grave four years. That is all there is of that. She swore, may it please your Honor, that she never knew or heard of her father's financial embarrassment, and yet she, in November, 1860, received from him the letter of November 28th in which he writes her, "I have been so pressed for money that I can't sleep o' nights. Neither Clapp nor myself can raise a single dollar, and the banks don't discount." She testified as I have stated, and letters contradicting her were produced. I have one written February 9, 1861. This is written by her father to her :—

"Box P. O., Boston, Feb. 9, 1861.

"Dear Eliza :—I have not written you so often as I should, because I have not been able to , and am obliged to be retired very much and take care of myself, that I may keep from being laid up. Though I am very much burdened with cares and anxieties, which I am obliged to neglect, for when I have upon my shoulders every ounce that I can stand under, another pound would crush me down, and if so, might not rise again like a young person full of vigor and health. This then must be my excuse. I deeply sympathize with you, as I expressed in a former letter, and send a paper as often as I can. I have nine lawyers and your Ma has two. You may judge then a little how many suits I have to defend, and duns too, without number. some on my own and some on your account."

Right at that point I noticed that the petitioners' counsel, in his opening, in order to make it excessively plain that the old man was the victim of domestic terrors, quoted that letter, dated in 1862, in which the old man says he was fighting for the last dollar. I should think he was, he had nine lawyers, it was a pretty tough fight. I wonder whether there are any such litigious gentlemen now, and whether the number nine is filled up. If it is not, there are more who would like to be counted in. He says he was fighting for the last dollar ; they say he was fighting to protect himself against his children whom he loved, and who loved him. Domestic infelicity !—professional infelicity, professional vicissitudes and the perplexities of nine lawyers piling on that one man in one day ! I wonder he didn't seek refuge in the Medford school-house, the seminary of West Medford, the shades of Mystic Hall, where Eliza W. was.

" I have nine lawyers and your Ma has two. You may judge then a little how many suits I have to defend, and duns too, without number, some on my own and some on your account. These are part of my feebleness (not medicine.) Besides, I have just got some friends to petition the Legislature"—

Here the old gentleman is trying to rescue himself from that horrid West Medford property, which was worth a million in Eliza W. Smith's estimation, and in which he didn't have a dollar's interest, according to Eliza W. Smith's testimony.

" I have just got some friends to petition the Legislature for a charter for an Agricultural Park at West Medford, and the committee have given the petitioners leave to withdraw their petition. I was in hopes to have done something through this charter with that hateful property,"—

Mind you, during all his life, that property which Eliza W. swore was the gem of his estate.

—" which has been the means of almost running me out at the little end of the *horn* just before I can get ready to die! If I could have gone to the Insane Asylum before I had gone to W. Medford, it would have been money in my purse, if not health to my body, but I was not possessed of " madness and malignity' to get me to the asylum, if I had tried, (and I am sure *I* never knew or heard of any of my ancestors or of blood relations that *were* so) but it was purely from the desire to be useful that carried me to Medford. You and your family are young and healthy, more to be prized than silver and gold, and we should look upon our adversities as real blessings, intended for our good, perhaps to ward off a greater evil, and make us more wise. If I should be sick, I will let you know of it.   Aff'y   FATHER.

" P. S.—I am told that the cold here this morning is 27° *below* zero ! I have not heard from Medford. It is thought there will be peace and quietness at Washington within 30 days—'so mote it be.'   GRPA."

Eliza W. is one of the parties who is prosecuting this suit, not a nominal party to the petition, but a witness who volunteered to come here, in constant attendance day by day, but a real party who expects to get $50,000 if this will is broken up. She is a party, she, who swore that her father never lent her a dollar, who swore that he never put a dollar into the West Medford property, who swore that her mother loved her ; no one of which things is true, because the documents here were shown to contradict it; she is a party, she, who swore that her father was alive in 1868, and that he told her about Isaac T. Smith, when in fact he had been four years dead in his grave, and away out of all her complications and vexations.

Another party to this suit is Hazen J. Burton, Jr. May it please the Court, there is something painful at the sight of a man standing in a court of justice and testifying, not according to his recollection, but as he wishes it to be. It is no pleasant duty to charge upon a man who has before him apparently a long life, either for prosperity or adversity, of usefulness or of worthlessness; it is no pleasing task, I say. to apply to him phrases which involve his character as an honest man, and as a worthy citizen. Hazen J. Burton, Jr., the son of old Hazen J. of 1848 memory, makes statements under oath in this court which have been proved to be the baldest lies that ever were sworn to or stated by man. He stood up here, sir, and swore, on being asked—and this shows the importance of the statement—" when after 1865 did you first have reason to believe that there was fraud in this case, what was the fact that attracted your attention?" "I first knew it when Judge Hoar told me in his office that he had evidence enough in his possession to indict Isaac T. Smith," Judge Hoar, at the time referred to, was counsel for Mrs. Thorndike in the suit which she was resisting, which these same adventurers had brought, he was counsel resisting their efforts to break the will of Mrs. Ebenezer Smith, and they came to his office, and this man swore that Judge Hoar told him that Issac T. Smith could be indicted at any moment. That testimony he gave here, sir, and I was surprised, I was taken by surprise, for I knew that if Judge Hoar said it he meant it, and it didn't cross my mind for an instant that the man would have the audacity and the wicked hardihood to stand here and swear falsely, when he knew the character of Judge Hoar would bear him down to eternal infamy, unless he confirmed his statement. The falsehood and perjury had not passed from his lips for ten minutes before the counsel for the respondents were fully informed as to the facts. Two days after, the next day perhaps, Judge Hoar goes on to this stand, and I ask him: " Did you ever tell Hazen J. Burton you had evidence enough to indict Isaac T. Smith?" And your Honor remembers his answer. He said " no, never: I never had any evidence upon which to indict him. Never had occasion to reflect on his character. I never knew anything against him, and I never told that man any such thing." There was the testimony of a man who stands as high as man can wish to stand in the confidence of this community or any. Ebenezer Rockwood Hoar, whose character carries weight against an army of Burtons. Why, they flee before his presence as the clouds before the morning sun. They can no more stand up. Did the whole family of Burtons swear that Judge Hoar made such a statement as that, they could swear it until they had sworn their souls to purgatory and nobody would believe it. Why, sir. then comes the younger brother to the rescue. Judge Hoar has ruined his brother's character for truth and veracity, he stands convicted in the minds of all who heard his testimony, he must stand convicted in his own mind, and in the judgment of this court, as a foul perjurer and a bad man, a man who goes out before his fellow-men, who will never trust him, knowing what he has testified to here. He is entitled to nothing but the maledictions, or rather the silent passing by of all good men and true. Having been so extinguished, so pulverized, so entirely convicted of either wilful perjury or a stupidity or ignorance of speech, which render his testimony in this matter entirely worthless, he brings his younger brother to confront Judge Hoar and to sustain himself. Well, there are two Burtons against Judge Hoar. Hazen J. Burton, Jr., had said that Judge Hoar had said that Isaac T. Smith could be indicted, (but he didn't say that the Judge said he was going to do it.) Judge Hoar swore that that was a falsehood, and the consequence was that that man perjured himself. Now he undertakes to rescue himself from that dilemma. How does he do it? He brings forward George S. Burton, his brother, a feeble youth, who knows little, and has testified to little in this case. I remember that the words " imperious nature " have been applied to my client, Isaac T. Smith. I should say that the imperious nature of Hazen J. Burton, Jr., may have overpowered George S., and he brings him up to the rescue. What does he say? He was there at the interview, the two boys were there in Judge Hoar's office, and he says if Judge Hoar hadn't testified as he had that morning he would have sworn to just what Hazen J. Burton, Jr., had sworn. I don't doubt he would. Lucky for him he didn't have the chance, lucky for him that he didn't go on to the stand before Judge Hoar's voice had been raised, and was thus saved one of the perils which await his elder brother, lucky for him that he didn't render himself a fit subject for the other end of the Court House, and that Judge Hoar's voice was raised to stop his downward career. He may thank God for saving him from the companionship of his perjured brother.

I pass from that exploit of that young man to another little piece of evidence. I don't know, but I am almost inclined to think, it is the spirit of Hazen J. Burton, Jr., that is controlling the course of this case and that his counsel is simply echoing his decrees. Hazen J. Burton, Jr., is one of the parties to this prosecution, he is first mate, his father being the captain. He is one of the parties who has been exhausting the patience and the time of this county and this court. He asked me one day, sir, — his counsel did for him — whom I was going to put on the stand the next day. Well, I have never tried a case more above board than I have this in all my life. I was simply watching a parcel of bad men, I knew that, — that was perfectly clear to me, — as bad as I ever knew. I knew them. Watching them I was perfectly contented they should watch me, and when they asked me whom I was going to call the next day I told them I was going to call Arthur G. Smith, who is the son of Eliza W. He is the man who, she said, stole her things out there in 1868, and of whom her father said she must not blame him because Isaac put Arthur up to it, and the old man had been dead four years when she said he said it, — been dead four years when he made this statement, been dead four years before the things were carried away. That announcement was made to them. I would just as lief they would know what I was going to do, so long as I could see what they were going to do. I thought I should detect them in some of their wicked chicaneries. And I did detect Hazen J. Burton, Jr., and can convict him of subornation of perjury or of an attempt to suborn perjury. I have argued, and the duty has devolved upon me to do so, that he is a perjurer, and I now argue that he is an attempter of subornation of perjury. He goes on to New York. We adjourned on Wednesday afternoon. Think now, after I had announced on that Wednesday afternoon that Arthur G. Smith was going to be brought on here by me if I could get him, on the very next night, or the night after, this man goes on to New York and he goes to the store of this cousin of his whom he is not proven to have seen for years and years.

Mr. Chandler: He saw him here a few days before. *Mr. Loring:* He saw him here once, and then Mr. Arthur G. Smith at that same time saw Mr. Chandler. Mr. Chandler told him he was going to break this will. *Mr. Chandler:* No, sir. *Mr. Loring:* Told him he was going to break the trusts, or something or other. *Mr. Chandler:* No, sir. You can put me on the stand if you want to know what I have said.

Mr. Loring: I don't want to put you on the stand, because I should expose so many things, which I don't want to do. He goes on to New York and he goes to this young man, this Arthur G. Smith, who, may it please your Honor, was here one day, and his statement corrects me. He was here at one of the former hearings to hear this testimony, he is the son of Eliza W., he has a talk with Mr. Chandler and with Hazen J. Burton, Jr. I didn't hear what the testimony was, because I was out of the room at the time, but Mr. Chandler's name was brought in. I tell these gentlemen what witnesses I am going to put on the stand at the next hearing, and I say I told them on purpose, because I thought they would do something they ought not to do. Hazen J. Burton, Jr., goes on to New York the day after, I will say, but I am not sure,—the record will show. He goes on to New York and hunts up this Arthur, at whose store he had not been before, whom I will venture to say he had not called on in all his life, he goes to Arthur G. Smith and says to him " I don't want you to go to Boston to testify against us, I want you to stay here in New York or else if you do go on, to go on and testify in our favor." There was talk about securing something to Arthur G. Smith. A certain $5,000 was named,—an assurance of guaranty from this man to him, that if he would not come on to Boston to testify —

Mr. Chandler: That is not so, Mr. Loring *Mr. Loring:* I haven't got through my sentence yet. He doesn't correct me when I say that this man tried to prevent his coming on here. *Mr. Chandler:* The whole thing is erroneously stated by you. *Mr. Drury:* The witness testified to it.

Mr. Loring: The gentleman says I am not stating the testimony as it is. He says he understands I don't. I suspect that the party who seems. as I have said before, to be running this case—his counsel acting as a sort of second mate —is the one from whom the understanding must come. I say, your Honor,— I challenge contradiction, I shall get contradiction I have no doubt, I challenge the proof of the contrary,—that young man went on and wanted Arthur G. Smith either to stay in New York or else, if he came on here, to come on and swear for him. Something was said about $5,000, something was said about guaránteeing to him a certain portion of the trust fund. Then, Mr. Arthur G. Smith did say this, this I remember : " I shall take no guarantees under any circumstances for any such a purpose. I am going on to tell the truth and I shall not be deterred from that by your suggestions or intimations." He was then told by this young man, " Well, if we lose this case we shall appeal it, we are not going to stop here." That didn't deter him. I will add one further fact. I asked him if he didn't go on to New York on purpose to see Arthur G. Smith ; he said he went on to see the counsel in that case of Eliza W. against her son Arthur, which happened in 1868, about the rubbish which he carried from Medford. Hazen J., Jr., is quite skilful and puts a lawyer to his trumps to get the truth from him. He does not get his skill from his father, because you can see through his father as you can through the broad daylight, he is empty, you can see what he is made out of. The young man learns his lesson well, he was not to be so easily handled, he said going on to New York to see Arthur G. Smith formed a very little portion of his visit. He didn't appear to have done anything while he was there but to have his interviews with Arthur G. Smith and to see the lawyers in this case. It was *very* little. Now your Honor remembers that that man who asks your Honor to believe him, that man who has dared to stand here and state to you under oath things that I argue cannot be credited for an instant, that man who swears he went on not to see Arthur G. Smith, not that that formed the slightest part of his purpose in going there, says, " I took a memorandum of the conversations which we had at the time." Well, if I go on to New York on a special business and I go to a man whom I never called upon before in all my life and I ask him in regard to a case which I am marshalling, and he tells me certain things and I set down those things in a memorandum book, it shows that it was a most singular co-incidence that I should have stumbled in there, it shows I thought a good deal of the object of that visit, it shows that that visit formed some part of the occupation of that day, and it was so important that I took a memorandum of it. Nobody asked him to show that memorandum. I had it on my tongue's end, but my tongue had been so active that I thought I would not. I referred to the headquarters of the leader of this " noble band " as apparently not on the saddle, but on the Stonington Line, between Boston and New York.

Mr. H. J. Burton, Jr. has apparently just returned from New York. Mr. O'Connor, that curiosity,—I am going to think of him over night before I say much about him,—saw this man ten days ago for the first time, had a letter from him since, and saw this man again last Sunday. He apologized the first time he went there for being there on Sunday, because he thought possibly Mr. O'Connor might be a good, piously-inclined Presbyterian, but the second day he happened to come Sunday again. Now what did he go on to New York for ? Why, sir, on the hearing before, Mr. Isaac T. Smith had been on here and told his story. Not the hearing before, but two hearings before. The hearing before was the time it was intimated Mr. Isaac T. Smith didn't care to come into the city. Mr. Isaac T. Smith would not come into this city, as I said, at the beck and call of these parties unless it was necessary for him to attend and meet their infamous charges. I think that the intimation that he did not dare to come is pretty well disposed of. But he had given, may it please your Honor, some strong testimony in regard to this will, and your Honor remembers that Mr. Chandler, at the last hearing, or the one before, said he was very anxious to cross-examine him, and if he didn't cross-examine him he should produce a large number of witnesses to prove by them what he should prove by him if he was here.— *Mr. Chandler :* Not " a large number." — *Mr. Loring :* Well. a small number. I take it back. He has had Mr. Smith, and not a small number of witnesses, but a number of small witnesses and all this morning's hearing was vouchsafed to Mr. Chandler, it was granted to him by the court, and we have no objection to it, and I wish he could have postponed it ten years and we should not have come here again. I didn't know what he wanted of Mr. Isaac T. Smith, but I was determined he should have a chance to try his hand on him. Well, he did, and he let him alone as quick as he did before. He was here before, and he came to spend two days, having learned, doubtless, from his counsel at this end what a protracted habit of mind Mr. Chandler had, and how he extended investigations which he made into a far distant and remote point,—so remote from the case that he was trying, that there was no knowing when he would get through the cross-examination of him. However, we gave him two days ; we put him on the stand and we examined him two hours, and, I should say, in about the same proportion, Mr. Chandler cross-examined him twenty minutes and dropped him. Burton goes on after hearing that testimony and we find him in close consultation with Mr. O'Connor ; he is one of the small witnesses whom Mr. Chandler brought us to-day. As I said before, I will pass him. I want one night to think of him. I will come back to him.

I have endeavored to give a correct account and description of the character of Hazen J. Burton, Jr. I know nothing about him outside of this case, except that he is a son of his father. I know of his father outside of this case, so do a great many others, perhaps many in the sound of my voice. The young men I have known nothing of. I have had to become acquainted with them since this cause began, and I am dealing with the facts as they appear here, forced so to do from professional duty, but not from any taste I have for any such mode of dealing.

I have mentioned George S., a feeble youth, who knew little and testified to little, who would have sworn that Judge Hoar said what his brother said he did if Judge Hoar had not sworn before him. The other party is nobody. That is all.

Those are the parties to this suit ; and having dealt with these I will conclude the few minutes left to me by commencing my consideration of the witnesses who support their case. They are the only witnesses who assail the will, Eliza W. Smith and Mrs. Giles. They are the only two people who were present at the time of the execution of the will, and no others who testify against the will were present. These two were present, and so was Margaret Patterson ; but Margaret Patterson, called by the petitioners themselves, says that the old gentleman was in his right senses, and that Isaac T. Smith helped his father to write his name, and so say we. So Margaret Patterson is with us. He called her, I doubt not he paid her, I am glad of it, we should have called her.—*Mr. Chandler:* Is there any evidence of that, that I paid Margaret Patterson? *Mr. Loring:* I say you called her and I have no doubt you paid her the witness fee. I have no idea that you did pay anybody anything else, I didn't intimate that you ever did. You may have, I think, too fine an appreciation of her character. So I count Margaret Patterson on my side.

Now I have considered Eliza W. Smith somewhat already as a party. I shall consider her somewhat more as a witness. She says that her father refused to sign this will, and that he said these words which the counsel for the petitioners adopted or used; whether he used them and she adopted them or whether she suggested them and he then adopted them, I don't know. But she swore that when Isaac came into the room and said to her father " here is your will," her father said feebly " my will, no" — I cannot imitate her, no man can, and then she says he relapsed into unconsciousness, and then that Isaac took his hand and wrote with it that name, and that the testator took no part in the writing and knew not that his name was being written. That is the testimony of Eliza W. Smith who stood by that table on that day, and she says that was what was done. It was doubtless her story which inspired this picture which I now exhibit from the National Police Gazette of January 18. It was doubtless this story which she must have told to the learned counsel for the petitioners when he framed his carefully and felicitously expressed romantic story with which he regaled us on the 4th of December. It was doubtless that story of Eliza W. Smith's which inspired this atrocious picture in one of the illustrated papers of New York. I offer it as illustration and as argument. It discredits, more than I can discredit, the abominable and disgusting exaggerations of this whole story. I point to that as discrediting what they say occurred there. I should say without reading anything, because it is not evidence, that this was the picture of a " dead man's signature (and perhaps Ebenezer Smith's), a wealthy and eccentric gentleman dies before he can sign his will and the eager heirs guide the fingers of the corpse to frame the coveted document." I think General Butler did announce the fact that this was signed by a dead man's hand ; — he said things as bad, if not worse. To prove that picture is a pretty serious matter. To make the opening speech which was made and not prove it is a more serious matter. The picture drawn I believe was inspired by the gross exaggeration of witnesses who must have misled the counsel, for I am not ready to believe that any member of the Suffolk bar could, with the evidence which has been really extracted, have thought he could prove what was said on the 4th of December here by the present counsel for the petitioners. I don't believe he would have drawn such a sketch had he not heard it from others, of course he must have heard it from others, and they were the witnesses to be produced. But I never in the whole course of my practice listened to direct testimony in some points supporting the allegations made in his romantic address, which so utterly melted away and turned to dross in the crucible of cross-examination. There was not enough left of the evidence given for the petitioners by Eliza W. Smith, Hazen J. Burton, Sr., Hazen J. Burton, Jr., Eben Smith (well, he didn't know anything) and **Mrs. Giles,** — there was not enough left of them to write their epitaphs, there was not enough left of them to bury, and as to their statements there was no occasion to argue this case, may it please your Honor. The arguments have been made as the case has gone on.

I have now reached the time of adjournment, and with your Honor's indulgence I shall have the honor of submitting what more I have, in as short time as possible, to-morrow.

(*Adjourned till* 10 *A. M., Wednesday. January* 22, 1879.)

January 22, 1879.

May it please the Court. I will now resume my argument at the point at which I paused last evening, at which time I was considering the character of the witnesses produced to support those accusations against my client, Mr. Smith, and against Dr. Thorndike, the client of my friend Mr. Drury. I was then considering the character and conduct of Eliza W. Smith with reference to this case. I had occasion to refer to certain statements of hers while on the stand, under oath, which were so utterly inconsistent with themselves, as to stamp her whole testimony with the character of absurdity, if not of wilful perjury. Why, she swore that with all her indignation and wrath at the great wrong which she had witnessed, she never spoke of it to a member of that family from that time down. On the morning of the day when her father, just at the point of death, was surrounded, as she says, by a wicked wife and two evil-minded children conspiring to defraud him, and to lead him to do an act which he would not have done had he been in his right mind, she stood there she says, amazed, stricken with horror, indignant, filled with a righteous wrath at the conduct of her mother and her brother and sister. And she said that, notwithstanding her indignation, notwithstanding her mental protest against such a transaction, she never uttered a word of it to a member of that family from that time down. Why, what is the character and mental and moral constitution, of that woman? Has she a moral constitution, or has it gone with her wild schemes and enterprises which she swears were so successful and prosperous, but which we have proved to have been so disastrous, if not infamous? For fourteen years that woman has known of this wickedness and never uttered a word of it to a mortal. She reaped the fruits thereof, she received $53,000 as the spoils of that battle, she denounced it to herself, but to the world she approved it, and when she says she did not approve it, she tells another falsehood under oath. Why I wonder if she knows the meaning of perjury? I wonder if her mind guides her in the comprehension of it, or whether she is blinded or besotted by the lust for that $50,000 which she says she is going to get if she breaks this will? I hope there is mercy somewhere and I hope there is grace to lead her to comprehend this wickedness and to repent it. If there is not mercy there is justice, and if there is not grace, there are the authorities of the law to put their hands upon such villainy, and even a woman is not safe from the righteous condemnation of a righteous Judge, nor from the solemn verdict of a jury sworn to try a case, be it of perjury or pilfering, and to find a verdict of guilty if the evidence so proves. She said she did not protest then, against it; and why? Mark, may it please your Honor. At this time she was standing there and had heard all that had passed and ~~was c~~ it all and inwardly condemned it all, and Mr. Chandler kindly—I dont think he intended to do a favor to us—put this question to her after I had extracted from her the evidence of her indignation and wrath; " Mrs. Smith, had you entered your protest at that time would your father have understood it?" " Oh, no, he would not have understood anything I said." I asked her if that was the reason she didn't protest? She said no, she was speechless. You remember the cross-examination of her upon that point, that condition in which she found herself by reason of that shock; speechless for a day and a half and never called in a physician although she had never been made speechless before in her life. If she had been struck dumb when she went upon the stand, when with the oath which she took before God that she would tell the truth,—had she with the first raising of her voice in this cause been struck dumb, she would have been saved from the infamous crime which I say she has committed here. I think from this day that woman who at sometime in her life has had a power to influence great men if not good ones, good ones if not wise ones,—I think from this day her power has ceased. I think she is shorn of all ability hereafter to mislead and misguide. I think she is known in this community at least, and that all men and all women are safe from her wild ways. When Mr. Chandler asked her if her father would have understood her if she had protested, she said " no." I asked her this question : " How at that very moment when you say he had lost all consciousness and sense, how at that same moment when his son asked him to sign the will, how did he then know enough to refuse to sign it?" Within the same minute that she said that the old man was so far gone, so nigh to his last gasp, that he would not have understood her if she had said " father, don't you do it," he understood his son when his son said " sign that will," and he said " no," meaning I will not. I asked her how it was that he did happen to understand Isaac when he would not understand her. And her reply was that it was Isaac's imperious nature that enabled him to rouse his father to a temporary consciousness. I asked her then if her nature, aroused by the wrath that possessed her, by the indignation that fired her heart hadn't imperiousness enough or energy enough to rouse that father. Her reply was " no, I was very sick, I had just got up from lung fever." If she has recovered from that lung fever, let her take precious care of her health hereafter.

This woman swore that this signature was written one or two days after Dr. Storer and Dr. Lewis held a consultation. She swore that she sent for these two distinguished physicians, and that they came. They did not come. That is all the answer to that. Dr. Lewis didn't come with Dr. Storer, and she didn't send for Dr. Storer, for Dr. Storer says Dr. Thorndike got him to come himself; and Dr. Storer also swears that he never held a consultation with Dr. Lewis in all his life. Now Dr. Storer is a gentleman and an honest man. No man, no woman can say aught against him or his character. He is a man upon whom the people of Boston rely in emergencies for good deeds, and he has them at hand. He is the wise physician, he is a friend of Dr. Thorndike, their characters stand on the same level, and far removed above the slanders and the vilifications that might be attempted to be heaped upon them by these bad people. Dr. Storer says he never consulted with Dr. Lewis; she says that he did. She says that Dr. Storer and Dr. Lewis met there on the 8th, and that the will was signed two or three days after. Dr. Storer was there on the 8th, but the will was signed before that visit, and she is disposed of there.

It seems to me, may it please your Honor, that that woman is insane, if she is not wicked. Her description of that horrid scene, which so paralyzed her, at her father's bed-side, is in entire conflict with the truth. The fact is she stood there by the bed-side of her dying father, one of the children who then was accepting his bounty, and ending all strife between them. She wanted this will made, she got $17,000 more by it than by the will of August, 1864. It was Sarah's codicil which had excited uneasiness in her mind. The will was drawn, the whole family was satisfied with it, not including the Burtons who never were included, beyond the sum of $500, by their grandfather,—and these children had nothing to do with that. I say, then, she had got her codicil as well as Sarah, and with apparent acquiescence pledged herself to harmony and peace from that time. By that will all dissension between the members of that family was disposed of as they understood it. When she says she was horrified she tells a falsehood. She came in from Medford on purpose to effect the making of that will. She horrified at that will! Why, in 1865, she conveyed nearly all her interest in that will to Edward Bangs, in consideration that her two sons, Thomas P. Smith and Arthur G. Smith, "shall abandon their opposition to the probate of the will of my late father, Ebenezer Smith, dated October 5, 1864." She horrified at that! Why, she was willing to change her estate, absolute under it, to a life estate for the sake of removing litigation which others had brought in their efforts to break it up. I need waste no more breath upon that. The facts give stronger argument, without comment. That conveyance which she made as an inducement to her children to withdraw their opposition, provided that the expenses of their lawyers should be paid, and that all other sums should be paid which were needed to buy off other litigants. That I didn't know, until I re-read this paper last night. She not only provided that the lawyers who were employed by Thomas and Arthur should be paid, but that all other sums should be paid out of her share of that property which were necessary to buy off other litigants. Well, she was spending a good deal of money to stop any opposition to a will which she now says she always did oppose, and she knows she never did oppose it in her life.

I have noticed the fact, may it please your Honor, that the only two witnesses of the scene of October 5, 1864, who support the petitioners by their fictions, or rather who attempt to support them, were Eliza W. and Mrs. Giles. This rule prevails, that if a witness contradicts himself or herself, his or her testimony is questioned; and if his or her contradiction is such as to convince one that there is no dependence to be placed upon anything which he or she says, that witness steps out of the case. Well, Eliza W. Smith stepped out of this case before she had been in it fifteen minutes, under the hands of the cross-examiner.

She travelled up to her eyes in filth and slander and perjury on the direct examination, but the instant she was touched by the cross-examiner she stepped down and out. She contradicts herself, she is all contradiction, and she is nothing if she is not contradiction. She cannot and did not state two sentences consecutively without the latter flatly contradicting the predecessor. She once had the power of persuasion, but she has lost all power of telling the truth, she has lost all power of statement except that power of statement which leads her to misstate, and so to state that you cannot make anything out of what she has said if you listen half an hour to her talk. In one breath she swears that her father never aided her save by his counsel and advice. Her father was her counsellor and adviser, but he never aided her pecuniarily, except that he may have given her five dollars, and perhaps at one time loaned her $500—, I don't think she said it reached near that sum. She swore distinctly that her father never put a dollar in the West Medford property, she swore distinctly that her father never aided her financially, and then the last statement that she made when she began to wander from the point to which I had called her attention in cross-examination, after she had answered my question as she pleased, was when she went off on a tangent to discourse herself, and what did she say? I was glad when she started, I knew she would get into trouble before she got through, and she said something which I had been trying to get from her in two days' cross-examination, and had failed utterly and entirely to get. I tried to find out from her whether she had ever drawn a dollar from her father, and she swore she never did. But here at the last moment, and in her almost farewell to the court, (my brother Chandler having recalled her for the pleasure of exhibiting her or of hearing some more of her chatter,) she said, on that little explanation which she made on her own hook, that *she always drew on her father as one would draw upon a bank*. Those were her words. I make no comment upon them. She swears his counsel was all his aid, and she writes for money, and for nothing else, savoring her petitions with what her father calls, in a letter which was read, written by him to her son Tom, who was her agent and financial man, " white-wash and soft-soap." I quote from his letter. She swears in 1879, that she was struck dumb and speechless by the dreadful crime committed by her mother, her sister, Mrs. Thorndike, and her brother Isaac T. Smith, and she gives the damning lie to this by her conveyance of September 20, 1865, to which I have just referred. And so her tongue continues to the end, in conflict with her long time previous prolific pen, swearing that she never owed her father one dollar, or not more than some paltry five or ten dollars, having given her father her notes, memoranda of which we produced in court, signed by her, for forty or fifty thousand dollars. Put those two facts together and reconcile them if you can. I remember once or twice, if not more, asking her, when such facts as those were brought together and presented to her, to reconcile them, and she said she didn't see that there was any discrepancy, she couldn't see that there was any discrepancy, any difficulty in reconciling them, there was nothing to reconcile. No, there was not. Nothing could be reconciled.

Well, I studied that character when she was on the stand and when I got through with my studies I didn't know anything about it. I could not fathom the mystery of her, except one thing, I knew she falsified to the last. The operations of her mind were peculiar to such a degree that they perplexed me, and I could not help thinking of her after I left the court-room. I shall forget her pretty soon I hope, I have got tired of the burden. I don't want to re-remember her, it is a painful spectacle, and a painful retrospect it will be to think of that bad old woman who comes here swearing to lies enough to send her soul—somewhere. She said she stayed day and night in her father's room from the time she came from Medford. She swore she stayed in that sick room day and night until the will was made, and then as soon as the will was made (she having got all she wanted) she left the poor old man to die,—left him to the tender mercies of people whom she denounced as conspiritors and bad,—left him to the tender mercies of the " wicked Mrs. Thorndike" and her wicked old mother whom she loved so well, nevertheless. She did leave that house, may it please your Honor, and she didn't stay there one night, because her mother wouldn't have her there. When she went there, she says herself—I extracted that from her,—that she and her mother did have some words, and she went away. And there is another time when she refers to the disposition on the part of the rest of the family to exclude her from the premises,—she said if she had spoken to her father at the time of the execution of the will, they would have put her out of the house. I don't blame them when they did put her out of the house, her who could ask the Rev. Dr. Neale, at the solemn service of her husband's burial, not to mention before the throne of grace the name of her mother who bore her. She is not a fit companion for christians and good people. She didn't stay there in her father's room at all. She was asked whether that will was read—I beg your Honor's note of that,—she was asked whether that will was ever read to her father, and she says she does not believe it ever was, she didn't see how it could have been, because she was in the room all the time from the time she went there until the will was made and she didn't hear it read, and her direct testimony was almost directly a positive statement that the will was not read, but upon Mr. Drury's cross-examination, or somebody's—it didn't make much difference who touched her, she always exposed something which she had tried to conceal by the direct story,—she said she couldn't tell whether the will was read or not, and it is true she could not because she didn't know anything about it.

The contradictions of Mrs. Giles in her testimony have been referred to. I have called your attention to some contradictions of Mrs. Smith in her own testimony, and I ask your Honor's attention now to the conflict which these two angels of mercy get into between themselves, how they cross each other's path at every turn. These two people are here to swear that this will was not signed properly; they are here to satisfy you that what Isaac T. Smith said on the stand here was not true; they are here to swear that he did what he never did do. Now can we trust them? Can we take them together as guides? I think your Honor has been satisfied that you will never be guided by either one separately. Let us take them together. Neither one of them as a single team is capable of pulling this load. Let us harness them together and see how they pull. Well, they pull right at cross purposes; when one pulls back the other jumps forward; and so they have been going along until they have lost all power. And thus they do it. Eliza swears her father said " no ;" Giles swears he didn't refuse to sign the will. Eliza swears to her own surprise at seeing the mother and Isaac and Mrs. Thorndike come into the room ; Mrs. Giles swears that she came into the room with the others and with the same purpose. Eliza swears she was speechless with indignation, and Giles swears they were all harmonious. And there are numerous other instances which, if my brother Drury sees fit, he will give the court, I have no doubt, and I wish he would take the case at this time to go on, but I have a little more to say. That is a wise proverb, may it please the court, that " liars should have long memories." When Hazen J. Burton, Jr., whose infamy I have sketched, concocted this story with the help of that aunt Eliza W., when he saw her for the first time for many long years, at the Essex House in Salem in 1876, he and she blindly put their necks into the noose which they contrived for others, and they have hanged themselves. These two thought that time had, with its ceaseless tide, wiped the footprints from its sands, but they were too deeply driven in, and as vividly as Macbeth saw the ghost of the murdered Banquo, they have seen these long-forgotten facts pointing their way to the horrors of their crime.

Edward D. Sohier, known to us all for his power of invective,—and I wish he occupied my place now, with his wondrous wit, his eloquence and his integrity,—he recorded upon a stray bit of paper the statements of Mrs. Giles fourteen years ago, and they are here to contradict her. I will not read them, I will leave that to brother Drury, if he chooses. Also, your Honor well remembers the testimony of Mr. Sohier on the stand, who produced this old paper which he hunted up among his waste basket or waste paper, and it was read to your Honor, and he testified and he contradicted Mrs. Giles utterly and entirely, and that is enough to ruin any witness. When a man of Mr. Sohier's clearness of perception, and high integrity, states distinctly that she said one thing, and she says another, that disposes of that witness just as thoroughly as the witness is disposed of who swears that Judge Hoar said on a certain day a thing which Judge Hoar comes and swears he never said. Judge Hoar and Edward D. Sohier are of themselves, when they testify to facts, enough to ruin the character of witnesses testifying to the contrary, and enough to ruin a case supported by those witnesses. And the two physicians who, on the 8th of October, 1864, consulted together, were alive to tell some facts. And so these two women put the signing of that will on the 9th or 10th. They both agree in that, but the will dates the 5th, and so this obstacle was to be overcome, and how was it? Confronted with this, Mrs. Giles dodged the issue by pleading ignorance of dates, refusing to swear to any ; while Eliza, more desperate, could only account for it on the supposition that Isaac had, out of all the lawyers of Boston—all strangers to him—happened to hit on the one man who was afterwards named by his mother or sister; that he went to him October 5th, and obtained a will which was in exact accordance with what happened to be agreed upon by the family in their conference, five days later; that he kept this magical will in his pocket from October 5th to October 10th, and then when it marvellously happened that exactly such a will, *verbatim et literatim*, was agreed upon, and the one man of all the lawyers in Boston, was named to draw the will, whom Isaac, by mystical foreknowledge, had divined would be named,—that then, on this 10th of October, with this will still in his pocket, he left the house and wandered around the streets of Boston for an hour or two, and then pretended that he had been to Rollins and got the will drawn. Does not this statement on its very face bear the clear impress of lunacy? Yes. Why, these petitioners have spent their strength in piling up statements about Isaac T. Smith. We have heard of his great, strong, imperious nature, of his force of character, of his power to intimidate and control, and yet they allow their principal witness, the pivot on whom their whole case rests, to prove her insanity by charging this man, as they and she depict him, with a proceeding so silly that I venture to say the petitioners' attorney, desperate as he is, will not venture to support it in his closing speech. I venture to say it merely, but I don't undertake to say what he will say. I will wait till he says it.

But there is another and more fatal contradiction, to which we now refer. Unless Isaac T. Smith was in Boston on the 10th of October, 1864, their whole story is shown to be a lie. They doubtless thought that after fourteen years, it could not be shown, except by his statement, which they were prepared to swear down, that he was not here. Now the difficulty of proving a date, after an interval of fourteen years, is well known to your Honor, and to all who have occasion to consider matters in the course of legal investigation. But that Providence which works for justice has, in a singular and striking manner, given us a proof which these falsifiers did not know of, and which they could not assail. The corporate records of the Metropolitan Savings Bank of the city of New York, made in the ordinary course of business,—proof of the highest order,—have been produced, and at the reading of the deposition of John Russell, cashier of the bank, the whole of this edifice of fraud and perjury, which these reckless blackmailers had erected, fell into ruins. Unless Isaac T. Smith was in Boston, October 10th, their story is a lie. That he was not here is proven, not only by his own oath, which, I submit, is sufficient to satisfy any intelligent man, but by the records of the bank in New York, which conclusively show that when they say he was in Boston executing this will, he was really in New York, attending to his business there. We might well stop here, and against their whole concoction of perjury or insanity, point only to this simple, unshaken record, which, like the touch of Ithuriel's spear, detects their plausible disguise and exposes the monstrous falsehood lurking underneath.

But before I conclude my consideration of the testimony given in by their witnesses, I desire to make a few feeble remarks upon the subject of Mr. O'Connor, who arrived from New York just in time to come in to the rescue of their falling fortunes. The petitioners' counsel had, with mighty pomp, at the last hearing, announced his intention of bringing witnesses here with regard to Mr. Isaac T. Smith. I think he said he could demolish him. He said that, as Mr. Smith was absent, and it was intimated that he never would make his appearance here again. This intimation was made for certain reasons best known to the counsel. He said that if Mr. Smith didn't come he was going to have some witnesses here from New York bearing down upon him. Well, Mr. Hazen J. Burton, Jr., made another trip over the New York and Boston road by way of Stonington, he made another excursion, he went on another hunt, and again on the Sabbath day, travelling round, he reaches Brooklyn. Whether he went into the slums and sought there for proper instruments of his wickedness we know not, but he succeeded in finding one from the heights of Brooklyn whom he thought it worth while to bring on here. I presume he paid that man's expenses, or, perhaps, promised to. I presume it cost him, however, the money that was needed to pay his fare from New York to Boston and his board and lodging while here, and it was a good investment for us. I say they brought over from New York Mr. O'Connor. And who is he? Why he is the deadly enemy of Isaac T. Smith. He is a man who got a thousand dollars of him in 1867 and paid him six cents on the dollar, although Mr. Smith and all the other creditors refused to accept the hundred cents which he offered them. He finally preferred to gratify them by going into bankruptcy and paying six cents on the dollar, and from that time he found Mr. Isaac T. Smith out. Up to that time he hadn't found him out and had thought he was a good man; and ever since that time he thought he was a bad man, because Mr. Isaac T. Smith told him he thought he was a swindler. That is all there is to that. Any man who occupies the position Mr. Smith does would be likely to make a few enemies. A man without enemies is almost an anomoly. It reminds me of the sentiment, "Be thou as chaste as ice, as pure as snow, thou shalt not escape calumny." No, not when there are O'Connors about. And the world is full of just such people ready to catch at the whispers or the cries of wicked men against their neighbors, and to carry them about in their pockets, perhaps get affidavits of them, and go to the bank over which the good man has presided for fourteen years or more and tell the directors that there is a will case going on here in Boston and they had better not have him for president. Shame on such a method of poisoning public opinion, and damaging, or attempting to damage, the characters of good men.

Mr. Chandler: No evidence of that, Mr. Loring. *Mr. Loring:* Of what? *Mr. Chandler:* No evidence of Mr. Hazen J. Burton, Jr., approaching the trustees and requesting them not to re-elect Isaac T. Smith as president.

Mr. Loring: I put Hazen J. Burton, Jr., and the man O'Connor in the same boat. What O'Connor did he learned from Hazen J. Burton, Jr., what he did Mr. Hazen J. Burton, Jr., did, I argue, and if anybody thinks he did not, they are welcome to the thought. If this O'Connor wasn't crammed to the muzzle with the foul slanders of Hazen J. Burton, Jr., and if he didn't discharge them into that bank meeting of directors because Hazen J. Burton, Jr., wanted him to, then he did it because he himself wanted to, and then he came on to Boston because he wanted to, and then he went on the stand because he wanted to, and then he testified because we wanted him to, and that was the time when we wanted him to do something and he did. It is not remarkable that O'Connor should be an enemy of Mr. Isaac T. Smith. Why, Hazen J. Burton, Sr., makes out the Lawrences, the Frothinghams, and James W. Page and old Mr. Sam. T. Coolidge,—I forget the others, but many more of the same character and class,—he makes them all blackmailers.

Mr. Chandler. No, sir. *Mr. Loring.* He said he was indicted that they might blackmail Mr. Ebenezer Smith, and force him to pay his debts. He went on to the stand and charged that long catalogue of worthy men, who were the pride of Boston at that time, and whose memory is cherished by all men now, and whose name and fame have given us a name abroad for integrity and honor,— Hazen J. Burton, Sr., goes on to the stand and swears that they blackmailed his old father-in-law, Ebenezer Smith. That is his testimony. *Mr. Chandler.* No, sir ; he specifies the ones, he doesn't bring them all in. *Mr. Loring.* He doesn't specify who blackmailed Mr. Smith. He specifies who perjured himself, that is the specification ; the charge of blackmailing he brought against the whole party ; the charge of perjury he brought against Mr. Samuel T. Coolidge of Coolidge & Haskell. *Mr. Chandler.* The charge of blackmailing was against the assignees ; the charge of perjury was against Mr. Coolidge only. *Mr. Loring.* The charge of blackmailing was against the creditors, who all attempted to blackmail Mr. Ebenezer Smith, and the charge of Mr. Chandler is not true. *Mr. Chandler.* You had better look at the short-hand reports. *Mr. Loring.* Look at your short-hand reports, and you will find it just as I have stated. It was not strange that Mr. Hazen J. Burton, Jr., going on to New York, could find some man who thought evil of Mr. Isaac T. Smith.

So, after the fearful announcement of his counsel, we waited to see what could possibly be raked up from all the slums and gutters of New York against Mr. Smith. The day came, and the court assembled,—and it is but doing justice to the petitioners' counsel to say, that he announced that his case was closed without producing any such evidence. But a suggestion coming, perhaps, from his worthy associate and client that there was a little more mud to throw, a Boston Judge and a Boston audience were regaled by the spectacle of O'Connor. And as he stepped upon the stand I feel assurred that the same thought struck your Honor as it did the audience and myself: Why here is a twin brother of Burton, senior ! In looks, in manner, in life, still more in character, the resemblance was complete. He didn't think well of Isaac T. Smith. He hated him as the devil hated holy water. Well, Mr. Smith's son took hold of him to cross-examine him, and he shook him as a terrier would shake a rat, and with the same results. He was left lifeless as a witness. Well, who is this O'Connor by his own confession? A bankrupt, accused of fraud ; president of a safe-deposit company, who was requested to resign, and did resign ; clerk in a life insurance company, who was discharged. No, he said he wasn't discharged—he was only requested to leave at once. This is a distinction as fine as that of the man who said he wasn't kicked down stairs, he was kicked at the top and fell down of his own accord. A debtor of Isaac T. Smith, whom he had paid six cents on the dollar; the applicant for a position in Mr. Smith's bank, which Mr. Smith as an honest man opposed giving; a trustee whom the depositors had tried to get a court to remove—in short, a sneak, a fraud, a worthless man, whose enmity is an honor to Isaac T. Smith. And this is the only testimony which by all their endeavors they have raked and scraped against my client. I wish them joy of their witness.

With one word more I leave them. They have given to this court falsehood instead of truth, or else the visions which issue from the ivory gate of dreamland. But I deny to them this latter excuse or palliation for their false swearing. They have testified under no delusion. They have substituted not dreams and imaginings for memory's truthful records, but the foul products of a desire to get gain. Money they call for, not heeding how so long as it is gotten.

And now, may it please the Court, I regard it as utterly unnecessary for me even to refer to the testimony which has been offered by the respondents, in order to establish the position of the executors,—evidence which presents such an accumulation of proof, that any lawyer whose mad desire for notoriety or for fees had not destroyed all honorable or honest instincts, would at once have abandoned a case so clearly built upon falsehood as this one. We have Dr. Thorndike, we have Isaac T. Smith, we have Arthur G. Smith, and we have John Russell. I cannot speak too highly in commendation of the character of Dr. Thorndike. His appearance on the stand was characteristic of that good man's character and career; plain, simple, straightforward, honest and good. No stain is upon his character, there is nothing against him, his testimony comes with that clear and distinct utterance which finds a parallel in the clearness of its truth. The husband of Sarah Smith, whose character was assailed by the Burtons in Judge Hoar's office, when the assailants and their attack received from that good man the indignant repulse which so outrageous an attempt or an insinuation deserved. Dr. Thorndike, who has stood through all this storm that has been raging about him, calmly and quietly waited until the call of duty should summon him, and then he came and told what he had to say. I need add nothing of praise to him.

Mr. Isaac T. Smith: I think your Honor will appreciate my sentiment when I say that I speak now not only as counsel for an esteemed client, but as a man who sees another man unjustly attacked, and who through long weeks has seen every means tried to injure that man—means so dastardly that only men who can abandon that "fair play" which even prize-fighters and bullies respect would have used them,—who has seen that man's life scanned by eager eyes to find a single blot, whether pertinent to this case or not, who has seen that man's character tried by a furnace heated seven times hot by a fire lit by avarice and malice, and perjury and madness, and who has seen him come out of all "without the smell of fire upon his garments." Surely, your Honor, I respectfully submit, it is due to you, it is due to myself, that the facts which these men have proved should be cited by me. These petitioners have poured their nitric acid of obloquy, hoping that base metal would melt, but Mr. Smith has come out refined gold. When he came on the stand his very appearance

II

shattered some foolish stories which had been circulated through the press about him. These stories were refuted, and they at least, if not their authors, slunk into their kennels and are heard of no more. I recall a description of him which I read in a morning paper after he appeared on the stand, the paper referring to the fact that he had been described by the petitioners' witnesses as an imperious man, overbearing and proud, and distant and arrogant. The writer in the newspaper said that he must have broken under time and events, that his strong and imperious nature had yielded, for he seemed a most amiable and agreeable gentleman, giving no signs of that cold and arrogant and hard nature which these petitioners attributed to him. The power of illustration which the petitioners' counsel has exhibited in his rhetoric he has sought to illuminate by the sketch which we see on the wall of the old man himself. That had disappeared, and I with pleasure look upon it this morning. It was put in here, and if your Honor noticed the resemblance between that man who is described by the petitioners' counsel as goodness itself and mercy and generosity, look at Isaac T. Smith's face, recall Isaac T. Smith's face, and see if you don't meet the same thing—that is all.

Why, what have the petitioners shown about Isaac T. Smith? They have shown that he was a good man and attended to his own business. He has not only been trusted by his fellow citizens, not only honored by his State, not only a man whose life his neighbors may respect, whose children may love and reverence, but a man whom a king selected as the agent of his government in this country. He has fulfilled the prophecy of the Bible: " a man who is diligent in his business shall stand before kings."

Mr. Chandler: Did he go to Siam? *Mr. Loring:* Why didn't you ask him that question when he was on the stand? *Mr. Chandler:* I prefer to put it to you now. *Mr. Loring:* He was his representative in this country. He is a man who by the unshaken testimony in this case could give up a great share of property, to which he was entitled not only by his father's love but by his father's gratitude, and which his father had given him in the will of August, 1864. He was willing to give up what his father, out of gratitude to him, had given him in preference to the other children, and on the 5th of October he gave it up for the sake of protecting that father's name even from a futile attack in the courts of law. Isaac T. Smith, on the 5th of October, 1864, drew the line which struck $15,000 out of his estate and put it in the pocket of Eliza W. If Isaac T. Smith had not consented to agree to this will which is now attacked, he would have been $15,000 richer than he is to-day. He is the conspirator who is trying to defraud the members of his family! He is the conspirator who, according to Eliza W. Smith, alias Gen, was perpetrating a foul crime for his own good. There was no crime committed and there was no good gotten by it. He practicing a fraud to take $15,000 out of his own pocket! He is a sensible man, he is a man of clear head, he is a man who manages the financial operations of the Metropolitan Savings Bank of New York, and he is not the foolish man to commit a crime to gratify somebody else, and at his own pecuniary loss. I will not enlarge upon that. I could, but I will not. The facts again argue themselves. He generously gave it up into the pocket of that very sister, whose mind, apparently unhinged by ambition and love of money, charges that sacrifice as a crime. I think she cannot be abetted therein by this tribunal.

Who was Isaac T. Smith? He did not go to college, but was educated at the military academy, Middletown, Connecticut. In 1834, at about the age of twenty, we find him going out as supercargo and confidential agent of our old East India merchants, who were very careful to whom they entrusted their millions to invest on the other side of the globe. Next we find him acting as treasurer of a company of which the Hon. Nathan Hale of this city was president, then for several years a successful merchant in New York, and agent of the Siamese Government, and then for over twenty-five years holding very responsible positions in a large moneyed institution in that city, and for the past fifteen years president of the Metropolitan Savings Bank, and director and manager in other financial corporations. He was also for several years a Commissioner of Emigration, a position of honor and trust conferred by the Governor only upon citizens of high character, having millions of money at their disposal and application. Then at the second election of Lincoln, when only men of unquestioned patriotism and intelligence were called to the front, he had the honor of being chosen by his fellow-citizens a Presidential elector. We find his name also connected as manager and director of several of the noble charitable institutions which adorn that city. Thus, during a period of forty-five years, we find him everywhere sought out and confided in and honored. And he is the man who is attacked!

May it please your Honor; the mutterings of this storm were heard a year or more before it broke. It could have been quieted for a time by the outlay of a little money, doubtless, only to have broken out again at another time, for the storms that these men have been raising have been quieted by money. I remember some testimony of Mr. Hazen J. Burton, Jr., which I will merely refer to. He says that in the settlement of the controversy over the will of his grandmother he directed his counsel to settle it but not to destroy his chance of opening it again if he wanted to. That is a magnanimous way of settling! That is honorable advice to give to a counsel, to advise him to make a show of settlement, but in reality to have the door open for farther litigation! So these gentlemen, these executors, became satisfied from past experience that it was idle to attempt anything excepting the examination of these people. There was no escape but their annihilation, and if they detected anything wrong to throttle them in their tracks by process of law. Christianity, education and civilization prohibit us from taking by the throat the man who slanders us, we turn to the process of law for our remedy and our hands are tied from inflicting that condign punishment which such men deserve. I think the whipping post has been restored in Delaware, or some place, and my impression is that its restoration has proved of great benefit in the effect which it has to stay certain vices. I conceive that there is one vice of which there is no more fitting punishment than the whipping post and the stocks. And these gentlemen, having nothing in their own characters or conduct to fear, Isaac T. Smith and Dr. Thorndike, determined to stand the shock and let the conspirators do their worst, and in taking this stand, may it please the court, I submit that these gentlemen not only adopted a wise part in itself, but performed a public service, a duty as citizens, in letting knaves understand that schemes of this kind will not bring them money. And now consider Arthur G. Smith's testimony. He is our next witness. He comes on here although Hazen J. Burton, Jr., tried to make a bargain with him by which he should be induced to stay in New York or else come on here and swear for him. I have called Hazen J. Burton, Jr., a perjurer and a suborner of perjury. I repeat the charge in connection with Arthur G. Smith for I am reminded of it, and I say that the attempt on his part to induce that man not to come on to Boston is simply of a character with the whole course of this case. Arthur G. Smith told him "I will not be induced by your guarantees or assurances, I am coming on to tell the truth, and," he adds, "to sustain the trust that was made." What does Mr. Burton say after Arthur G. Smith has told his story? Why he is called by Mr. Chandler to rebut him. Mr. Chandler made two or three attempts to rebut. He called on George S. Burton to rebut Judge Hoar's testimony. How did he rebut it? He said if Judge Hoar had not testified as he did he would have sworn just as his brother did. I remarked it was fortunate for him he heard Judge Hoar before he did testify like his brother. Another attempt is made upon Arthur G. Smith. He comes on here from New York and gives important testimony for the respondents, and the petitioners' counsel seeks to damage his testimony by showing that the witness once struck his brother. The petitioners' counsel asked him with an air of satisfaction and delight, "didn't you jump over a table and strike your brother?" "Yes, and I would do it again if he struck my sister." That is the attack which is made on Arthur G. Smith! He was asked if he wasn't tried in New York. He is not much acquainted with the process of law, and he said he was tried. They asked him if he wasn't tried for carrying off those papers, and he said "yes." When I showed him the records of the courts of New York, he was reminded of the fact that that was the record of the trial. And what was it? Why, your Honor, he was not tried in the courts of New York. Mrs. Smith, alias Gen, sued him in the courts of New York and judgment was rendered there against Mrs. Smith and in favor of Arthur G. That is the only trial he had. And Mr. Chandler called up to my mind again by that little question the existence of that judgment, which is proof enough, with Mrs. Smith, alias Gen's, testimony here, to cause her indictment for perjury, a conviction of perjury, followed by punishment. The testimony from Arthur G. Smith then bore upon Mrs. Smith's talk with him in 1864 when this will was offered for probate. Mrs. Smith has sworn here in 1879 and 1878, that when that will was made she was shocked, and she afterwards opposed it and wanted it to be broken down, thought it ought not to be set up. Well, Arthur G. Smith, (I will not read his testimony, but it was distinct and direct) swore that Mrs. Smith urged him to abandon his appeal and made an agreement by which his counsel fees were paid, and he was paid a hundred dollars, and the property was put in trust to Mr. Bangs; and she told him that that will could not be broken, that her father knew just as well what he was about as he (Arthur) did then when he was talking with her and that it was all absurd to attempt to attack it. That is what this woman said in 1864. And now she comes here armed with all the weapons which a corrupt nature and a designing imagination can invent, and stands up here and swears that that was not so. And she swears, I think, for her own amusement, she certainly swears for her own destruction. Arthur tells what she said and did in 1864 and 1865 and nobody will contradict it excepting Eliza W. Smith, she is a contradiction, as I have said, in herself *per se.* She is nothing if she is not a contradiction, and so she cannot contradict anybody.

Our evidence, may it please the court, the story of Mr. Isaac T. Smith, in regard to that scene at the signing of the will, I have no doubt impressed itself upon your Honor's mind with vividness and distinctness, and that it freed your mind from any question as to whether that will was properly signed. Isaac T. Smith came from New York, and, went to his father's house, he learned that his father had executed a codicil, and for some reason Mrs. Thorndike declined to show it to him; he went to Eliza out in Medford and she came in to see if she could not see the codicil. Eliza saw, and urged the making of a new will. The will was drawn by Mr. Rollins on the 5th of October. Mr. Rollins swears so. Isaac T. Smith says that on the 5th of October he went to the house with the will which he had drawn, and took it to his father and read it to him; that he then showed it to his mother and sisters, and it met with their approbation, and then he took that will into the room where his father was; then the family came into that room, witnesses were sent for, Mrs. Giles, Margaret Patterson and Andrix A. Foster; and the old gentleman took his pen with which to sign that will, and being feeble at that time he found difficulty in controlling the pen and it made a spattering, " then," says Isaac, " my mother said Why don't you assist your father, Isaac," and thereupon after he had written part of his name Isaac puts his hand upon his father's feeble hand and guides it to its conclusion. That is Isaac T. Smith's story about that, and that man, the petitioners' counsel, dares to stand before this court and say that that spattered signature needs no argument to pronounce it a forgery! Why, may it please the court, a forger usually attempts to imitate. The forgery that has been sketched before this court by this counsel's predecessor, if not by him, was that wicked, heinous forgery of taking a dead man's hand and writing his name to a will. Humanity is shocked at the suggestion of such an infamy. The human mind fails to comprehend it in all its enormity,—that the son of a good old father who had been kind to him and to whom he had been kind, that the son of that good old man who had always been true to his son, and to whom this son had always been devoted, that he who had stood by his father when his fortunes were being shattered by the fall in values, and poverty was hanging over his head, when his property was in the hands of a sheriff,—as my brother Drury offered to and did prove,—and was about to be sold, that this man who had stood as I say at his father's right hand as his defender, his protector and his supporter, that he who was his father's only living son, performing the filial duties of a son, that this son took his father's hand as he lay dying and unconscious, as bad as if dead, took that father's hand and just as his father was about leaving this world of woe to an eternity beyond, and committed this crime at the death bed of his father! That is the first crime which Isaac T. Smith ever committed in all his life; that is the first sin which he is known to have been guilty of. Well, a man never becomes wicked in a day, and it would take a long lifetime of atrocities to embolden the man and make him wicked enough to do this deed. To stand up before heaven, and with all the fear of a righteous judgment hereafter, and to do the deed which he is said to have done then, and now to have sworn that he did not,—why the duplicity of his offence finds no parallel in the annals of criminal record. There is a wickedness and a corruption, there is a hardness of heart and a degradation of soul attending the commission of such an offence that finds a parallel only in the like traits of character that are exhibited by the family of Burtons in this court.

I submit, may it please the Court, that before Isaac T. Smith shall be found guilty of the crime this counsel dares charge him with, the sun will stand still in the heavens, and the thunders will cease to roar. No, may it please the Court. No man can command that power of oratory and that elegance of diction and rhetoric, by which any testimony which has been brought into this case can be made to cast a shadow or a show of suspicion of guilt upon Isaac T. Smith. I know that no lawyer can use the English language with such convincing force as to persuade your Honor that my client, Mr. Isaac T. Smith, whose life up to the 5th of October, 1864, bore the record of an honest and righteous man, became on that day the vilest of sinners, and became on this last month the blackest of perjurers.

Had I not occupied so much of the time of the Court, it would gratify me personally to dwell a little more upon this spectacle which we have had before us. We have proved, may it please the Court, the substantial facts; that Mr. Isaac T. Smith was not in Boston on the 10th of October, as they swear he was; that the will, this paper, which they say was drawn on that day, and signed on that day, was not drawn and signed on that day by him because he was in New York. I pass the attempts, paltry and petty, and aimless and ineffectual, to attack that deposition; the deposition is here, and John Russell's testimony is here, and he confirms Isaac T. Smith. We prove by Isaac T. Smith what part he took in the signature to his father's will. I simply submit, as a matter of law, that the facts which he states constitute a lawful signing by the testator. I should say, furthermore, that had Isaac T. Smith written his father's name himself, without having his father's hand in his, had taken the pen and written his father's name, and then his father had acknowledged that to be his signature, and asked Mrs. Giles and Margaret Patterson and Andrix A. Foster to come and witness it, and they had witnessed it, and he had told them that it was his will, it would have been his signature and his will.

Mr. Chandler: No doubt of that.

Mr. Loring: I get no aid, may it please the Court, from the assent given to my proposition by the counsel for the petitioners. That would have been his will. This was his will. If this will had been rejected in the Probate Court, may it please your Honor, Isaac T. Smith would have been worth $15,000 more than he is. He had no motive to do such a thing. He hadn't the power to do such a thing, because if he did not have an imperious nature, he had a good conscience, a sense of right and goodness, he had the fear of God before his eyes, and he always has had; and that is what has made a good man of him. And he didn't forget the presence of his God as he stood by the bedside of his dying father. He didn't then for the first time break from the control of that holy influence which has evidently guided him through a long and active life, making him to stand before the people as a counsellor and friend, making him prominent among the good men of New York city, a dispenser of its charities, an honor to his name, and a credit to the place of his birth and of his adoption.

And now, may it please the court, I have done. The feeling of respect which naturally comes over me as I apprehend the inadequacy of these remarks is tempered by the knowledge that the high character of my client and the justice of my cause more than overbalance the weakness of their advocate, and that the decision will rest with you, sir, who both by training and inclination judge not from words but facts. It is one of the boasts of our civilization that it leads men to give up that natural impulse which prompts us to redress wrong by violence, and restrains that feeling which tempts us to grasp a liar and slanderer by the throat, and controls that instinct which would lead us, when insults so wanton and slanders so foul are hurled against the character of the living and the memory of the dead as the petitioners and some of their witnesses have dared to utter, to " put in every honest hand a whip and lash the rascals naked through the world." Civilization and religion teach us to lay aside our weapons, to control our just resentment, and to leave retribution to those tribunals which we have erected as the emblems of that righteous God who administers impartial justice. On that justice we rely—firm, secure, majestic. And we ask your Honor, as its representative, to render a decision so clear and decisive that it shall form both a punishment and a compensation —a fitting punishment to these base assailants, a high vindication of these innocent defendants.

What retribution is not due to those who, through unhallowed lust of gold, have violated every sentiment of family pride, every spark of honor, every instinct of decency? What deep infamy should fall on her whose lying lips have not only accused a brother and sister, but have overleaped that sacred bound which shields a parent's memory? " Taint not thy mind, nor let thy heart contrive against thy mother aught." That mother has not been spared by her, was not spared during her life, and since her death her memory has not been held sacred. Well for that daughter had it been, had she remembered this. The sentiment of pity leads me to hope that her infamy is palliated by want of reason. Insanity has been pleaded as a defence when one is tried for slaying the body; let it also mitigate, though it cannot cover, her crime in attempting to slay innocent character.

And that young man upon whose shoulders rests so much of the guilt of this black proceeding; who, by every means which baseness could prompt and brazen hardihood could execute, has endeavored, even when he saw his worthless case was lost, who when, as he told Arthur G. Smith, he threatened an appeal from what he felt or feared must be your Honor's verdict, has endeavored to stain the reputation of men who towered above him like "Hyperion to a satyr"; who, in this court and out of it, has lied and slandered and backbitten, trying, like the snake he is, to sting the heel since he cannot reach the heart :— Let your Honor's words, I pray, fall upon him with such a weight of warning that they may go through even the callous covering of his heart and teach him that, in this court at least, "Corruption wins not more than honesty."

So much for the guilty,—now one word for the innocent. I think I may be permitted to say that it is the duty and privilege of your Honor,—for it is a privilege as well as a duty to vindicate innocent character unjustly assailed—to give a decision which they can forever quote as a conclusive answer to these calumnies. In this proceeding and in this court my clients could not ask money damages, and it is well that it should be so. There are some injuries that money can compensate. If a thief steals my purse, if a ruffian assaults my person, I can go into a court of law and ask for money to repair the damage; but character is a plant of slow growth—"There doth a good man garner up his hopes," there either he must live or bear no life. And they who wickedly assail reputation commit a deeper and a blacker crime than they who wound the body or pilfer the purse.

We ask you therefore, may it please your Honor, not only to dismiss this petition, but to vouchsafe your reasons therefor, that where these people have sowed their lies we may scatter the good seed of your Honor's decision. Libel suits against these people would be barren victories. Indictments would punish them without benefiting us. No, sir. I ask in behalf of Isaac T. Smith, I ask in behalf of Dr. Thorndike, what, I think, I have a right to ask, and what, I think, no honest man can more highly value — the clear decision of an upright judge.

And with your Honor I leave my client's cause, confident of the result of your deliberations; and I beg to be thankful for the time and attention which have been given me, and if I have, by what I may have said, aided the court in arriving at the conclusion at which I arrive, the memory of it will be pleasant.

Closing Argument of Wm. H. Drury, Esq.,

Counsel for Dr. Wm. H. Thorndike,

JANUARY 22, 1879.

May it please your Honor:

During all the time of the Court which this case has occupied since it was begun, in May last; in all the appointments for hearing which have been made; through all the postponements and delays; in all the preliminary hearings upon the various motions and questions which have come before the Court; through this long trial upon the merits, listening to the statements of counsel, the examination of witnesses, and now in the final argument; your Honor has exhibited a patience which will ever be remembered by us with profound gratitude and respect. And I now ask your further indulgence, which I am all the more diffident to ask, because I feel that your Honor is willing to grant it, while I perform this last duty to my clients, and present my final argument for your consideration.

The real defendants in this case, may it please your Honor, are Hazen J. Burton, Jr., and those who have counselled, aided and abetted him. They are on trial here. This case was first presented in the shape of an attack, unexampled for bitterness and malignity, aimed principally against a woman who is now dead. A petition was filed in this court May 6, 1878, on the back of which appeared the name of Benjamin F. Butler, the substance of which petition was as follows :—

First, that Ebenezer Smith, possessed of a fortune of $300,000 and upwards, died intestate October 12, 1864;

Second, that prior to the death of the said Ebenezer Smith, Sarah W. Thorndike, (put at the head), Isaac T. Smith and Eliza W. Gen, (alias Smith), children of Ebenezer Smith, entered into a wicked conspiracy to defraud and cheat Hazen J. Burton, Jr., and George S. Burton, at that time minors, sons of a deceased daughter of the said Ebenezer Smith, from obtaining their shares of his estate to which they would have been entitled as his heirs-at-law in case of his intestacy;

Third, that in pursuance of said conspiracy, said conspirators caused and procured the name of Ebenezer Smith to be forged upon a false and fraudulent instrument dated October 5, 1864, purporting to be the last will and testament of Ebenezer Smith;

Fourth, that said conspirators fraudulently procured said forged instrument to be attested and signed by three persons as witnesses;

Fifth, (here is where Dr. Thorndike comes in), that said conspiritors, together with Dr. William H. Thorndike, one of the executors named in the forged instrument aforesaid, and well knowing these facts, and aiding and abetting in them, in further pursuance of said conspiracy, fraudulently caused and procured said forged instrument to be proved and admitted to probate;

Sixth, that upon an appeal from the probate of said will, taken to the Supreme Judicial Court by the guardian *ad litem* of the petitioners, a compromise was made, in pursuance of which a final decree was entered in said case sustaining the probate of said will, and their said guardian accepted and received for them $5.000 in satisfaction of their claim against the estate of Ebenezer Smith, said guardian being deceived and misled thereunto by the fraudulent doings of said conspiritors, and being wholly ignorant of the facts in the premises;

And *Seventh*, that said Hazen J. Burton, Jr., and George S. Burton were, by the fraudulent acts of said conspiritors, done secretly and concealed from them as aforesid, defrauded out of their lawful share of Ebenezer Smith's estate, such share amounting to about $60,000.

This was the substance of the allegations in the petition as far as it related to the will of Ebenezer Smith; and I call your attention to the enormity of the offences which are therein charged;—offences some of which would have been felonies by the statute law of this Commonwealth, and these persons, who are charged with having committed them, would have been liable to sentence for ten years in the State Prison. and the offences are not outlawed to-day in regard to Isaac T. Smith, who is subject to indictment for the crimes with which he is charged, if he is guilty of them, and if any Grand Jury could be found to bring in an indictment.

Mr. Chandler: The statute of limitations saves them. *Mr. Drury:* It does not save him, not Isaac T. Smith. He is subject to indictment. And why don't these men who are clamoring here go to that Grand Jury, as Judge Hoar told them to go with their former blackmailing case? Why don't they go to that Grand Jury and have Isaac T. Smith indicted, if they mean what they say? *Mr. Chandler:* Because the statute of limitations prohibits it. *Mr. Drury:* Because they lie, because they do not mean what they say, and the statute of limitations does not prohibit an indictment. I say, your honor, that the alleged offences, some of them, would have been felonies, and the others would have been crimes in themselves morally as bad as felonies;—a conspiracy to defraud, carried out by forgery, pursued by fraudulently procuring a forged instrument to be witnessed, further pursued by imposing upon a court by false testimony,—publishing a false and forged instrument whereby a forged instrument was falsely proved and procured to be admitted to probate,—and crowned with success by obtaining the great stake of $60,000, out of which two helpless minors were unjustly and wickedly defrauded.

To these charges relating to the will of Ebenezer Smith, was attached another bitter and malignant attack upon a woman alone, relating to the will of Eliza Smith, the widow of Ebenezer Smith, charging Sarah W. Thorndike, by means of undue influence upon her mother, and by other wicked and atrocious means, with cheating the petitioners out of about $40,000.

The substance of this petition was published at the time by the procurement of the petitioners, as I have good reason to believe. At the return day of this petition a hearing was appointed to take place on the 18th of June, and I appeared here with witnesses intending to go to trial; but the petitioners were not ready. Thereupon, upon my application to your Honor, the petitioners were ordered to file affidavits of the evidence which the petitioners alleged in their petition that they possessed, upon which they relied to sustain the charges which they had made. Affidavits were accordingly filed in court on the 29th of June, having previously been furnished to the newspapers for publication, together with some other affidavits which were not filed; and they first appeared at great length in the Sunday papers of June 30th, preceded in one paper by the startling words in large type: "The Root of all Evil." "100,000 and some Boston reputations involved." "Signing a will on the threshold of eternity." "A harrowing story by a defrauded daughter."

Mr. Chandler: Is that in evidence? *Mr. Drury:* Public history and common knowledge. And thenceforth this case became a public sensation,—a matter of common knowledge and public history now. On the 8th of July I appeared before your Honor and asked that a hearing might be had the next day upon a motion which I should make to dismiss so much of the petition as related to the will of Eliza Smith. The case was excessively annoying and distressing to my clients, because of this publicity, but they had no fear of the result in court; and to show their confidence in their case they did not fear to entrust it to my hands against the great and glorious Butler; for they knew that

"Thrice is he armed that hath his quarrel just,
And he but naked, though locked up in steel,
Whose conscience with injustice is corrupted."

I had a week in which to read the affidavits which the petitioners had been on a "still hunt" preparing for a year and a half, with the most noted lawyer in the country and his numerous assistants to aid them and to represent them. General Butler appeared here in court, greatly to my astonishment. I did not even attempt to rebut the affidavits by a single word of evidence. I took occasion, however, to sift them, and with nothing but law and argument on our side to meet that part of the case, after a hearing which occupied a whole day, in which the distinguished counsel for the petitioners occupied two-thirds of the time and did two-thirds of the talking, it was decided that they had not made out any case as far as the will of Eliza Smith was concerned. That part of the petition was dismissed and the petitioners were routed, and they found that there were blows for them to receive as well as blows to give.

The other part of the petition relating to the will of Ebenezer Smith came on for trial September 3d, and the petitioners were asked simply to comply with the law, and show their good faith, by paying back the $5,000 received from the estate of their grandfather, before proceeding further, which they failed to do. General Butler stepped out, and the present counsel for the petitioners stepped in. And his first step was to ask that the petition which his clients had filed be dismissed without prejudice, frankly confessing before your Honor here in court that he could not sustain the charges which were therein made. I opposed the application as vigorously as I could, because I wished to hold these petitioners to the monstrous charges which they had made, and which they confessed through their counsel that they had been guilty of making, without the ability to prove them. The application to dismiss without prejudice was denied. Counsel next asked leave to amend the petition by striking out everything therein relating to the will of Ebenezer Smith and substituting therefor the amended petition upon which this case is now on trial,—a comparatively mild petition on which I at first thought I should advise my clients not to go to trial, because it contained nothing that was not comprehended in the reasons of appeal on which the case went up to the Supreme Judicial Court fourteen years ago. But Isaac T. Smith, especially, was very desirous for an investigation of the case as thorough as possible, and my clients thought, on the whole, it was better to have the matter decided as soon as possible. The motion for the repayment of the $5,000 was withdrawn, the decree thereon waived, and we consented to go on as if the motion had not been made. The case came on for trial December 4th, and the counsel for the petitioners made an opening argument reviving everything which he had abandoned, everything which was contained in the first petition and a great deal more that was not in it,—some of the groundless talk of Benjamin F. Butler,—an argument fairly entitled to the credit of containing more groundless charges, false insinuations, fictitious statements and perversions of fact than are often found condensed together into the same space.

I repeat now, your Honor, that Hazen J. Burton, Jr., and George S. Burton, their counsellors, aiders and abetters are upon trial here, and are the real defendants in this case. Unless they have sustained, or given reasonable and probable cause for, the monstrous charges made and published, they stand guilty of prosecuting a wickedly malicious case and prostituting a court of justice to the foul and base purpose of giving protection to the utterance and publication of the foulest kind of slander. Considering what a strong case any counsel of decent ability would have told them they must make out to upset a will fourteen years after it had been admitted to probate, considering this whole case, the way the old case was settled fourteen years ago by a family compromise, and the way in which the case has been prosecuted, the way in which the charges have been published, if they have not shown to the satisfaction of this court beyond a reasonable doubt that all these defendants are the grossest criminals, guilty of the enormous crimes charged, then these petitioners are themselves morally guilty of a great crime, and deserve to be consigned to infamy for the rest of their lives and to receive the contempt of all honest men. If they have imputed to persons of good character and standing the foulest kind of crimes, without adequate cause, they must expect that I shall, in the course of my argument, characterize them as they deserve.

We have been patiently waiting, your Honor, and I have no doubt you have been patiently waiting, and the public has been patiently waiting, to see the counsel for the petitioners come down out of the clouds into which he soared in his opening argument, and sustain the charges which he therein made, and "give to airy nothing a local habitation and a name." But have they justified themselves? Have they proved what they have charged? No, they have not. It would be too charitable to say that those charges are the ravings of a madman, or even the inventions, visions and dreams of a wicked, diseased, distempered and distorted imagination.

This case, your Honor, has attracted infinitely more public attention, and received far greater notoriety, than it ever deserved. This is not an important case intrinsically, but is important only as made so by publicity. It is a great noise about nothing. I suppose the reason why at one time some thought it was so important was that the name of a very noted lawyer was attached to the petition. We were to be treated to something startling, highly interesting and sensational. A large estate, grown to be worth perhaps a million dollars, which had been settled a dozen years, was to be unsettled. The public mind was prepared by newspaper articles to believe that one of the foremost physicians in the city in reputation for character and ability, his wife and his wife's brother, a prominent gentleman in New York of high reputation, and holding various offices of trust and responsibility and honor, were to be convicted of conspiracy, forgery and various other crimes, and brought down out of their high positions, dishonored and disgraced before the world. Here was food for scandal. Would anybody have the audacity, it was thought, to make such an undertaking, try to do what had been done, and make such charges, unless they could be sustained by extraordinary and most conclusive proof of enormous crimes committed by four persons feloniously combined together to cheat the dead and the living? But it has all fallen flat. We have now heard everything that could be raked and scraped from the four corners of the globe to support these charges, and it is now doubtful whether this case ought to be treated with serious consideration.

Instead of meeting the Great Mogul whom people thought we were to encounter, we find this case was merely begun under the shadow of his great name, with a view, probably, of striking terror to us and giving notoriety to the case. His name is on the old petition and that is all, and his name is all that now gives their case whatever dignity it has. The lion's skin is there, but the lion is not there. His name was used simply as a bugbear, and perhaps it is one of those many bricks, which he is famous for keeping, which fall far short of their mark. I myself, your Honor, never expected to meet General Butler in court in this case. Nobody was afraid to meet him. My clients knew that I, or anybody else, could carry their case to success against General Butler and the devil combined. I did not believe, really, that he had anything to do with the case. I believed that the work was done under the shadow of his name by somebody who was putting that name to the base use of giving weight to foul public slander against honest and respectable persons. I believed this for several reasons.

First, I believed that he, at least, was enough of a lawyer to have some conception of the difficulty of the work which was undertaken, if undertaken seriously, and that he would have sense enough to know that it could not be done. True it is, the greater and more difficult the work to be done, the more need of a powerful man to do the work, but you will always find that a powerful intellect generally has discretion to know what is impossible, and for that reason we find men of the weakest mental power undertaking impossible and the most difficult enterprises. Hence I believed that the work was undertaken either by men who did not know what they were doing, or else by men who thought that this onslaught, coming in such a way, with the aid of the newspapers, behind a powerful name, charging monstrous crimes, creating public scandal, would drive the parties accused to make a compromise and buy off the accusers.

Another reason why I believed that the bearer of that name on the back of the old petition either did not knowingly have anything to do with the case, or would not, after an investigation of the facts, have anything to do with it, was that I did not believe that he would lend his name to making such charges against such people, unless they could be substantiated beyond a reasonable doubt by most extraordinary and conclusive proof, and I knew this could not be done in this case. Whatever may be said against General Butler, he is not totally depraved. It is evident that the courts of justice could be made by irresponsible and unscrupulous persons the most oppressive means for the gratification of private malice and for the purposes of extortion, and that one great protection against the prostitution of the courts to such purposes is in the character of the legal profession ; and any lawyer who has not such a sense of justice that he will not engage in such work, is not fit to be a member of the profession. Whatever may be said in a petition filed here is privileged. A man can accuse another, in such a petition, of all known crimes without a shadow upon which to base the accusations, and yet the person making the accusations cannot be indicted for publishing a false and malicious libel. The newspapers can publish the accusations, and neither they nor the authors of them be liable to an action for libel. Hence I did not believe that an eminent public man, renowned as one of the ablest lawyers in the country, would have so little sense of justice as to lend his great name to the prostitution of a court of justice to the purposes of foul calumny, malignity, revenge and extortion, and by the aid of his name give to false and monstrous charges a dignity and weight which they would not otherwise have.

I find I was correct in coming to these conclusions. When General Butler came into the court in this case he was as ignorant of it as the babe unborn. He floundered around here, got everything wrong end first, drew on his imagination for facts, and whatever was whispered to him by his lieutenant who sat beside him, came out in such a perverted shape that nobody could tell what he was up to. All on account of his ignorance of the case. And then again, when the hearing in regard to the payment of the $5,000 came up, he knew nothing about the case. He actually said if I would show that his clients were paid $5,000, he would give up the case. And when the compromise was shown to him he was completely confounded, saw he had no case, and was as good as his word,—went out of court in disgust and never appeared in the case again.

This proceeding, brought forward in this way under the name of one man and prosecuted in court by another, reminds me of an anecdote which I will relate to the court, although I once had occasion to relate it elsewhere. Once upon a time a traveller entered Philadelphia on the cars and went to the front of the depot, thinking he would procure the best conveyance he could find to take him to the house of a friend in a fashionable quarter of the city. He wanted to go in good style. He saw standing across the street opposite the depot door an elegant conveyance, a superb pair of high-spirited horses, well equipped, and a very stylish carriage, on which sat a slick and nicely dressed driver, who shouted to the traveller asking him if he wanted a carriage. This elegant conveyance was just what the traveller wanted, and even surpassed his expectations. He had a little luggage, so he handed his check to the driver and waited for him to go round to the rear of the depot where his luggage was; and pretty soon the traveller, left there by the driver to reflect upon the elegant appearance which he would make going to the house of his friend, had his expectations greatly let down by seeing this same driver come up to the door with an altogether different conveyance,—a pair of lean, miserable, ill-harnessed horses, tied to a shabby old hack. The driver jumped down from the seat, opened the door and told the traveller that his carriage was ready. "That," said the traveller, "is not the carriage which I engaged, I engaged that elegant conveyance which you had across the way." "Yes," said the driver, "that is the carriage that gets the business; this is the carriage that does the job."

And that is the way in which the public has been treated in this case. The thing promised has not been the thing furnished. The expectation of the public was aroused by the promise of that old, superb and white-plumed war-horse, drawing after him like a chariot of fire his old thundering petition, spreading dismay in every direction. That is the carriage that gets the business. I will not carry out the parallel exactly. But this great public expectation was to be disappointed by mere child's play,—the appearance on the scene of action of a youth trundling his little wheelbarrow petition, and flying his paper kite of an opening speech. That is the carriage that does the job.

But because so much expectation has been raised, although there has been such a falling off, letting down and disappointment, and because there has been so much sensation created, the respondents deem it important to demonstrate this completely, as far as possible, so that it may be seen what a trivial case and what mere child's play this is.

Now then I come to the case. I promised in my opening argument that we would go further than the law required, and would show all that would be required to establish the will of October 5, 1864, as the last valid will and testament of Ebenezer Smith,—to establish it *de novo*. It is provided by the laws of this Commonwealth in General Statutes, chapter 92, sections 1, 2 and 6, that " every person of full age and of sound mind " may dispose of his property by his last will and testament in writing; and no will shall be valid unless it is in writing and signed by the testator, or by some peison in his presence and by his express direction, and attested and subscribed in his presence by three or more competent witnesses.

I shall consider first the question of testamentary capacity. Was Ebenezer Smith, at the time of the execution of that will, of sound mind? What is the legal meaning of the term "of sound mind?" It is well known that a greatly enfeebled mind may be a sound mind, within the meaning of the law. If Ebenezer Smith had sufficient mind to remember his immediate family and property and to understand what was done, he was legally of sound mind, although very sick, and his mind greatly enfeebled. Now to show the utter absurdity of the idea that he was not at the time of the execution of that will, legally speaking, of sound mind, I will refer to a few cases of contested wills in which this question has been considered of how much mind a man must have to make a valid will. Now I will refer to the case of *Hathorn* v. *King*, 8 Mass. 371. At 11 o'clock in the forenoon, the testatrix, being then very ill, gave directions as to preparing her will, and she continued sinking until 6 o'clock in the afternoon of the same day, when she executed the will. and at 8 1-4 o'clock, 2 1-4 hours afterwards, she died. The will was sustained, apparently against the opinion of the attending physicians as to her sanity.

The case of *Stone* v. *Damon*, 12 Mass. 488, is to this effect: If a lunatic under guardianship be restored to his reason, he may make a will. although the letters of guardianship be unrepealed.

The case of *Breed* v. *Pratt*, 18 Pickering, 115, where the decision is given by Shaw, C. J.: The testator was a man of peculiar character and habits, and had long been under guardianship, as a person *non compos mentis*. and during all the time of his guardianship, and at the time of making the will. the executor, (being the principal devisee and having married the testator's daughter who had deceased without issue before the making of the will), was himself the testator's guardian. The heirs-at-law contested the will, but the will was sustained. the court holding that a person under guardianship as *non compos mentis* may make a will, if he is in fact of sound mind at the time of its execution, and at the same time holding that the fact of the guardianship was *prima facie* evidence of insanity and incapacity to make a will. and made it incumbent on the executor to show beyond a reasonable doubt that the testator had such mental capacity and such feedom of will and action as are requisite to render a will legally valid. With that great burden upon the executor, the testator being a man like that, — under guardianship, — the executor having been the guardian and being the principal devisee, to the exclusion of the heirs-at-law, that will was sustained. and there is the decision of Chief Justice Shaw sustaining it, in the 18th of Pickering.

Another case I will refer to is *Reed's Will*, 2 B. Monroe. (Ky.) page 79. The probate or county court rejected the will, and it went to the Court of Appeals. The only litigated question was that of testamentary capacity. The opinions of all the subscribing witnesses, and of some other witnesses, were that the testator was of unsound mind. He was more than 80 years of age, had been a peculiar man, and was so afflicted with palsy that he could not write, or even feed himself. But the Court of Appeals gathered from circumstances and some other evidence that he was rational enough, for a person of his great age, and sustained the will.

Another case to which I will refer your Honor is the case of *Van Alst* v. *Hunter*, 5 Johnson's Chancery, page 158, where Chancellor Kent gives the opinion of the Court as follows:

" The testator was between 90 and 100 years of age when he made his will, but it is well understood that age alone will not disqualify" (I am using his words) "a person from making a will, provided he has a competent possession of his mental faculties. 'A man may freely make a testament, how old soever he may be, for it is not the integrity of the body, but of the mind, that is requisite in testaments.' This has been the law in every age. The law looks to the competency of the understanding; neither age, nor sickness, nor extreme distress or debility of body will affect the capacity to make a will, if sufficient intelligence remains." " The will of such an aged man ought to be regarded with great tenderness." " The failure of memory is not sufficient to create the incapacity, unless it be quite total, or extend to his immediate family or property. The want of recollection of names is one of the earliest symptoms of a decay of the memory, but this failure may exist to a very great degree, and yet the solid power of understanding remain."

I refer also to the case of *Stevens* v. *Vancleve*, 4 Washington Circuit Court, 262. (My law library brought into court in this case consists of only about two books).

The testator in this case was in bed when he made his will, having been struck with palsy, which entirely disabled one-half of his body. He was rather imbecile before the stroke of the palsy. On the other side a great number of witnesses were examined, who deposed that the memory of the testator was greatly impaired, even before the last stroke of the palsy ; that he would ask foolish questions, and enquire the names of his former acquaintances who called to see him. Upon one occasion, he enquired how a particular acquaintance of his was, and being answered that he was dead, he, not long afterwards, expressed a wish to see him, At another time, he mistook one of his nieces for a grand-daughter who had long before been dead. Many similar instances of a great decay in his memory were stated by these witnesses. After the last stroke of the palsy, they never heard him speak, although he would sometimes make a noise, as if he desired to speak; that when they called to see him, he lay in a state of insensibility, with a vacant stare, and apparently unconscious of anything, neither speaking to nor noticing those who addressed him, not even his own daughters. That he was entirely childish, as well as helpless; and was treated as if he had been an infant. These witnesses all concur in opinion that the testator was at no time, during his last sickness, competent to make a will, or to transact any other kind of business, and that his mind and judgment were entirely prostrated. His hand was guided also in making the signature. Here is what the Judge says as to the meaning of the terms " of sound and disposing mind and memory" : " He must have memory. A man in whom this faculty is totally extinguished cannot be said to possess understanding to any degree whatever, or for any purpose. But his memory may be very imperfect; it may be greatly impaired by age or disease. He may not be able, at all times, to recollect the names, the persons or the families of those with whom he had been intimately acquainted ; may at times ask idle questions, and repeat those which had before been asked and answered, and yet his understanding may be sufficiently sound for many of the ordinary transactions of life. He may not have sufficient strength of memory and vigor of intellect to make and to digest all the parts of a contract, and yet be competent to direct the distribution of his property by will. This is a subject which he may possibly have often thought of, and there is probably no person who has not arranged such a disposition in his mind before he committed it to writing. More especially, in such a reduced state of mind and memory, he may be able to recollect and to understand the disposition of his property which he had made by a former will, when the same is distinctly read over to him. The question is not so much what was the degree of memory possessed by the testator, as this—Had he a *disposing* memory? Was he capable of recollecting the property he was about to bequeath; the manner of distributing it, and the objects of his bounty? To sum up the whole in the most simple and intelligent form,—Were his mind and memory sufficiently sound to enable him to know and to understand the business in which he was engaged at the time when he executed his will?"

I will refer now to the case of *Burger* v. *Hill*, 1 Bradford, 360.

" The testator's dissolution was near at hand; he was incapable of moving his limbs; his hand was nerveless, so that he could not write his name, and he spoke with difficulty. His condition of body and mind showed physical and mental prostration, loss of active and originating power, of attention and connected thought, with sufficient intelligence, however, when the faculties were aroused and fixed upon any particular point." A doctor who saw him the day before gave the opinion that he was idiotic. A clergyman who saw him a few minutes after the will was executed, testified that his mind was weak and wandering. The will was admitted to probate. And this is the summing up of the Judge:—"The judicial interpretation given to these terms (soundness or unsoundness of mind and memory) leads to the established proposition that mere imbecility or weakness of understanding or memory is not sufficient of itself to disable a person to dispose of his property by will; if he be not totally deprived of reason, he is the lawful disposer of his property."

I will next refer, and finally refer, to a case which has received a great deal of criticism, I admit, in consequence of the conclusion arrived at in regard to that particular case, although I think it is sustained by all the authorities which are cited in that case. I refer to the case of *Stewart* v. *Lispenard*, 26 Wendell, 255, not as an authority but because it is an illustration or an example of what a will has been admitted to probate after it has been thoroughly contested. That case went first through the Probate Court and was rejected; went up to the next court and was formally rejected, I think without any hearing; went up to Chancellor Walworth, he considered it and rejected the will; finally it went up to the Court of Errors, and there were some three or four hundred pages of testimony and arguments of counsel, and the will was set up, in the face of so much against it. And besides that, the general opinion was, and almost everybody believed, that the person who made that will was an idiot. And her father in his will, (Alice Lispenard was the name of the testatrix) had this clause :—

"And as it has pleased Almighty God that my daughter Alice should have such imbecility of mind as to render her incapable of managing or taking care of property, my will further is, that she be allowed for her maintenance the sum of five hundred dollars annually during her natural life."

" In *support* of the application to admit the will to probate, it was shown that until the age of eight or nine years Alice had as much intellect and intelligence as children generally, and partook in the sports and amusements of children; that she learned to spell and could read a little in the spelling-book, but was inattentive, and her father would not permit her preceptress, employed as a teacher in the family, to insist upon her applying herself to her studies, and after an ineffectual effort at a school in the neighborhood to educate her, all attempts in that respect were abandoned. Her temper was very bad; she was sullen and obstinate, would cry when her play-mates offended her, run in and tell her father, who would coax her and indulge her in all her whims. Her parents did not attempt to control her; on the contrary, she controlled her parents, giving them no rest until they yielded to her wishes. She was permitted to drink as much strong beer as she liked, and subsequently wine and brandy. She soon became daily intoxicated. This course of conduct was continued during the lifetime of her father, and whilst she resided with her brother Leonard she was still indulged in the use of strong drinks, but not to the same extent as during the life time of her father."

Then it goes on in further support of the will. Habits changed, she got under kind treatment of her brother-in-law; he gave her little occupations to do, such as keeping the key of the closet in the house, running of errands,—a girl 35 years of age treated in that way.

"There were many witnesses examined on both sides; those called in opposition to the granting of probate generally expressing the opinion that she was *wholly incapable*, whilst those produced in support of the application for probate, expressed the opinion that she was *fully capable* to make a will. Most of the former class formed their opinions of the mind and understanding of Alice, from her appearance, peculiar manner and deportment, as exhibited previous to her removal to the house of Mr. Stewart, when she was looked upon and treated as an idiot, they having had no conversation with her, deeming her incapable of conversing rationally on any subject; whilst the opinions of many of the latter class of witnesses were formed after her removal to the house of Mr. Stewart, where she met with kindness, attention and respect, and was treated like a rational being. Several of these latter witnesses stated that their impressions as to the state of the mind of Alice when they first saw her were very unfavorable, but from constant intercourse, and frequent and familiar conversation with her, these impressions had been removed, and they had come to the conlusion that, though her mind was not naturally strong, she possessed ordinary reasoning and discriminating faculties, and in confirmation of their opinions, many of the facts above detailed, showing that she was endowed with *reason* and *understanding*, were related by them."

Here is a little of the opinion in the case : "To establish any standard of intellect or information beyond the possession of reason in its lowest degree, as in itself *essential* to legal capacity, would create endless uncertainty, difficulty and litigation, would shake the security of property, and wrest from the aged and infirm that authority over their earnings or savings which is often their best security against injury and neglect. If you throw aside the common law test of capacity, then proofs of wild speculations or extravagant and peculiar opinions, or of the forgetfulness or the prejudices of old age, might be sufficient to shake the fairest conveyance, or impeach the most equitable will. The law, therefore, in fixing the standard of positive legal competency, has taken a low standard of capacity; but it is a clear and definite one, and therefore wise and safe. It holds, (in the language of the latest English Commentator,) that ' weak minds differ from strong ones only in the extent and power of their faculties ; but unless they betray a total loss of understanding, or idiocy, or delusion, they cannot properly be considered unsound.' "

So we see, may it please your Honor, in what cases wills have been admitted to probate when contested, and what has been determined to be sound mind. Now let us apply the law to the case of Ebenezer Smith. These persons were of rather weak intellect, even when in good health, generally unlearned and illiterate. But Ebenezer Smith, up to his last sickness, is admitted on all hands to have been one of the keenest men who ever lived in Boston, long-headed, far-seeing, of very strong character, of indomitable will. Mr. Clapp, the petitioners' own witness, he himself being a very smart man, who has come in contact with a great many smart men, says :—" He was the smartest business man I ever came in contact with since I have been on the list of action ;" and this is the current of all the testimony of any account or value. Here manifestly was a mind which might have been greatly enfeebled, and still perfectly sound, in the legal meaning of that term.

Now let us see what was the mental condition of Ebenezer Smith when that will was executed. But first, on what day was it executed? We have some very positive testimony upon that point, — not negative but positive, — which I will briefly sum up, as to the day on which it was executed. *First*, the will was dated October 5th. This alone raises the presumption, the legal presumption, that it was executed October 5th. It is written evidence, not subject to the defects of memory. *Second*, the charge upon the day book of Mr. Rollins who drew the will is as follows : — " 1864 October 5th, Ebenezer Smith to drafting your will *this day*." Mr. Rollins says " my general rule is to put down the charge the very day the service is performed. I have no doubt whatever that the will was drawn October 5th, 1864." And here I will make just a little excursion. I will make just one digression, as it occurs to me now, and that is this, and I may forget it if I should let it go, that the charge for making that will is to Ebenezer Smith ; it was drawn for Ebenezer Smith, Isaac going to Rollins's office as his agent, and in the course of the case we shall see that he was his agent and went there for his father, and Rollins made the charge for writing the will to his father. Now to come back to this evidence of Rollins contained in his book and in what he says of his general habit. This is better evidence than mere unaided memory, and it enables Isaac to fix most positively the day on which it was executed ; because he swears very positively that he took the will as soon as drawn, went directly to the house, and it was executed on that day. *Third*, Isaac, was comparatively a stranger in Boston, who had not lived here for 30 years, — had been here very seldom, at no time more than a day or two. Somebody told him to go to Rollins and have the will drawn. Isaac says it was Eliza. Eliza says it was Sarah ; but Sarah did not know Rollins, and Rollins says he never saw Sarah in his life. On the other hand, Rollins had been the attorney of Eliza's husband and was her attorney in the settlement of her husband's estate. At any rate, on being told to go to Rollins, he went out, ostensibly to have the will drawn, returned with the will, said he had been delayed because Rollins was out, and the will was executed on that day. Even Eliza says so. To make this out any day later than October 5th, it is necessary to construct the absurd theory that when told to go to Rollins, Isaac already had the will in his pocket, and that his going out was a mere pretence, and that he was roaming about the streets of Boston to kill time, until about time enough had elapsed for drawing a will. And what conceivable reason or motive for such a pretence? And then consider the remarkable coincidence that out of the thousand lawyers of Boston, Isaac, a stranger in the city, should already accidentally have hit upon the very lawyer to whom he was afterwards told by his sister to go and should beforehand have got him to draw that very will in those very same terms ! It is absurd. So circumstances prove that the will was executed on the 5th, and circumstance and probability add weight to Isaac's testimony. *Fourth*, Dr. Thorndike testifies that he is able to fix the date of the execution of the will of October 5th by the date of the execution of the codicil of October 1st, in this way : — that the codicil was executed Saturday evening October 1st ; Isaac arrived Sunday morning October

2nd; on Monday he tried to see the codicil of Sarah, but could not, and went out to see his sister Eliza; and on Tuesday she came and brought a nurse who was not acceptable to Mrs. Ebenezer Smith, and that evening Dr. Thorndike engaged Mrs. Giles, and took her to the house; and on the day following, which was Wednesday, the will was executed, and Isaac went to New York that evening. Dr. Thorndike further testifies that Isaac did not return to Boston until October 12th and was not here between the 5th and 12th. Here is Dr. Thorndike's testimony on two points: — that the will was positively executed on the 5th, and that it could not have been executed later with the presence of Isaac, because he was not here. *Fifth*, It is conceded that Isaac did go to New York October 5th. There is no doubt whatever about that, and Isaac testifies that he was not thereafter in Boston until the 12th. *Sixth*, Edward D. Sohier's minutes of the statement of Mrs. Giles, taken down 14 years ago, show that she went to Mr. Smith's house the night before the will was signed, and she went to Mr. Smith's house October 4th. *Seventh*, now here is evidence enough already, six sources of positive evidence, circumstantial and that of witnesses, six sources already, followed up with the seventh which was not necessary to get, but which is stronger than all the rest. The records of the bank in New York show that Isaac was in New York on the 6th, 7th, 8th, 9th, and 10th of October 1864. There is the evidence on the date on which that was executed, and yet I suppose you will hear this counsel of the petitioners, against that, undertaking to argue to your Honor, and to insult you with argument, to show that that will was executed on the 9th or 10th of October 1864, on the worthless testimony of that miserable Giles woman.

And against all this evidence is the evidence of an ignorant woman, Mrs. Giles, on her direct examination; she depending upon bare memory for four-teen years, unaided by any memorandum, having no special interest in the will. On cross-examination she says in one place that she will not swear positively that the will was not executed the day after she went to Mr. Smith's house, and in answer to cross-interrogatory 144 she does not feel willing to swear positively that the will was not executed on the day Isaac went to New York, the day after she went to Mr. Smith's. She swears positively, however, that it was executed after a consultation of physicians at which Dr. Lewis was present, but it has been conclusively shown that there never was any such consultation, Dr. Lewis having called alone October 5th. So she is contradicted by her own statement taken out of her own mouth by Mr. Sohier fourteen years ago when her memory was fresh, by which she fixes the execution of the will October 5th. And this uncertainty of memory which she shows on the cross-exami-nation, she naturally would show, or any other woman who had any honesty in her nature, even a particle of honesty in her nature, would be compelled to show upon any kind of an examination. *Mr. Chandler:* Were those notes of Mr. Sohier put in evidence? *Mr. Drury:* Yes, sir. Don't you wish they had not been? *Mr. Chandler:* Not at all.

Mr. Drury: It is as certain as anything can be established by human testi-mony, that that will was executed October 5th, and it cannot, with any reason, or with a particle of doubt, be contradicted. Now I have dwelt carefully on this point, because if it was executed October 5th, the whole theory of the petitioners as to Ebenezer Smith's mental condition at the execution of the will is destroyed. They set out to show that it was executed on the 9th or 10th of October, as the very foundation of their case, and I find upon reading the counsel's opening argument that he did state positively that it was executed on October 9th or 10th, and in just the next sentence to the one in which he tried to dodge the question of the dates. He has utterly failed, and his case is shown to have been built upon a mere shadow.

Now the will having been executed on October 5th, what was Ebenezer Smith's mental condition upon that day? You have heard Dr. Thorndike's testimony as to the nature of Mr. Smith's disease, and its effect upon his mind. He has treated a great many similar cases. No respectable physician could be found to stand up here and contradict his evidence upon that point. He was Mr. Smith's regular physician, and had been for thirteen years, and had been frequently consulted by him, was his confidential medical adviser. Mr. Smith's mind was not diseased, Dr. Thorndike said. The uncontradicted evidence in this case shows that he was gradually growing feebler and feebler; that he was feebler on the 8th than he was on the 7th, feebler on the 7th than on the 6th, feebler on the 6th than on the 5th; and on the other hand he was stronger on the 5th than on the 6th, and so on down to the day of his death. So then, according to all the evidence that there is in this case, not disputed in a single iota, Ebenezer Smith was in a better condition upon the 5th of October than he was three days afterwards on the 8th. Now we have very good evidence from a witness whom the petitioners cannot contradict, and they called him themselves,—they had to to sustain a part of their theory,—and he, Dr. Storer, a regular physician of high character, testifies as to Mr. Smith's mental condition on October 8th, and he is corroborated by Dr. Thorndike. Dr. Storer's day book, your Honor, has this entry :—" Oct. 8, 1864, Ebenezer Smith, Allston St., Dr. Thorndike, $5." He had known Mr. Smith a great many years. In their younger days they had belonged to the same lodge of Odd Fellows, and they talked about the old times, and had a very pleasant conversation. And Dr. Storer now gives this testimony : —

"I didn't see but that he conversed as he always did; his mind seemed to be clear, and he was very much as I had seen him about. I went away with the idea that his mind was as clear as it ever was, as clear as minds usually are."

And Dr. Thorndike says :

"On the day Dr. Storer called, Mr. Smith was perfectly rational. They had some pleasant conversation."

Mrs. Giles, the principal witness for the petitioners, upon whom they rely chiefly for the support of their whole case, says on direct examination :—

"When I went there he seemed to be conscious and talked; he talked the next day, and the day after; he told me about his coming to Boston, and gave me a history."

On the cross-examination she says :

"When the consultation of physicians took place, after they had pronounced his case hopeless, he asked them whether there wouldn't be a chance for him if they took off his leg up to his knee. The day after I arrived there he asked me to keep strict watch of the table drawer in front of him, in which he said valuable papers were deposited. His mind seemed quite clear up to the time of the consultation. He talked with me and Dr. Storer at the time of the examination. Between the time of my going there and the time of that consultation he gave me a history of his first days, when he came to Boston; said he was a mere boy, came with a pack on his back, and walked most of the way. We talked some about his sickness. He spoke about the Masonic Lodge. In the morning, before the consultation, he told me who were coming, and requested me to be present."

Now if your Honor please, all this is said of a man who, before his last sickness, was a man of great intellectual power,—not a lunatic, not a weak minded man, but a man in whom the reasoning faculties were largely developed. His affectionate grandchildren have such reverence for the memory of their dear old grandfather that they would like to make him out an idiot, if they could find anybody idiot or knave enough to so testify. This testimony, I say, is given concerning a man of high intellectual and reasoning power, as he appeared with his mind unimpaired by the disease which weakened and enfeebled his body. This was his condition October 8th, three days after the will was signed. But his condition October 5th was much better than on October 8th. The nurse cannot by any possibility, or by any stretch of her imagination, or by any distortion of her memory, make him unconscious until the 9th or 10th. If the will was executed before October 9th, she is utterly at fault. It being, then, a fact established beyond reasonable doubt, (I am going through this whole case on the evidence, and I am going to clinch every point in the same way that I have this as I go along,) that the will was executed October 5th, what are the facts bearing upon his mental condition on that day, and at the time of the execution of the will,—that hour, that minute, that second? *First:*—His condition three days afterwards on October 8th, when, upon all the testimony, testimony uncontradicted and unquestioned, he had been gradually growing feebler and feebler. *Second :*—The testimony of Mrs. Giles, the petitioners' principal witness. A great deal of the talk of Ebenezer Smith and of his conversation of which she speaks must have taken place after the 5th. And she said expressly that his mind seemed quite clear and he talked quite freely on the 5th. *Third :*—The statement of Mrs. Thorndike,—I believe that has been ruled out? I don't know whether it has been ruled out or not. I offered it. Counsel once said I might put it in, he didn't object to it, but when I went to put it in he did object.

McKim, J.: What is that? *Mr. Drury:* That is the statement of Mrs. Thorndike. *McKim, J. :* That is not in. *Mr. Drury:* Is not in? *McKim, J.:* No, I dont remember its going in. *Mr. Drury:* Well, then, I will say, *Third :* — The testimony of Isaac and the statement of Mrs. Giles taken down by Mr. Sohier 14 years ago, all to the effect that he called upon each of his family present and asked each if they were satisfied, which fact shows a great amount of carefulness and deliberation, clear comprehension, knowledge, memory, recognition of members of his family and the nature of the matter then in hand. *Fourth :*—The testimony of Dr. Thorndike, who appeared on the scene of action just after the will had been executed while Mr. Foster was present, and heard a pleasant conversation between Mr. Smith and Mr. Foster, and Mr. Smith's pertinent answers to questions put by Mr. Foster to him, giving a clear recognition of Mr. Foster, carrying his mind and memory back to their younger days and calling up pleasant reminiscences of the interest and enjoyment which they both mutually took in music. That a pleasant conversation did take place upon that solemn occasion between those two old men,—and it was a striking thing and would naturally impress itself upon a man's mind, because they were both old men,—that that conversation between those two old men did take place, is further testified to by Isaac, is contained in the statement of Mrs. Giles which Mr. Sohier took down, and to clinch it all, Mr. Sohier remembers that Mr. Foster, a man highly esteemed, of excellent and irreproachable character, testified fourteen years ago as to that same conversation substantially as Dr. Thorndike has related it. *Fifth :*—Two of the witnesses of the will testified under oath,—Andrix A. Foster and Margaret Patterson,—that they were of the opinion that Mr. Smith was of sound mind when the will was executed ;—Mr. Foster fourteen years ago in this court; and Margaret Patterson also fourteen years ago in this court, and again before your Honor since this case came to trial. Against all this evidence there is absolutely nothing but the evidence of Eliza W. Smith, who, by the falsehoods too numerous to mention shown in the course of this investigation to have been uttered here by her, is totally discredited and shown to be unfit to be believed under oath, and discredited by her own son who swears positively that she made an altogether different statement to him fourteen years ago ;—there is nothing, I say, except her worthless testimony and the bare opinion of Mrs. Giles,—that opinion, however, based upon facts which even she herself related, which facts, together with her total misapprehension as to the time when the will was executed, and her confusion of all the occurrences which took place while she was at Mr. Smith's, utterly discredit her opinion, so that she is discredited by the testimony of all and even by the testimony of herself.

Was Ebenezer Smith, as alleged in that petition, when that will was executed, of unsound mind by reason of old age, sickness and other causes? What *other causes,* if your Honor please? They have tried to make out that he was drunk.

Mr. Chandler: No such charge as that, Mr. Drury. No such word has been used. *Mr. Drury:* "*Dosed with whiskey as a dernier resort.*" *Mr. Chandler:* Yes, sir. *Mr. Drury:* What does that mean? That doesn't mean drunk! There was no insinuation of drunk there! Oh, no. "A rose by any other name would smell as sweet." I don't care whether you call it drunk or "dosed with whiskey," you did make the charge that he was drunk. *Mr. Chandler:* Oh no, sir. You didn't hear it from me. *Mr. Drury:* And that he was made drunk by these alleged conspirators. *Mr. Chandler:* There is nothing of the kind in the language. You are getting wild. I think we had better adjourn, your Honor, and take a little rest. *Mr. Drury:* I would rather go on, your Honor, if you can preserve order. What evidence is there of it? Even their witness, young Ebenezer Smith says that he was with his grandfather 19 nights and until Mrs. Giles was engaged, that

"I never put a drop of whiskey in the glass while I was there. I always left the glass with about the same quantity as there was the night before. He didn't take half a glass in all while I was there."

What does Mrs. Giles say? She says that she was in the room night and day, that nobody else gave him any whiskey while she was there, that Mrs. Ebenezer Smith would bring in two-thirds of a tumblerful which would last 24 hours, that at first without assistance he would take a swallow out of the tumbler once in three hours or so, when he was taken with spasms of pain, that after he became weaker she herself would give him a spoonful or two at a time with a spoon on the occurrence of such spasms, and she adds:—"I don't think the man was drunk, of course not, he didn't take whiskey enough for that."

Now what other causes? What is that intended to cover? I supposed that was intended to cover this whiskey charge.

And besides all this testimony as to his mental condition, this direct evidence, the legal presumption is in favor of the sanity of the testator, and if there is any doubt upon this point, we are entitled to the benefit of the doubt, and for that proposition, your Honor, I refer you to the case of *Baxter* v. *Abbott*, 7 Gray, 71. Now all this evidence discloses not only testamentary capacity, but a high degree of testamentary capacity. On all this great preponderance of evidence, together with the legal presumption of sanity;—the opinions of eminent physicians based upon his appearance and conversations three days after the will was executed, and on the very day and hour on which it was executed,—on the very hour and minute; the opinions of two of the subscribing witnesses of the will; his deliberation and carefulness when the will was before him,—calling upon his wife and children and asking them each separately if they were satisfied, and then calling for his spectacles; his conversation with his old neighbor about the good old times; the powers of memory which he exhibited, doing what a man of sound and reflective mind standing on the brink of eternity and facing the boundless and unknown future would naturally do,—casting a lingering look behind, taking an account of his past eventful life, talking, soliloquizing and thinking of his boyhood, his manhood, his trials, his struggles, his achievements, his disappointments and his transgressions, and considering his whole life in the retrospect, before yielding his soul to the tender mercy of his God;— on all this testimony, I say, your Honor, not depending entirely upon the frail and naked memory of witnesses carried back behind a period of 14 years, but corroborated by records which were providentially made at the time and saved, can your Honor, can anybody, have any possible particle of doubt that when the will was executed Ebenezer Smith was of sound mind in the legal meaning of that term and perfectly capable of making a valid will?

Recess till 2 15 P. M.

May it please your Honor: I now come to the next point. Here we have a mind abundantly capable to make a valid will. Did he make it? Was the will duly executed by Ebenezer Smith? Here is a will which has been admitted to probate, which has stood 14 years, under which an estate of a quarter of a million dollars has been settled and distributed, purporting to be the will of Ebenezer Smith, purporting to have been signed by him, and actually attested by three competent witnesses. The first evidence and the best evidence upon the point of the due execution of the will, and I may say evidence which ought to be conclusive at this late day, 14 years after it was recorded, even against the testimony of the three subscribing witnesses is the evidence which the instrument bears upon its face. I refer to the certificate of attestation :—

"The above instrument was signed, sealed, published and declared by the above-named Ebenezer Smith, as and for his last will and testament, in the presence of us the undersigned, who, at the request of the said Ebenezer, and in his presence, and in the presence of each other, have subscribed our names hereto. Signed, Andrix A. Foster, Anna G. Giles, Margaret Patterson."

And here I will make just a little digression to go over a point which I omitted and overlooked, and that is that that word "*fifth*" day of October is in the handwriting of Mr. Rollins, that it was put in by him and not put in afterwards, he put it there, Isaac didn't put it there. The man who is alleged to have been instrumental in having it executed on the 9th or 10th didn't put it there, he didn't date it back, it was put there by Mr. Rollins who drew the will.

Now considering that certificate as evidence of the due execution of the will, I will say that it seems to me that the value of evidence which depends upon the memory of witnesses diminishes with the lapse of time. Such evidence grows weaker and weaker with age. Who can remember accurately all the details of a transaction fourteen years after it occurred? But in the ratio in which human memory grows dim and faded with the lapse of time, and the evidence depending thereon grows weaker and weaker, in that same ratio with the lapse of time the evidence borne on the face of that instrument grows stronger and stronger. The legal presumption is that the certificate is correct. If there is any doubt about its truth, we are entitled to the benefit of the doubt. We start with the presumption in its favor. Fourteen years after the certificate was signed, one of the witnesses who signed it impeaches her act and throws discredit upon herself by saying her act was false. *Secondly :—*The next evidence upon this point : The three witnesses testified under oath fourteen years ago in this court ; able and eminent counsel were present and conducted the examination,—Mr. Sohier and Mr. Willard, counsel for the executors, Dwight Foster for the very petitioners who are now here, Charles Levi Woodbury for Thomas P. Smith, Hazelton & Ware for Arthur G. Smith and his two brothers, Eben and Alexander. Here was everything calculated to bring out the truth. The parties represented by Hazelton & Ware and Dwight Foster,—yes, and by Charles Levi Woodbury, were opposed to the will. The witnesses were carefully examined. A shrewd, careful and capable Judge presided at the examination. In that decree is implied the finding, (that decree admitting the will to probate) that the will was signed by Ebenezer Smith, or by some person in his presence and by his express direction, and attested and subscribed in his presence by three competent witnesses. This evidence which we here find in the decree of the Judge also grows stronger and stronger, and has gained cumulative power year after year with the lapse of time since the decree was made.

Now it would be extremely dangerous to allow such evidence, furnished on the will itself and by the decree of a capable Judge after hearing the witnesses under oath in court when their memories were fresh and soon after the will was executed, to be overthrown by any evidence depending on bare memory fourteen years afterwards. I appeal to all human experience of which we know when I say no human memory is sufficiently retentive so that it can be safely relied on to give accurately all the details of a transaction fourteen years after it occurred. It may retain parts substantially, but not the whole. Let us take a few out of the many instances too numerous to mention which have already occurred in the course of this trial. Dwight Foster, although confident from circumstantial evidence that he was present fourteen years ago in the Probate Court at the important hearing in which he was greatly interested, although he says the strong inference is that he was here and that he believes he was here, yet has not the slightest recollection even of having been present. Edward D. Sohier, a man of powerful intellect, remembers but very little of that hearing, but one thing struck one element in Mr. Sohier's character,—the bringing up of that scene of those two old men, Ebenezer Smith about to die and old Mr. Foster, talking on that solemn occasion about their interest in music, about singing at the Park Street Church, and about the Handel and Haydn Society. Dr. Thorndike, one of the executors of the will, a party greatly interested in the hearing, remembers hardly anything about it except that he was here. Compare the utterly contradictory statements of Mrs. Giles and Eliza W. Smith, the two principal witnesses of the petitioners, as to what actually did take place upon the occasion of executing the will. All this illustrates, and in fact all human experience illustrates, how unsafe it is to rely upon human memory after its impressions have become rubbed out and worn out by the processes to which it has been subjected after a period of fourteen years.

Now no record was made at the time of all the details which took place in that room on the occasion of making this will. The only record evidence we have of what took place is that which is borne upon this certificate on the will—the certificate of attestation—and the statement of Mrs. Giles taken down out of her mouth by Mr. Sohier fourteen years ago as to Mr. Smith's calling upon his wife and children and asking them if they were satisfied, and the few other incidents therein recorded. One thing, however, is certain,—that Isaac T. Smith aided in making that signature. I discard the preposterous idea that there was any intentional wrong in that act, because Isaac knew that by the making of that signature he was deprived of a large portion, which proved to be over $15,000, out of his father's estate, and that the will gave him considerably less than he would have received as one of his father's heirs-at-law, even. Another thing is certain:—The three subscribing witnesses saw that signature made. That they saw it made is certain, although Mrs. Giles says in her affidavit that the other witnesses were not present and did not see this signature made. She has not testified differently in the course of this examination, nor in her deposition, but this is one of the numerous errors in her testimony. In the same affidavit she says that she was the first witness to sign, and that the others did not see her sign. But here upon the stand she says that Mr. Foster was the first to sign, as in fact it appears on the face of the will. Margaret Patterson here upon the stand says she saw the signature made. Mrs. Giles in her statement taken down by Mr. Sohier says that Mr. Foster came in before the signature was made. Mr. Foster so testified here fourteen years ago. And Eliza W. Smith,—even she testifies that Mr. Foster was present. Isaac so testified. So that the fact is established beyond any reasonable doubt in spite of the worthless testimony of Mrs. Giles. Eliza says that Isaac placed the pen in his father's hand and was standing upon his father's left, that Mr. Smith could not control the pen and the pen began to slide upon the paper, when Isaac stepped round to the right, took hold of his father's hand, and the signature was made. Now this may be true, although it comes from a lying witness, one who has been proved to be a lying witness, and is not entitled to much weight, but she is the witness of the petitioners and not ours. If true, it shows plainly that Isaac supposed that his father was able to, and that he would, write his name alone without assistance, and that he stepped round from the left to the right to assist in doing what he saw his father was trying to do himself with difficulty. In some respects this is consistent with the testimony of Isaac, who says that he was standing on his father's left, and his mother called his attention to the fact that his father was finding difficulty in writing his name and suggested that he aid his father, that, (as was perfectly natural, moved by natural impulse), he stepped around to his father's right, his father's hand was moving in the act of writing, he took hold of his father's hand, felt his father's hand moving under his and assisted his father in writing his name. Now I don't care whether that signature looks like the handwriting of Ebenezer Smith or not. It would be wonderful if it did even if written by him alone—written at that time when he was in such feeble health. I have seen a signature of a man written when he was sick, and I know that no expert under heaven, by comparing it with the genuine signatures of that man written when he was well, could say positively that it was written by the same man simply from its appearance. I repeat, I don't care whether that signature resembles the handwriting of Ebenezer Smith or not. I don't care if but very little of Ebenezer Smith's body went into that signature. I don't care if the degree of bodily power which Ebenezer Smith put into that signature was equal to only the one-hundredth part of the bodily power put into it by him who guided Ebenezer Smith's hand. A will is not the offspring of a man's body, but of his mind. I don't care whether his body went into the signature or not. If his mind went into it, if his will, his willingness, his acquiescence or his consent went into it, I am satisfied. If the signature was made in that way with the consent or acquiescence of Ebenezer Smith by word or act, it is his lawful signature, and none but a naturally base, depraved, wicked and malignant heart could perceive any wrong in it. This guiding of a testator's hand is a very common occurrence, because a great proportion of the wills which are made are made when the testators are in feeble health and near their decease, towards the end of their lives, when men begin to think of death and the disposition which they wish to be made of their property after they are dead. If the testator directs another to sign his name, it satisfies the law, it is legally valid. If another writes the testator's name without his direction and the testator makes his mark, it satisfies the law, it is the testator's signature. If the testator's name is written by another and the testator traces over it with a dry pen, it satisfies the law and is the testator's signature. So if the pen is held in the testator's hand and another with his consent, express or implied, by word or by act, takes hold of that hand and exerts the power used in writing his name, it is the testator's lawful signature. *Stevens* v. *Van Cleve*, 4 Washington, C. C. 269. I will cite this case which I have already cited in the previous part of my argument :—

"The submission of the testator, who, in relation to this part of the case, is to be considered as fully cognizant of what he was doing, to have his hand directed so as to write his name, was at least equivalent to an express direction to another to sign his name, for it cannot be denied that under the statute the direction to subscribe the name of the testator may be given by him by signs, as well as by words."

That, your Honor, is a case which is cited in every decent text book upon the subject of wills, and has been cited with approval by a great many courts, and I don't believe that it was ever cited with disfavor by any court,—an important case, because it is exactly what was done in the will of Ebenezer Smith. Was that signature affixed, in the way in which it was, with the testator's consent or acquiescence? As I said before, and as this case which I have cited shows, consent may be implied from acts as well as words. He was of sound mind and perfectly conscious of what was done, as I have already shown from the evidence. He was doing all he could to execute that will. He asked each member of his family separately if they were satisfied, said it was all right, called attention to the fact that it was necessary to have three witnesses, called for his spectacles with the will before him, and began to write his name and found difficulty in writing. If Isaac had stepped up and said, "Father, shall I assist you?" and his father had nodded his head, this would have been equivalent to an express direction, although without the utterance of a word. If Isaac had stepped up without saying a word and taken hold of his father's hand and offered to assist him, and his father continued on moving his hand and coöperated with Isaac, this would have denoted consent and acquiescence, without the utterance of a word by either. The direct evidence on this point goes certainly to this extent. Isaac so testifies, and to his credit it may be said, he does not testify to more than he remembers. The testimony is as distinct as can naturally be expected 14 years after the event. Now, if your Honor please, experts in penmanship have been produced for the purpose of showing that the signature was not written by Ebenezer Smith, but was written by Isaac. The experts could not tell from the appearance of the signature how it was written, and a good reason why they could not was because they had no experience in signatures written in that way. Mr. Sawyer acknowledged he was not an expert in regard to a signature written in the manner in which we claim that was written. When I asked him to write his name and then let me try to write the same name with him, he said he was not an expert in that line. He did not undertake to say it was not written in that way. The unnaturalness of the writing and the inconsistency between the different parts, spoken of by Mr. Sawyer, if they show anything, go to demonstrate that it was written in the manner in which we claim it was written. Mr. Phippen never examined a signature of a man written when aided by another. He says it was written with so much ink that he cannot tell which hand prevailed. He thinks that if two persons should attempt to write the same signature with the same pen and at the same time, the result would be the same as appears on the will. His idea that the signature is an imitation of the handwriting of Ebenezer Smith sustains the idea that the power of Ebenezer Smith was put into that signature. The expert testimony, as far as it is of any value, is in our favor. Two witnesses who knew Ebenezer Smith as well as anybody, and were as well acquainted with his handwriting as anybody, two witnesses called by the petitioners themselves, give evidence in our favor. Mr. Clapp, for 25 years the confidential business agent of Ebenezer Smith, who saw him write a great many times, and was well acquainted with his handwriting, says that in his opinion, that is the characteristic signature of Ebenezer Smith. And Mr. Rollins, who was the counsel of Ebenezer Smith for 10 years and did a great deal of his business and had seen him write a great many times and was well acquainted with his handwriting, gave the same opinion as Mr. Clapp, under oath.

So then we have the evidence of the certificate, of the decree of the Judge who presided at the hearing 14 years ago, and the testimony of Isaac corroborated by two experts called by the petitioners themselves, and by two witnesses also called by the petitioners themselves.

"That spattered signature needs no expert to stamp it as a forgery," was the triumphant declaration of the counsel for the petitioners in his opening argument, but that same spattered signature, your Honor, is the lawful signature of Ebenezer Smith; all the experts in this world cannot disturb it; and it will stand valid till the end of time—in this world.

So then, on this evidence alone, thus far related, we have a will which comes within the requirements of the statute law of this Commonwealth;—a will signed by Ebenezer Smith when he was of full age and sound mind, and attested and subscribed in his presence by three competent witnesses. Those are all the requirements of the statute law of this Commonwealth.

Ebenezer Smith knew and was fully conscious of what was transpiring. He understood that he was making a will. In fact everybody present so understood. That was the business in hand and openly declared to be the business in hand. Everything was above board. The subscribing witnesses were sent for, and they understood that they were present, for the purpose of witnessing the execution of a will. It was not necessary that Ebenezer Smith should have said in so many words "this is my will." It is not a necessary part to the validity of a will that it should be declared by the testator to be his will. The witnesses may not know that it is a will and it will be valid. All this is well known law in this Commonwealth and is given at full length in the case of *Osborne* v. *Cook*, 11 Cushing, page 532, where all the authorities are brought together, the English authorities and the American authorities, and the law declared by Judge Thomas, who knew pretty well about wills,—that the matter of declaration is not an essential part to a will. It is not necessary that a man should say in so many words "this is my will," or in any words or by any act "this is my will." And it was not necessary for Ebenezer Smith to say to the witnesses "I wish you to attest this." All this is implied by the acts, surroundings, and circumstances of the time. A request may be conveyed by a look, even, as well as by a word. Here is the testimony of Isaac :—

"Q. Who sent for Mr. Foster? A. I think my father said, 'who is going to witness the will, whom have you got?' and it didn't seem to have occurred to them till then. Then they said, 'Mr. Foster keeps the store round in the neighborhood, perhaps he will step in.' Q. State what took place between him and Mr. Foster. A. He said, 'I am very glad to see you Mr. Foster; I am always glad to see my neighbors.' Mr. Foster said, 'I am sorry to see you so ill, Mr. Smith, and I am asked to come here to witness your will, and I hope it is not an indication that you think of passing away!' And my father replied to him pleasantly, he was much obliged to him for coming. There was a little unimportant conversation, not of much account."

There certainly is enough in that to indicate a request to Mr. Foster to witness a will, and the other witnesses were there for the same purpose. In the request to Mr. Foster, to anyone of them, is implied the request to them all.

But this is not all there is on this point. And before leaving this branch of the subject, I will refer to one other piece of testimony bearing upon the truth of the statements contained in that certificate of attestation, also bearing upon the various parts of this case, testimony which I regard as of great importance, and of far greater importance than all the testimony of witnesses which depends upon their bare memory. I mean the character of Andrix A. Foster, which completely refutes the idea that he would have put his name to a false certificate, gives weight to the testimony which he gave here in court 14 years ago, gives weight to his opinion of the sanity of the testator at that time given, and blasts the idea which was thrown out by the counsel for the petitioners in his opening argument that Mr. Foster committed perjury at that time of giving his testimony. And this is of tenfold importance, because it gives tenfold weight to the legal presumption that he at least duly and properly attested the will, because the law is this : If an attesting witness to a will has since deceased, proof of his handwriting is *prima facie* proof that he duly and properly attested it. *Nickerson* v. *Buck*, 12 Cushing, 332. And that is a case which it would be well to read in connection with this case, as showing what request is necessary on the part of the testator to be made to the witnesses to make their attestation valid. No other case which ever came into this court ever so clearly demonstrated the importance of having good substantial persons and persons of high character and intelligence as witnesses of a will. If all three of those witnesses had been persons of such high character as Mr. Foster, this petition would never have been heard of or thought of. Take the will of August 13, 1864, bearing the names of William Minot and Moody Merrill as witnesses, and the codicil of September 2, 1864, bearing the name of the Rev.

Rollin H. Neale as a witness. Nobody of any sense would dream of saying, in our day, of a will bearing the genuine attesting signatures of those men, that the will was a forgery, or that the certificate of attestation signed by them was untrue. If the genuine signatures of those men were on a will, we would know that it was not a forged will. This illustrates very well the weight which character has on a question of this kind. Andrix A. Foster was a very respectable man of fine personal appearance, carried intelligence in his very presence, a man who closely resembled the Rev. Dr. Kirk, for whom he was often taken, a man of fair education having taught school in his early life, of good general information and intelligence, well known, having many friends and acquaintances. He was also a religious man, actively interested in the Mount Vernon church of which he was a member. He was a man of unsullied reputation for truth and honesty, of unswerving integrity, firm character, and in every way above reproach or suspicion. Andrew Cushing, superintendent of city Missions, a man of high character and intelligence in this community, a man belonging to the same church as Mr. Foster, who for 25 years had known him intimately, and had seen him every day for the last 15 years of his life; Edward D. Sohier, one of the ablest and most upright men in Massachusetts, who had known Mr. Foster for a long time before this will was offered for probate, and who knew him quite a while afterwards; Simon Burnett, who had always known Mr. Foster as long as he knew anybody, and his partner in business for more than 30 years; — these men have given testimony of the kind of a man that Andrix A. Foster was, and if necessary we could bring a hundred good men to give testimony to the same effect. Can anybody with a good heart, can anybody even with a black and wicked heart, knowing the reputation and character of Andrix A. Foster, look at that photograph and say that the man who is portrayed in that picture ever signed his name as witness to a forged will, or that he signed a false certificate in regard to the execution of a will, or that he ever committed perjury or gave perjured testimony in support of it? And I would ask anybody to look at that man as he is portrayed there, a good likeness, and answer. The countenance fits his character and his character fits his countenance, — a countenance bearing the stamp and the superscription of the Most High. And here is the testimony of Mr. Sohier which I will read, because it bears both upon the soundness of the testator's mind, and upon his testamentary capacity, and upon the question of the due execution of the will.

" Mr. Foster testified, (these are Mr. Sohier's words) that he was sent for to come in and witness a will, and on going into the room he spoke to Mr. Smith, to see whether he was perfectly conscious, asked Mr. Smith if he knew him, Mr. Smith said he did, ' you keep a provision store in Howard St.' After that the will was signed, and the witnesses signed, and then they had a conversation—some few words between Mr. Smith and Mr. Foster in regard to singing either at Handel and Haydn or Park St.—but I cannot now recall exactly what it was. Mr. Foster said he was satisfied Mr. Smith was conscious, and knew what the transaction was—what he was performing—from this conversation. I recollect that of Mr. Foster very well, for I had known him for a long time, and remember him. He was a man highly respected, of good reputation, an intelligent man I thought. I never heard a word against his reputation. I heard that he was a man quite esteemed, and I always considered him such. I knew him for several years afterwards."

That is the kind of a man Andrix A. Foster was. That is what he said in court under oath. That is what he put his name to; and to show how much weight that is entitled to, let me read a few words of Judge Washington in the case of *Stevens* v. *Vancleve*, to which I have already referred, in the 4th of Washington Circuit Court Reports:—"There are few men so ignorant as not to know that a person *non compos mentis* cannot make a valid disposition of his property by will, and that his signature to the will attests its due execution."

How do the petitioners meet this testimony in regard to Mr. Foster? Why, they show that he witnessed the will of Amasa Winchester, which was opposed in some way but sustained and admitted to probate, and they try to show that he said that he had witnessed some will or other besides that of Amasa Winchester and had his doubts afterwards whether or not the man was conscious. It is not shown that this was said of the will of Ebenezer Smith, but if it had been, it would not be evidence, and for this, your Honor, I refer to the case of *Baxter* v. *Abbott*, 7 Gray, 71, which, being very short, I will read. I ask your Honor to look at that decision. I have it written here among my papers somewhere, but I don't know where I have laid it. I would like to have your Honor look at it, not because it is necessary, but to show how incompetent any such evidence would be even if it had been uttered in regard to the will of Ebenezer Smith, and could be fixed upon his will. There is also the further testimony offered by the petitioners that Mr. Foster when he left the room of Amasa Winchester, after having witnessed that will, said "the deed is done, the will is made and signed and witnessed;"—no doubt calling to the fertile and frenzy-rolling mind of the counsel for the petitioners the words of Daniel Webster at the Knapp trial:—"The deed is done. He has done the murder. No eye has seen him; no ear has heard him. The secret is his own and it is safe;"—or perhaps suggesting to his mind the words of Macbeth, blood stained and guilty, coming from the chamber of the murdered Duncan, "I have done the deed." This perversion deserves to go into the same category with that other infamous perversion,—the perversion of the words of old Ebenezer Smith written in April, 1862, with which he was repelling what was to him a bore:— "I must fight or be robbed of the last pound of flesh and last dollar."

Here, then, we have a will duly executed by a man of sound mind. This is all that is necessary to show to entitle the will to probate if offered *de novo*. From the due execution of a will made by a man of sound mind, the legal presumption arises that he understood the contents, in the same way that it arises from the due execution of a deed by a man of sound mind. In the case of a will, however, this presumption may be rebutted, but it can be rebutted only by evidence; and what evidence is there, I ask, to rebut that presumption and to show that Ebenezer Smith did not understand the contents? Now there is no evidence whatever, except that which has already been overthrown and demonstrated to be worthless, by which they sought to impeach Mr. Smith's testamentary capacity and the due execution of the will. So then the legal presumption which is in our favor stands unrebutted. On the other hand, we have gone further than was necessary, without resting upon this presumption alone, and have shown affirmatively that the presumption is correct. In truth and fact he did understand the contents, and we have shown it. If before the will was drawn Ebenezer Smith gave instructions as to the terms of the will, or if the terms of the will were proposed to and understood and adopted by him, and afterwards the will was drawn embodying those terms, then in the contemplation of law he understood the contents of the will, whether, after it was drawn, it was or was not read to or by him. So if a man directs a will to be made in a certain way, or if it is suggested to him that a will be made for him in a certain way, and he understands and adopts the suggestion, and afterwards the will containing some variations from the way directed or adopted by him, is brought to him and read to or by him and he understandingly adopts the will, it satisfies the law. This was determined in the case of *Hess's Appeal*, 43 Penn. State, 73. Indeed, if without any suggestion made or adopted by the testator, a will already made is brought to him and read to or by him, and he understandingly adopts it, this satisfies the law. And that was held in the case of *Constable & Bailey* v. *Trefnell & Mason*, 4 Haggard's Eccl. Reports, 477. It is not necessary to the validity of a will that the idea of the will should have originated with Ebenezer Smith. And in that case which I have cited Sir John Nicholl says:—

"It is no part of the testamentary law of this country that the making of a will *must originate* with a testator, nor is it required that proof should be given of the commencement of such a transaction; *provided*, I repeat, it be proved that the deceased completely understood, adopted and sanctioned the disposition proposed to him and that the instrument itself embodied such a disposition."

Also the case of *Jones* v. *Jones*, 14 B. Monroe (Ky.,) 464;—an exception to this instruction given to the jury was sustained: The instruction was that the jury ought to find against the will unless it was drawn up by the testator's request and desire. Exception to this was sustained, and the Court say:—

"A testator might adopt a paper drawn up by or at the instance of the parties interested in its provisions, and if he did it understandingly, the mere fact that it had not been drawn up at his instance or request would not of itself render the will invalid."

The idea of the will, as I understand the testimony, did not originate with Ebenezer Smith. He had already made a testamentary disposition of his property which was then existing giving his furniture and one-third of his estate to his wife, one-third of the balance to his daughter Sarah W. Thorndike, $1,325 to relatives who were not heirs-at-law, $1,000 to the Burtons, and the remainder to his son Isaac and his daughter Eliza W., in the proportion of two-thirds to Isaac and one-third to Eliza. The daughter Eliza who, with her insane love of quarrel, had been the cause of a great deal of trouble, threatened to destroy the family peace if the then-existing testamentary disposition remained The testator's two other children and his wife, tired of the dissension with which the family had been rent in previous years, desired peace. And for the purpose of pacifying Eliza it was proposed to Mr. Smith, substantially, that he make a new will giving the widow the same as before and placing the three children on an equality. Mr. Smith was at first reluctant to do this, because it would prejudice his son Isaac, but that very son was present acquiescing in the change to his own prejudice, and so the testator seeing that his son was satisfied to make a sacrifice, consented to the making of a new will. The will was drawn, substantially in accordance with the change proposed, and was adopted by Mr. Smith. The testator's brother, sister, nephew and nieces, to whom in the prior will of August 13, 1864, he had given small legacies, amounting to $1,325 in all, were left out of the new will; and they, if anybody, are the only persons in this world who can, with any justice whatever on their side, complain of the new will; but he had himself cut them down considerably in the will of August 13th, 1864, from the amounts which he had given them in his will of May 2, 1859. The will was drawn embodying these directions of Mr. Smith, or at least these suggestions made to Mr. Smith and adopted by Mr. Smith. Isaac took the new will to his father, and read it over to him carefully. His father was perfectly conscious, clear in his mind and able to comprehend the terms of the will, and especially was he so able, since it so nearly corresponded with the terms of the disposition which he had theretofore recently made. Mr. Smith understood it; he knew also that it was prejudicial principally to that son who was reading it to him; he knew that it was made in the interest of family peace; and when afterwards it was brought in for him to execute, and he learned from his wife and from each of his children that they were satisfied, he was satisfied and adopted the will. The statement of the nurse that she was in the room all the time and does not remember the conversation of Isaac with his father, and does not remember the reading of the will, is mere negative evidence from a discredited witness who had no interest in the matter, and there was no reason why she should remember it. She was the night nurse and might have been asleep, and very probably was out of the room.

Mr. Chandler:—She was the day nurse, Mr. Drury. *Mr. Drury:*—Well, a person cannot live day and night without sleeping. I say that is impossible, for nurses or for anybody else. No human being who ever lived could live without sleeping either day or night. She was the night nurse. If the evidence on this point were evenly balanced so as to leave a doubt whether or not the will was read to or by him, or its contents understood by him, we are entitled to the benefit of the doubt, because the presumption is that it was either read to him or that he understood the contents in some way.

So then, we have the legal presumption unrebutted, and besides this, the uncontradicted evidence of Isaac that he talked the terms over with his father and read the will to him, strengthened by the absence of any possible or sanely conceivable motive to impose upon his father to give him $15,000 less than the prior will gave him, and the overwhelming testimony that Mr. Smith adopted it clearly in the presence of his wife and children. Is it to be supposed that all the powers of darkness combined can disturb a will like that after it has stood for 14 years? What *sublime* stupidity a man must have to think it possible!

We now have all the elements of a valid will affirmatively proved. We have proved some things not necessary. We have a will duly executed by a person of sound mind with an understanding of its contents. And the first seven allegations in the petition are now disposed of, and we come to the eighth, which is this :—" That the said instrument and the supposed signature thereto of the said Ebenezer Smith were obtained and procured by collusion, by fraud, by undue influence and by force."

Was the will procured by undue influence? The allegation or claim that it was, it would be incumbent upon the petitioners to prove by a preponderance of evidence, if the will were now offered for probate by the respondents for the first time. The presumption of law here is that it was not so procured. The burden is upon him who asserts undue influence. No evidence whatever has been produced for the purpose of showing, or tending to show, that the will was procured by undue influence. The theory of the petitioners has been, and is, that Ebenezer Smith was not susceptible of influence, that he had no mind which could be influenced, that he had no testamentary power, that he was not conscious, that he had no part in the will any more than if he had been dead, that the signature was not his and was not made by his direction, and that, although there was breath in his body, and although he was not physically dead, he was, as far as that will is concerned, dead and beyond the power of influence, due or undue. It is therefore unnecessary to consider the question of undue influence, and yet. inasmuch, as the whole theory of the petitioners in regard to the questions which I have thus far considered is completely overthrown, and inasmuch as the allegation of undue influence is made, although not supported by an iota of evidence, I will consider that question as if the burden were upon us. I voluntarily assume the burden of that.

If the counsel for the petitioners were to state the case of his clients in the strongest way in which it could be stated, I think he would abandon the first seven allegations in the petition altogether, and put his whole power into the eighth allegation alone. He would admit that Ebenezer Smith had sufficient testamentary capacity to make the will, and that the will was duly executed by the testator with a knowledge of its contents. He would if he had the instincts of a gentleman and a decent regard for his professional honor and character, honestly acting for the true interests of his clients, and spurning to gratify their malignity ;— he would, I say, offer an apology for, and would abandon, his statements concerning conspiracy, forgery, intimidation, force and fraud, and his numerous perversions of fact, and his talk about the cell, rinsing the cup for fear of poison, primogeniture, threats of guardianship, being robbed of the last pound of flesh and last dollar, manoeuvreing so as to cut off the Burton branch from their inheritance, imprisonment, burning of papers, dosing with whiskey, and all that kind of talk, which only serves to weaken his case. He would try to reconcile his case with honesty of purpose and intent on the part of the wife and children of Ebenezer Smith, because a court naturally and instinctively revolts from the idea of crime and wickedness. All these charges of crime made by the petitioners, all this talk of wrong doing uttered by and for them, are only signs of weakness and signals of distress, and throw suspicion upon their case ; for what court would not rather believe all the charges false than to believe them true, and reconcile all our acts with honesty than with guilt? If the counsel for the petitioners were to state the case of his clients in the strongest possible way, and in a way to commend their case to the greatest possible favor from a court of justice, he would say, what has been conclusively proved, that there was no fraudulent influence, no force, no collusion in procuring that will from Ebenezer Smith; for nobody of any sense, nobody who is not a knave, can now have the idea that any of the family of Ebenezer Smith was acting with a fraudulent intent and purpose, that any of them had anything but an honest intent and purpose. All this may have been true, and yet there may have been undue influence of some kind. Undue influence may have been consistent with honesty. Ebenezer Smith was in feeble health, gradually but surely approaching dissolution, and his life was fast flickering out. He still had remarkable powers of memory, reason and mind for a man in his physical condition. He remembered his past life and related a great deal of it either in soliloquy or to his nurse, he reasoned with his physicians, he remembered and recognized the members of his family and his acquaintances, he had a care about his property, he had what the law recognizes as a sound and disposing mind and memory, and had a sufficiently clear idea of the disposition which he wished to be made of his property. But he was in a condition in which he was much more susceptible of influence than when he was in health, the influence of kindness and persuasion, the claims of kindred and benevolence, the influence arising from sense of obligation and good will and affection. He was in that condition in which the law is inclined to treat him with tenderness and to throw around him every protection from undue influence of every kind, so that he might have the utmost freedom of will. Now was there the honest overcoming of a disposing but weak mind by a mind or by minds powerful and strong, whereby that instrument became, not the will of Ebenezer Smith, but the will of those who were honestly acting upon him? That is the strongest way to put the case of the petitioners, I believe, or would be, if the will were now offered for probate for the first time, and were not fixed by the stability of 14 years. All this is perfectly consistent with honesty of purpose and intent, and the sneer of a sneak cannot make it otherwise. If the counsel for the petitioners were to take some such ground as this, he would then be in a condition to use with great effect one of the ideas advanced in his opening argument, if that idea were based upon fact, which it is not. The idea to which I refer is this: — "The will which we now dispute is of itself conclusive proof that it does not speak the views of justice, the benevolence, the affections or the inclinations of this fond grandfather. On the contrary, it is so repugnant to, so unmistakably in conflict with, the life-long sentiments entertained by Mr. Smith, in that it cuts off these pet grandsons with a paltry $500 out of about $500,000, that we might confidently rest our case upon the proof of this alone." But unfortunately for the petitioners there is a short and complete answer to all this, as well as to the idea of fraudulent influence, coercion and fraud, and that answer is this: If that will had never been made, these pet grandsons would never have received more than the same paltry $500 each, and each of the persons upon whom it is sought to fix undue influence, Isaac, Mrs. Ebenezer Smith and Sarah, would have received more, and the person upon whom it is principally charged would have received upwards of $15,000 more. We can conceive a man doing something bad for the sake of gaining something; we can even conceive that a man would commit forgery for the purpose of gaining $15,000. You can find a motive there. But when we are told that a man commits forgery for the sake of cutting himself off of $15,000, we say we do not believe it. Why, that illustration which Judge Hoar used would be very pertinent here. I think that was suggested by an anecdote, which I have heard elsewhere, of a priest who was trying to make a boy comprehend what a miracle was. The priest said to the boy " Suppose that somebody should tell you that last night at midnight he saw the sun directly over his head?" "Why, I would say he lied," said the boy. The priest said " But suppose *I* told you so?" " I should say you were drunk," was the boy's reply. I dont care who says it of any man who ever lived, I don't believe that there was ever a man lived, — it would be a miracle, may it please your Honor, — who would commit the crime of forgery for the sake of taking $15,000 out of his own pocket and throwing it away; and if anybody should tell me that a man did that, I would say that the man who said it was either a liar or was drunk at the time he conceived that idea.

Was there then this undue influence, this honest overcoming of a weak mind by a strong and powerful mind, so that that will was the will of those persons who were acting upon Ebenezer Smith? Did not Ebenezer Smith have perfect freedom? It would not have been a great restraint upon him for that son to have gone and said to him " Father, I want you to cut me down in your will, I don't want you to give me so much as you have given me, my sister is making a fuss, she threatens that she is going to destroy the peace of the family after you are dead; now I think the best way to do will be to make us equal." Suppose he fell in with it, do you suppose that would be any sign of undue influence? And that is all he was asked to do,—he was asked to diminish Isaac's share and increase Eliza's,—and if the undue influence was exercised upon anybody it was upon Isaac. His mother and sisters wanted him to give way for the sake of peace, and he consented to do it.

Now this argument is unanswerable, unless the prior will of August 13th can be successfully attacked. Has there been one particle of evidence in the course of this trial, your Honor, to impeach that will of August 13, 1864? Did he not understand the contents of that will? Did he not sign that will? Was not that will witnessed? Was he not of sound mind when he made that? Was there any undue influence upon him when he made that? What evidence of it? By whom was this undue influence exercised? It could have been by no one but Isaac. It was not exercised by Mrs. Ebenezer Smith, because when she found out the contents of it she was not satisfied, it was not in accordance with her wish. Eliza W. did not exercise any undue influence, although she had as much influence over her father as anybody. She exercised no undue influence, because the giving to her of only one-quarter of the residue and giving to Isaac one-half, was not in accordance with her wishes. Sarah did not exercise any undue influence upon him, because it was not according to her wishes, and she afterwards procured a codicil which was in accordance with her wishes, giving her one-third of the balance left after setting aside the portion to the widow. Then there is no one left but Isaac. Who else could have influenced him. It was not the Burtons who influenced him, because they got only $500 each, and it was not in accordance with their wishes. Nobody interested in that will of August 13th, could have exercised any undue influence upon him, except Isaac. And we have to adopt the absurd theory that Isaac, living 250 miles away in New York City, exercised undue influence upon Ebenezer Smith to the prejudice of his wife and his children who were right here at home with him, and also to the prejudice of his affectionate grandchildren whom he was visiting every day, according to their story, and who must have had as much influence as anybody upon him, if he had the affection towards them to which their father has testified so strongly. Isaac, 250 miles away, exercised that influence upon Ebenezer Smith against all the influence of his grandchildren, and his grandchildren's father, and the grandchildren's father's fourth wife, and the testator's own wife, and the testator's own two daughters!

Now what evidence has there been in this case of any undue influence in regard to that will? Not a particle. The silly stuff of Eliza W. about the guardianship may, perhaps, be considered as evidence of undue influence, if your Honor gives a feather's weight to any testimony which has come out of the mouth of that witness. Isaac was not here at the time she speaks of,—had not been here in August.

Against all this, if your Honor please, we have the acts of Ebenezer Smith himself shown by his letter written to his son, sending to his son a long draft in his own handwriting, which must have taken him a day or two to write, of the will of 1859, and the codicil thereto, and a draft of the proposed changes; and now that eleven sheets of closely written writing,—he sends that to his son Isaac, and at the same time sends him a proposed draft of the will of August 1864, and that draft is as follows:—

"I give to my brother Samuel Smith and to my sister Sally Smith of Peterborough, New Hampshire, $200 each. *Second.* I give to each of the five children of my said brother $50 each, and $75 to the widow and children of my deceased nephew Eli Smith. *Third.* I give to Noah, John and Elmira Smith $400 in trust for my four neices, namely, Asineth, Eliza, Elmira and Sarah Ann."—You notice he made a change there from that proposition. Instead of giving them $400 in trust, he gives them in the will outright $75 each. "*Fourth.* I give to each of the three children of my deceased sister Phoebe Seaver $100 each, namely, to Isaac T. Smith of New York in trust for Zachariah Seaver $100 and to Ebenezer Seaver of Boston $100, and to said Ebenezer Seaver $100 in trust for Charlotte Seaver. *Fifth.* I give to my wife"—(he doesn't say how much.) "*Sixth.* I give to Ebenezer, if living, $100." "George Alexander, dead,"—that is the seventh clause. "*Eighth.* Right. Interest Burton boys, Harriet. *Ninth.* I give to my son Isaac half residue"— and a word I cannot make out. "*Tenth.* I give and devise two undivided quarters to Eliza and Sarah. *Eleventh.* Question. *Twelfth.* Right. *Thirteenth.* Question. *Fourteenth.* Isaac and Eliza." That clause fourteen is in regard to the debts of Isaac and Eliza. "*Fifteenth.* Right. *Sixteenth.* I appoint Isaac T. Smith to be my legal representative to decide upon all matters overlooked, doubtful or not clearly expressed in will, or otherwise, with full power to decide." There he proposed in that will to make Isaac T. Smith his sole executor, and to give him full power to do everything that was not fully expressed in that will. Now in fact when he made the will, he made Isaac, Edward Bangs and William Minot executors and trustees with no such power.

The eighth clause in the will of 1859 which Ebenezer Smith marks "Right" in his own draft for his own proposed new will, is as follows: "Eighth. When my grandsons Hazen J. Burton, Jr., and George S. Burton, children of my deceased daughter Harriet, shall severally attain the age of 21 years, I give to each of them on his attaining that age $500."

And the letter written by Ebenezer Smith on one leaf of the long copy, which he himself wrote, of the will and codicil of 1859 is as follows:

"BOSTON, July 25, 1864.

DEAR ISAAC:—I cannot write any more now, I am very tired, but simply to say that whatever suggestions you have to make will be thankfully received, and let me have them immediately, that I may close the will without delay.   Yours affectionately.   FATHER."

There we find Ebenezer Smith writing to his son Isaac, 250 miles away, urging upon him to make suggestions immediately, telling him that any suggestions that he may make will be thankfully received. Well, now let us see. Is there any sign here that any suggestions were made to the favor of Isaac? This gives him one-half of the residue. These are the suggestions which went with this, and in this he appoints Isaac his sole executor and legal representative to decide upon all matters overlooked and made doubtful. In fact, when he makes the will, he adds two other men to the executors. Now is there any evidence from that of any undue influence on the part of Isaac? Is it not on the contrary, evidence that he was soliciting Isaac to make suggestions to him in regard to the making of his will? And we find afterwards among the papers of Ebenezer Smith, in his own handwriting, a full draft of the proposed will, wherein he makes this distribution which is proposed here, and gives the Burton boys $500 each. There was a great deal of work in regard to that will which was done by Ebenezer Smith,—copying of that long will and codicil of 1859, writing the will of August, 1864, in his own handwriting, also this draft which he sent to Isaac. Then another thing;—the names of the witnesses upon that will of August, 13, 1864, William Minot, Moody Merrill and Luther L. White, ought to be conclusive evidence of its due execution, and they are men who would not knowingly have been party to the making of a will brought about by any undue influence. It was drawn by William Minot. Isaac had nothing to do with it. It was drawn in the office of William Minot in the handwriting of Moody Merrill, drawn by this same William Minot who drew his will and codicil of 1859, and who was his regular attorney in all matters in regard to his wills.

Well, now may it please your Honor, what is the best evidence of what a man's free will is? The best evidence of a man's testamentary declarations are not the words which are floating in the air for 14 years and remembered by an interested witness, but the acts of the testator himself which he has put down in legal form and in solemn form in accordance with the law; and what do we find that his previous testamentary declarations were? Wherein do we find, that in that will of October 5, 1864, there is evidence that Ebenezer Smith's mind, as it had been made up for years, as it had been declared by himself privately, was warped and twisted in any direction, or that he didn't have absolute freedom of will? Wherein does that will differ from the will of 1859? There in those wills and codicils is the best evidence of his previous testamentary declarations. In a great many cases in the English Reports, the English Ecclesiastical Reports, you will find this matter brought up: What were the previous wills? Wherein does this differ from his previous testamentary declarations? This has usually been the inquiry where undue influence, or fraud, or anything of that sort has been alleged, and that has always been regarded as evidence of the greatest weight, if the Judges see a uniformity in all the testamentary dispositions of a man taken together, or some change which can be reasonably explained when it is compared with the previous testamentary declarations. Now here we have the will of October 5, 1864. It is almost exactly like the will of 1859 except in one or two particulars,—it leaves out the relatives outside the family, and gives to the wife absolutely one-third instead of the life income of one-third, and says nothing about the debts of Eliza and Isaac. Those are all the changes from the will of 1859. That man also made a declaration on the 16th day of May, 1859, and that declaration shows what a fond old grandfather Ebenezer Smith was, because, his son Alexander having died after May 2, 1859, he, in order to show the love which he had for his pet grandsons, the children of his son George Alexander, gave them $5 each, and did not take the trouble to find out whether George Alexander had any children or not,—didn't know whether he had any or not. That shows the affection of the man for his grandchildren. It shows what Chancellor Kent says in that case of *Van Alst* v. *Hunter*, to which I have already referred, that the affections of an old man grow dim as the generations from him recede. They were two generations off, he was an old man, locked up in himself, secret, and nobody could find out from mere talk with him what his will was.

Even if Isaac did exercise undue influence in the will of August 13, 1864, what was the effect of that undue influence? Not to prejudice the Burtons. They had no reason to complain. Well, suppose they go back to the will of 1859, how can they attack that? How can they account for that in 1859, wherein he gave them only $500 each? What answer is it possible for any man to make to this argument? That statement of the wills which I presented to your Honor in my opening argument (see statement on pages 18 and 19) is perfectly unanswerable: it cannot be answered. When an able lawyer like Dwight Foster, and an honest man, took their case in 1864, and saw the true state of things with two wills right behind that to fall back upon, he would not be guilty of longer prosecuting a case to upset a will fortified like that, especially after it had been compromised and they had received five times as much as that testator ever, in any legal testamentary declaration which he ever made, intended that they should have. Now, if your Honor please, look at the action of that man's mind as it is displayed there upon that page of the statement of wills where it can be seen at a single glance. Can your Honor see, can anybody see, any sign of undue influence in that? There is the record of that man's mind, and there is the best evidence of what that man's mind was for years, stamped there, fixed there, so that we can read it, down to these remote times, 14 years after the old man died.

(Adjourned till 1 o'clock, Thursday, January 23, 1879.)

Jan'y 23, '79.

May it please your Honor: Before I continue my argument in the line in which I was going at the adjournment yesterday afternoon, I will cite to your Honor a case which bears upon a part which I have already gone over; — the case of *Wilson* v. *Beddard*, Simon's Reports, Volume 12, page 28.

"The will in this case was made the day preceding the testator's death, and when he was extremely ill. He signed it, not with his name, but with his mark; in doing which his hand was guided. The depositions of two of the attesting witnesses taken in the suit, tended to impeach the testator's competency. Those witnesses having died, their depositions were read at the trial. The Court say: "Next it was contended that what the learned Judge said, with reference to the testator's hand being guided when he made his mark to his will, was not law. The Judge said that it was necessary that the will should be signed by the testator, not with his name, for his mark was sufficient if made by his hand, though that hand might be guided by another person; and in my opinion, that proposition is correct in point of law. For the statute of frauds requires that a will should be signed by the testator, or by some other person in his presence, and by his direction; and I wish to know, if a dumb man, who could not write, were to hold out his hand for some person to guide it, and were then to make his mark, whether that would not be a sufficient signature to his will. In order to constitute a direction it is not necessary that anything should be said. If a testator, in making his mark, is assisted by some other person, and acquiesces and adopts it, it is just the same as if he had made it without any assistance. It is observable, too, that before the mark was made, the testator made some faint strokes on each of the sheets. My opinion, therefore, is that the observation made by the learned Judge on this part of the case, was quite correct in point of law, and therefore, it affords no ground for granting a new trial."

Mr. Chandler: That was where the statute required a direction only? It didn't say express direction. It says direction. *Mr. Drury:* Yes, I think so. I don't care what it says. You have a good opportunity to comment upon it, if you can find any consolation out of that case, or out of the statute.

Another point which I will call up, bearing upon the date of the execution, to make it ten-fold stronger: The bank records were not attacked, and I want to ask why Mr. O'Connor did not attack them, if they were attackable? He was eager to find something against Isaac T. Smith, and was looking at that draft book of the bank, presumably to see if he could not in some way injure him. He was glad of the opportunity to come to Boston to testify against him, and if the records could have been attacked we should have heard of it.

The case of *Baxter* v. *Abbott*, which I mentioned yesterday and could not find, 7 Gray, 71, is this:—

"It cannot be given in evidence against the will that one of the attesting witnesses, who testified in the probate court to the testator's sanity, and has since deceased, declared after the probate, that he wished to live to unsay what he had said, and that the testator was insane."

Even if Andrix A. Foster had said of this will of Ebenezer Smith what they are trying by an inference to make him say, it would not be admissible in evidence.

And another thing: I forgot to speak of the testimony of Mrs. Eliza W. Smith in regard to the reading of the will. She says, "I have no reason to think the will could have been read to father, but still it might have been." As to his recognition of Mr. Foster she says, "I don't think he recognized Mr. Foster, the whole thing was very confusing. If there had been any remark by Mr. Foster, I shouldn't have noticed it."

I come now again to the subject of undue influence, and upon that point, I will call your Honor's attention to the case *Williams* v. *Goude*, 1 Hogg, 581 :

"The influence to vitiate an act must amount to force and coercion, destroying free agency —it must not be the influence of affection and attachment,—it must not be the mere desire of gratifying the wishes of another, for that would be a very strong ground in support of a testamentary act. Further, there must be proof that the act was obtained by this coercion,—by importunity which could not be resisted,—that it was done merely for the sake of peace,—so that the motive was tantamount to force and fear."

This decision is by that same great Judge whom I have cited before in this case, Sir John Nicholl. And the will of October 5, 1864 was executed, not that Ebenezer Smith might have peace, but that there might, after he died, be peace among his descendants, his children, and he made it willingly without any restraint, not for the sake of buying his own peace, but for the sake of peace after his death. I say this, anticipating any perversion which may come from the counsel who is to follow.

The only testimony upon which any attempt has been made to impeach the will of August 13, 1864, has been the testimony of Eliza W. Smith, who says that the first talk of guardianship was ten years before her father's death — it might have been 15 years. Now this is perfectly laughable to those who know and remember what kind of a man Ebenezer Smith was, or anything about his character. The idea that anybody was so insane as to let the idea go into his head that it was possible to get that man under guardianship, is perfectly absurd. And then she says he used to say "They will put me under guardianship if I do this or that," when repelling some advances of hers. The next time that she heard of guardianship was when her father came out there to West Medford the last time before his death, and told Eliza that Isaac had been on, and had made him make a will, and "Isaac made me promise not to tell you what he has been doing. If I tell you, I am to be put under guardianship. My word is passed not to come to West Medford but once." I leave that alone to answer itself. If the absurdity of a statement is sufficient answer to it, there could not be a greater degree of absurdity than that statement, and hence there could not be a more complete answer to it than to leave it to answer itself. The idea that Isaac forced his father to make a will and made him promise under penalty of guardianship not to tell Eliza and not to go to Medford, and that this dread of guardianship took such a hold of the old man that he went right out to his gabbling daughter at Medford and committed the very act which was to bring the dreaded consequence upon him! We know in what mint that idea was coined, for there is only one in the world capable of leaving such a stamp:

There has been talk of the Insane Asylum, of there having been talk of putting Ebenezer Smith into an insane asylum. Now I see where that idea originated. Here is a letter which Ebenezer Smith wrote to his beloved daughter Eliza, dated February 9, 1861, and I wish to call your Honor's attention to this clause in that letter :—

"I was in hopes to have done something through this charter with that hateful property which has been the means of almost running me out at the little end of the horn just before I can get ready to die. If I could have gone to the *insane asylum* before I had gone to West Medford it would have been money in my purse, if not health in my body. But I was not possessed of 'madness and malignity' to get me to the asylum if I had tried, and I am sure *I* never heard or knew of any of my ancestors or of blood relations that were so."

That is pretty good evidence in regard to the man's hereditary insanity,— would be very good, particularly if they had started an idea of hereditary insanity in the family.

The petitioners have undertaken to show by the testimony of their father, and of themselves, that the relations existing between Ebenezer Smith and the Burtons were very cordial. He spoke of the cordiality and tenderness with which Ebenezer Smith treated his daughter Harriet. I have no doubt she deserved to be treated with all a father's tenderness, but something,—her husband probably, his disgrace,—had alienated him from her even during her life, and that sad letter of Harriet Burton to her father is like a voice from the grave which comes up here 25 years after it was written, after she has been in the ground, to confute and confound her own husband and her own sons, — yes, and her own sister whom Harriet in that letter charges with being the cause of the " awful gulf" which existed between her and her father. If there was this " awful gulf" when Harriet was alive in 1853, is it to be supposed that that gulf narrowed rather than widened after she had gone? And there was then her presence to induce him to these cordial relations with his grandsons. These sons, this husband, this sister of Harriet Burton, are the only ones to tell of these cordial relations. If, in-fact, Ebenezer Smith did tell old Burton to keep his children away from his house, depend upon it it was done in order that they might keep away and because he did not want to see them there any oftener than he could help, or anywhere else. When he met his son-in-law the meeting was " clandestine, as Mr. Clapp terms it, and secret. He did not wish it to be seen that he was on terms of any intimacy with Mr. Burton. The theory of the relationship with the Burton family, the cordial relationship, is entirely fictitious, and I think can be demonstrated conclusively to be so. They build up a theory on the testimony of Hazen J. Burton, Sr., and other worthless persons. Then from that for a basis they reason that the will is inconsistent and untrue ; and they must say the same of the wills of May 2, 1859, and of August 13, 1864, which give them just the same amount of money. Now I reason in just the opposite direction. I start from just the opposite point. I place my foundation upon the testamentary acts and declarations which Ebenezer Smith put down in writing with all legal solemnities, deliberately, and calling good men to stand around him and give attestation to his acts and declarations. From this I reason conclusively that the theory of the cordiality existing between the Burtons and Ebenezer Smith is untrue. They say: When there was all this cordiality which we have shown, would he have made those wills freely? I say: When we know that he did make those wills freely, was there this cordiality? They say that the theory of cordiality contradicts the wills. I say the wills contradict the theory of cordiality. And I ask your Honor which starts upon the better foundation?—I who stand upon the wills which are unchanged and unchangeable, under the hand and seal of Ebenezer Smith, sanctioned by every solemnity; or they, who construct a theory out of their own minds and build upon that? If their theory is not untrue, then we are compelled to come to the conclusion that it was out of his regard and love for his grandchildren that Ebenezer Smith did not give them money, that he thought money would be a curse to them, that their fond old grandfather thought he was granting them a blessing in not giving them money to spoil them as he had spoilt his *sons*. The same as he did not wish to spoil them with education as he had spoilt his sons with education.

Their theory, too, of the benevolent character of Ebenezer Smith contradicts their theory of this cordiality. If he was such a benevolent man,—and I don't say whether he was or not,—if he was cordial and benevolent to strangers, then that proves that he was not cordial to these Burton people, because he did not give them money; unless upon the supposition, which I have just made, that he thought he was doing them a favor by not giving them money.

Who was this Ebenezer Smith of whom we are talking? What kind of a man was he? What kind of wax was this which for five and one half years, the latter part of his life, could be formed into any shape desired? What do their own witnesses say about him in this respect? Joshua W. Clapp, who probably knows more about the character of Ebenezer Smith than any other man now living in Boston, from his confidential relations with him for 25 years, and the witness of the petitioners, a very able man himself, who has encountered able men, has drawn this graphic picture of the character of Ebenezer Smith:—I asked him this question:

"Now in regard to the peculiarities of Ebenezer Smith, what was the striking peculiarity? If you were going to describe the striking peculiarity of that man, what would you say it was,—you said he was a very peculiar man?" A. Yes, sir. Well, the most striking characteristic of him was, he was very slovenly, and very neat. One day he would be Apollo Belvedere, and the next day you would think he was the Rag Picker of Paris." Q. "What I mean is mentally?" A. "I think he was shrewd and sharp, far-seeing and far-sighted, I think he was as keen as a brier, I think he was the smartest business man I have come in contact with since I have been on the list of action. He could see farther into a trade than any man I saw, and his prophecies were wonderful, and they have come true since his death and during twenty or thirty years contact with him." Q. "Was he secretive? What I mean by that is secret?" A. "Yes, sir: I think that he was. I think he admired to be." Q. "Rather misleading?" A. "I think, sir, that you would be deceived in him very easily indeed." Q. "He would make one man think he was doing one thing and another man he would make think he was doing the opposite thing?" A. "I think Ebenezer Smith was an honest man, but I think he had peculiar ways of manipulating his doings in such a manner as to make it none of your business to attend to his business, and if you attempted to get anything out of him, I don't believe you would succeed very well." Q. "If you undertook to find out what he was about?" A. "I don't believe you would find it out" Q. "Was he a man of firm purpose?" A. "I always looked upon him as being a man of indomitable will and industry and perseverance, up early and late, studying all the time." Q. "Was he a man that could be easily controlled?" A. "I would as soon undertake to control the north wind as control him."

That is the kind of a man Ebenezer Smith was as described by their own witness.

And what does Mr. J. W. Rollins, also called by them, say? His counsel for ten years, who knew him very well and had occasion to know pretty well what kind of a man Ebenezer Smith was as regards to firmness says:—"Remarkably firm man; anybody who called him stubborn would not be guilty of slander; very firm: not easily intimidated; very strong character." Dr. Thorndike speaks of him in the same manner. And Eliza, even, felt obliged to say that he was a very tenacious man. Mr. Loring asked Mr. Clapp: "Don't you remember once, Mr. Clapp, that he left $50,000 on deposit in one of the banks here in Boston and would not touch it, although it was not drawing interest for several years,—that grew out of the Boston and Maine controversy?" "I remember it well," says Mr. Clapp, "I was interested in it for 14 years." That is the kind of wax that could be formed to suit anybody's purposes for the last five and a half years of his life, either by fear or by persuasion. A man tenacious of his rights, as he showed by employing nine lawyers at a time.

Now we have to start with, if your Honor please, the legal presumption that the will was not procured by undue influence. To attempt to sustain the theory of undue influence, the petitioners must abandon the first seven allegations in their petition altogether; they must suppose that Isaac T. Smith was voluntarily doing a thing which was creditable to him, and yet they must go from that supposition to the absurd supposition that the same man was actively striving by undue means to force his father to deprive him, Isaac, of a large share of his estate which proved to be over $15,000; that Isaac's mother and sister Sarah were doing the same thing, though not so much to their prejudice, yet to their prejudice, and that the only one who was not using undue influence was his sister Eliza who was benefitted by the will at the expense of all the rest over $17,000; they have to attack the testamentary capacity of Ebenezer Smith for the last five and one-half years of his life, Ebenezer Smith whom their own witnesses describe as one of the ablest of men; they have to break through that whole line of wills and codicils which are exhibited upon that statement, those wills and codicils prepared at his request by honest men and men of high standing and ability, and attested by respectable witnesses; and they have to construct a theory wholly at variance with the conception of Ebenezer Smith's character as conceived by every disinterested man, and I may say even as conceived by themselves.

Now I pass by for the present that ear-trumpet allegation in the petition, the 9th I think it is, which I will refer to again.

Thús far I have endeavored to place the evidence before your Honor in such form that it could be seen without the trouble of reading all that testimony through, and thus have been extracting, as it were, the wheat from the chaff. All this evidence shows,—*First :* That Ebenezer Smith when he executed that will was of sound mind. *Second :* That he made the will and duly signed it, and it was duly attested by three competent witnesses. *Third :* He understood what was done, and understood the contents of the will. *Fourth :* He had perfect freedom of will, and the will was not procured by undue influence.

This case, thus far, completely refutes the idea of conspiracy to defraud the Burtons, for we know that the will did not affect them one dollar ; refutes the idea of forgery, for it prejudiced no one but him who is charged with the forgery, and there is not the presence of any conceivable motive for forgery, the act was done openly and above board ; it refutes the idea of procuring a false will to be witnessed, for the same reasons, and the witnesses saw what was done and were not imposed upon ; it refutes the idea of the publication of a false will, or procuring its probate by perjury or imposition upon the court, for it would have been a benefit to those who propounded the will, if it had been rejected, and especially a benefit to him who is charged with having been the principal offender ; and it refutes the idea that the Burtons were cheated, for the will did not deprive them of a single dollar.

Did ever a more groundless case come into court? Was ever a case prosecuted with greater malignity and in a more aggravating and cruel manner, or in a manner better calculated to wound the hearts, distress the feelings, injure the health and shorten the lives of innocent people, to whom an attempted stain upon their spotless character and lives is worse than the dagger of an assassin in the heart? Do not the movers in this case deserve to be blasted to eternal infamy?—for they are worse than the assassins of lives, they are the assassins of good character and reputation which are the immediate jewels of the souls of the upright, dearer and more precious to them than life itself.

And is not our case proved already, may it please your Honor? I have endeavored to aid the court to come to a conclusion without difficulty, and to comprehend the monstrous character of the prosecution of this case. This case has occupied a great deal of my time for months. I have thought about it a great deal, and I felt it my duty, not only to my clients, but to your Honor and to the community which has been outraged by the petitioners in their prosecution of this case in this outrageous manner in which it has been prosecuted and published. This case concerns every innocent man and woman, and ought to receive such a judgment that every innocent man and woman will be encouraged and every guilty man and woman rebuked. I knew that your Honor's time has been greatly occupied with the many and increasing duties which your office requires, and I trust I may have the satisfaction of feeling that I have saved some of your Honor's time hereafter by putting the evidence together.

This case is invulnerable thus far at every point. I feel that the case is won. Ordinarily I should be content to stop here, but my object is not merely to win this case, but to show that it is without the shadow of foundation. It is important to my clients that this should be shown, and that the character of the whole case brought against us should be set forth in its true light. I proceed to perform that duty, and this will have some bearing perhaps upon questions which will be raised hereafter in this court after the case is decided.

Strong as this case is on the grounds which I have already gone over, the strongest part yet remains. This is a small part of the case. I have been arranging the evidence in its proper order, and concentrating and summarizing it, so that the court might see that the will was a valid will in itself. But suppose your Honor to be convinced that there is no more question about the validity of that will than about the validity of the best will that was ever made; that would be the weaker part of our case. Suppose it were an invalid will originally, we have a ground of defence which would be just as strong as if it were the most valid will ever seen or made.

We are not here, your Honor, for the purpose of propounding a will. We are here to show why a will propounded 14 years ago should not be disturbed. We are here talking about a will which was admitted to probate 14 years ago, and which has stood 14 years undisturbed. If so much could have been said in its favor 14 years ago when originally offered for probate, how much stronger the argument against revoking at this late day the probate which has stood so long! Says Pollock, J., 2 Hurlston & Norman, 623 :—"It is a maxim of the law of England to give effect to everything which appears to have been established for a considerable course of time, and to presume that what has been done has been done of right and not of wrong." But the counsel for the petitioners undertook to say, when this case was begun on the 4th of December, that we could not have the benefit of that 14 years, and he has cited I don't know how many out of the 134 authorities which your Honor is to have the pleasure of reading in support of that proposition. And how absurd it is! Why, he hugs a delusion, and it is hard to get it out of him. He had that delusion that he could file interrogatories in this Probate Court, and he put in here a brief of 22 pages to show that you could file interrogatories to an executor just the same as you could to parties in an ordinary action at law, and we had to be here and argue the A B Cs of law, because we saw him so persistent in it, and I don't know but what he may be persistent in this yet. But to save your Honor any thought or looking up any authority upon it, I will just call attention to the cases which he has cited upon that point, which I know do not sustain what he contends that they do. The first case which he cites on the brief is *Collier* v. *Idleys'* Executors, 1 Bradford, 94. That is a New York case decided at a time when the statute provided that if allegations were made at any time within one year, the heirs might call upon the executor to prove the will anew, to prove it *de novo*, a decision made under a statute, and it was decided that the original probate could not be brought up as *prima facie* evidence. That is the law also in England where they had (I don't know how it is now) the proof by common form and the proof by solemn form or after citation. The heirs, or those not cited, could call upon the executor at any time to prove the will anew, and he had to proceed just as if it had never been admitted to probate. And these cases are cases bearing upon that. Now don't we know that here in this State of Massachusetts we can rely upon the probate of a will? Don't we know that an executor cannot be called upon every week to begin *de novo* and set up a will? Don't we have common sense to know that you cannot keep executors trotting through this court in that way forever?

Mr. Chandler: That is admitted. *Mr. Drury:* Well, I am glad to see one idea of common sense enter the head of the counsel for the petitioners. I don't know what the object is of citing these criminal cases upon that point. I know what the effect of them is, and that is, that the probate is not any answer to a criminal indictment. That is very well known.

Mr. Chandler: Did you know that you had got hold of the wrong list of cases? *Mr. Loring:* Perhaps you got hold of the wrong one, when you gave it to us as the one you relied upon.

Mr. Chandler: If I made a mistake, I will look out for it. Brother Drury has got hold of the wrong list of cases. The cases are put under their several heads. You have got hold of the wrong head. *Mr. Drury:* The head is, " De novo, will to be proved anew." Is not that the right head?

Mr. Chandler: That is the right head for those cases. *Mr. Drury: Rex v. Buttery.*

Mr. Chandler: Your point is you are speaking about the lapse of time? *Mr. Drury:* I am talking about this absurd idea that here in this Commonwealth we are obliged to prove a will anew 14 years after it has been admitted to probate, which we know to be very absurd. We know very well that the admission of a will to probate, if it is forged, is no answer to a criminal indictment. Nothing that takes place in a civil case can be brought as a defence to a criminal indictment brought by the Commonwealth. And inasmuch as this is the law, I ask the counsel again, and I ask the petitioners, why don't they indict Isaac T. Smith?

Mr. Chandler: Because the statute of limitations saves him. *Mr. Drury:* The statute of limitations does not apply to Isaac T. Smith. It applies only to those who have been residents of this Commonwealth six years. Gen. Stats. c. 171, § 20.

What difference does it make now, your Honor? I say we rest upon the probate of that will. What difference does it make now at this time whether that will was valid or not in law? I don't care, as far as the legality of that is concerned, whether that will was or was not originally valid. I don't care if it had been a piece of brown paper, or if it had been the affidavit of Eliza W. Smith— false as hell—if it had been admitted to probate as a will in the way this was. If it had been admitted to probate under the circumstances under which this will was admitted it could not be disturbed. Was there any fraud in the admission of that will to probate? Was not everything about that will known which ought to have been known? Was there any concealment which would vitiate that probate? If not, then was the time to contest it, after this Court had appointed a guardian for the petitioners to look out for their interests.

That was the time to oppose it. And I wish to call your Honor's attention now at this point to what must have struck everybody interested in this case,—the conspicuous absence of Andrew N. Burton, the guardian *ad litem* of the petitioners at the time when that compromise was made. I heard this long list of witnesses of theirs come here and testify, and I kept wondering why doesn't Andrew N. Burton come here and testify? When the case was closed for the petitioners, I called their counsel's attention to that fact then, and said I, "Are you not going to call Andrew N. Burton?" Andrew N. Burton, the witness of all witnesses who should have been produced, was not here, and was conspicuous by his absence. They brought the guardian, Lyman L. Harding, who had nothing to do with that compromise, who was not appointed until after the compromise had been made and the will had been admitted to probate, the letters testamentary issued to the executors, who had nothing whatever to do, who knew nothing about the case. They had Lyman L. Harding here to testify, and yet the very man of all others, whom this Court had appointed to look out for the interests of these minors, has not shown his head. Have they proved, as the burden is upon them to prove, that there was anything in the circumstances of the execution of that will, or in the probate of that will, which ought to have been known, which was not known? Have they proved it, when they have kept this Andrew N. Burton away? If he knew it, it binds them. And he does not come here to say that he had no knowledge how the will was executed. What evidence have we of the proceedings here in the Probate Court? Now here are these witnesses who have testified about it; Eliza W. Smith, Anna G. Giles, Ebenezer Smith, Arthur G. Smith, Dr. Thorndike, Edward D. Sohier and Dwight Foster. All three of the witnesses to the will were examined when it was offered for probate. Eliza says the examination was an hour or so. Giles remembers at one time that she was not asked whether Mr. Smith was conscious in her opinion, and then again she answers that she was asked that question. She undertakes to remember not only what questions were asked her, but what questions were not asked her. Put a particular question to her, she will say " No, I was not asked that," but she says, " If I had been asked if I saw Ebenezer Smith sign that I should have said no. I saw his son Isaac take hold of his hand,"—and all through that,— " and he was not conscious at all any more than a dead man," and all that stuff. If it did come out here fourteen years ago, they knew it. If it came out fourteen years ago in this court that Mrs. Giles thought he was unconscious at the time, if it came out here in this court that Isaac guided his hand, that binds these petitioners, because they had counsel here at that time, they had a guardian *ad litem* at that time, for this very case who had been appointed by this Court at that very time for over ten days to look out for their interests. If it came out in this court, it was the neglect of their guardian *ad litem* that he didn't know it. Young Ebenezer rather thinks he was here, but is not exactly sure whether he was or not. Arthur was here; he says he thinks Dwight Foster was here. Dr. Thorndike does not remember anything about it, except that Mr. Sohier and himself were here. And Mr. Dwight Foster does not remember, has not the slightest recollection, very poor memory, that he was here, and yet I will see what he says :—

"My belief is I must have been at the hearing in the Probate Court when the will was offered for probate. I understood it was a question whether he possessed testamentary capacity and whether undue influence was exercised over him. I called on the witness Foster and enquired as carefully as I could as to the circumstances of the execution. I probably was present in the Probate Court. I asked Mr. Foster carefully about the execution and the signing. No recollection of seeing Giles and Patterson; cannot say whether or not they were brought to my office. I don't know whether or not I ever saw the other compromise, have no recollection of it." Then looking at the petition for the appointment of Andrew N. Burton as guardian *ad litem*, he says, "The inference is very strong that I attended the hearing in the Probate Court." It was negligence if he did not, which negligence is not to be presumed of a man, a lawyer of the reputation and standing of Dwight Foster, afterwards a Judge of the Supreme Court of Massachusetts. "I got the impression from what Foster said," he adds, "that I had a chance of contesting the will, and assented to the compromise because, while I thought it quite possible a jury would not find the last will properly executed in consequence of the exceeding feebleness of the testator, yet there were prior wills which gave my clients no larger provision. I made all the enquiry I knew how to make at the time. I should suppose the signature would naturally excite enquiry among those interested in the will. The statement of Mr. Foster was that the testator was exceedingly feeble and weak, but he thought he understood what was taking place at the time. I had no information of forgery in the technical sense, but thought there was some evidence of procuring the signature of a man who had not testamentary capacity."

Does anybody mean to say, your Honor, after a case has been litigated in this court once, with this evidence as given now, evidence of this kind, after everybody has forgotten what evidence was related, after everybody has forgotten what they knew, does anybody soberly mean to say that we, when that probate is attacked, are compelled, and have the burden, to establish that will anew? Too absurd to think of! Does your Honor suppose that a will could be palmed off upon you in which the testator's hand had been guided, without your learning the fact? Do you suppose that would be possible in the case of yourself? Would it be possible in case of any Judge, or anybody fit to be a Judge of the probate court of the county of Suffolk? And Isaac Ames was that. "Did you see him sign it," you would ask. You would even ask if he signed it without any assistance. You would ask all the particulars, and you would do that, your Honor, with one of the witnesses, even when there was no contest. But if there were any opposition, you would be very careful to bring out every fact, and especially with such a signature as that. The idea that Isaac Ames, looking at that signature, did not ask how that signature was made is perfect folly. There are his checkmarks as he called each witness; he pencilled them on the left, as he always did. And the idea of supposing that a lawyer like Dwight Foster, seeing that signature, being here as he was from every inference, and we might presume that he was here, because it has not been proved that he was not, — the idea that Dwight Foster saw that signature without finding out from those witnesses when they were on the stand here under oath how it happened to be made in that way is another absurdity. And then we have to suppose that Mr. H. L. Hazelton and Darwin E. Ware, who were then of the firm of Hazelton & Ware, did not call attention to that. We have got to suppose that that will ran the gauntlet of so many lawyers, and that the fact was, not brought out, that the truth was not brought out, as to the manner in which that signature was made, on an examination which took place an hour or so !

The witnesses to that will, as I have shown your Honor in a previous part of my argument, knew everything about the making of that signature, which was of any importance for them to know. After having proved that the will was duly executed, the executors were not obliged to go any further. There was nothing to conceal, the witnesses were all here ; and we know just as well as if we had heard them yesterday, we know that it came out, we know that it must have come out, we know that it would have come out under a capable Judge, we know it would have come out under your Honor and any other Judge of probate, just how that signature was made. But I call the attention of your Honor to what Mrs. Giles says. Now this is another point which affects her credibility. We find all these other witnesses saying they don't remember whether such and such questions were asked or not. But we find this Giles woman ready to answer any question that is asked her, and she does it positively almost every time, and almost before we get the question out of our mouth. And we know your Honor cannot tell what questions were put to any particular witness who has been examined in the course of this trial during this past month. If your Honor were called upon to do it, if I were to ask you, was this witness asked that question and was he asked that and that, and were I to make some supposed question, your Honor could not tell that. No human mind can tell it, unless you take it down. Perhaps the substance could be told, perhaps the effect of the testimony could be given, but the idea of remembering what questions were asked and what were not asked and of relating them, even of the witnesses of a month past, — it cannot be done. You can tell some things, you can pick out some things. Now there is Mr. Clapp's testimony ; anybody can remember that, almost give it off word for word in that graphic language which he used. I don't suppose he meant, when he said Ebenezer Smith was like Apollo Belvedere, that he sometimes appeared in the streets naked ; he only meant by that, that sometimes Mr. Smith appeared very well dressed. An unhappy illustration, probably, but that was what the meaning of it was, — sometimes very neat and at other times very slovenly. There in Mr. Clapp's testimony was something which would strike anybody, but the idea of remembering all the details of testimony, carrying it down from year to year for 14 years in the memory of a nurse is perfectly absurd. However, whether the circumstances came out in regard to the execution of that will or not, due care would have brought those circumstances out. If they were not brought out, it was not our fault. We concealed nothing ; there was nothing to conceal. It would have been a benefit to Isaac, yes, a benefit to the extent of $15,000 and over to Isaac, it would have been a benefit to Mrs. Ebenezer Smith and to Sarah, if the will had been rejected, for if the last will was invalid, the prior will was not revoked. If it was not valid as a will, then it was not valid as a revocation of the prior will. So of each will behind it. It falls back upon the other. If the last will is not valid as a will, it is not valid as the révocation of a will.   Then Dwight Foster thought there was a good chance of contesting that will.   It was kept in the Courts, and in the Supreme Court one year, and it came on for trial finally in September and October 1865, as shown by the 'summons to the witnesses ; and Eliza W. says she went to court herself, and was called up there in court to come and sign this compromise which was made ; it was signed in the court room on the very day of the trial, and I presume that the witnesses testified there in court.   I know this, that the jury did find there, as it appears by their verdicts which I have shown your Honor, and which are in the case, that a jury did find upon each and every one of the three issues which were presented to them, and the verdicts are signed by the foreman of the jury who found, *first*,—that the will was signed by Ebenezer Smith or by some person in his presence and by his express direction and was attested and subscribed by three competent witnesses in his presence. Then there was the issue of undue influence found in favor of the executors ; and there is one other, I forget now what the issue was,—oh, was he of sound and disposing mind and memory? And they found he was ; and that appears and there is evidence there to establish that fact, and the Judge presumably instructed the jury, although there was not a formal trial, to find a verdict in favor of the executors.

Well, after being a year in court, after Judge Foster had had every opportunity to find out everything to be known about that will, it was settled by a family compromise in which all the heirs-at-law of Ebenezer Smith were represented,—a family compromise.   And here is what our Supreme Court say of a family compromise, in *Leach* v. *Fobes*, 11 Gray, 506, a case in Equity : —

" The agreement set out in the bill is of a nature which is entitled to the highest favor at the hands of a court of equity.   It is the result of a family compromise of a controversy which had arisen between the heir-at-law and devisee of a testator concerning his sanity and free agency at the time of making his last will.   Such contracts are not against public policy.   On the contrary, as they contribute to the peace and harmony of families and to the prevention of litigation, they will be supported in equity without an inquiry into the adequacy of the consideration on which they are founded."

Mr. Chandler :—Read the next sentence.   *Mr. Drury :*—You can read it. That is all I have written here.   *Mr. Chandler :*—I shall have to if you don't. *Mr. Drury :*—You can do it if you want to.   That is what a family compromise is in a court of equity, even, where they even decreed a specific performance of the compromise.   If entitled to the highest consideration in a court of equity, then how much higher consideration it is entitled to in a court of law and in a Probate Court.   I didn't bring over the Law Library with me, so I cannot read the rest of that.   If you have it among your hundred volumes I will read it.

Mr. Chandler :—I haven't it.   I shall have it here when I make my closing argument.   *Mr. Drury :*—I shall be very happy to hear it again, and have it impressed upon the mind of the Court.   In *Ward* v. *Ward*, 15 Pickering, 511, it was held that a Probate Court was authorized to take notice of and conform to an agreement among some of the heirs, in the final settlement of the account of the executor, in relation to the testator's personal estate, instead of conforming with the provisions of the will. Every immediate heir-at-law was present and represented, and the counsel for the petitioners may cite all the cases in the Newgate Calendar, or elsewhere ;—such a compromise is valid, made ten times more so by acquiescence for 8 or 10 years after these petitioners became of age, and their keeping the money ; and made a thousand fold more valid by keeping the money after they intended to begin and had begun litigation.

So then we have not only a will which is valid in itself, but the probate of a will which would be good and conclusive now even if the will had not been valid.

Look at that case, your Honor, which has been brought here by these petitioners. See what a beautiful fabric they have built, only to see it come tumbling down in ruin upon their heads. A fabric built on the confessed ignorance of experts, testifying about matters of which they confessed they never had experience ; on the bare unaided memory of an ignorant woman, a nurse, as to the date of an event which took place 14 years ago ; upon the visions and dreams of Hazen J. Burton, Sr., and Eliza W. Smith ; and upon the desires, malignity and pretended suspicions of Hazen J. Burton, Jr., and his brother, who are capable of conceiving that a man would commit a series of monstrous crimes without a conceivable motive, merely to deprive himself of $15,000, and that man such a fool as they would make him out, who has been honored in both hemispheres, honored by his fellow citizens, by his city, and by his State, and is so now,·against whom nothing could be found, against whom no respectable person could be found to say a word, nor any person whatever could be found to testify, until, after raking and scraping New York, they had been obliged to go down into the slums and bring up the disreputable O'Connor, covered all over with the nastiness of his vile character and reputation, whose good opinion of an honest man would be defiling to that honest man and make that honest man say, " What evil thing have I done ? Get thee behind me Satan "—and whose worst opinion of an honest man would be that honest man's best recommendation which that O'Connor could give. " Birds of a feather flock together," and these vultures of society, Hazen J. Burton, Sr., and this O'Connor, whatever his initials are, have come together to await the hoped for disinterment of the remains of old Ebenezer Smith. As Joseph Cook has quoted in the last lecture which he delivered in Tremont Temple : " ' The costliest unclean beast,' Thorold Rogers says, ' that society can keep in its menagerie, is an unpunished commercial rogue.' " ·This is the foundation upon which that fabric was constructed.

Against such a case are the instincts of justice, revolting from the idea of crime, the good character of the accused, the suspicious and the worthless character of the accusers, the validity of the will which cannot now be reasonably doubted, the maxims of law, every presumption, and presumptions which gain strength and cumulative power with the lapse of time, the knowledge obtained and easily obtainable 14 years ago as to all the circumstances attending the execution of the will, the decision of this court and the decision of the Supreme Judicial court which have stood 14 years, and a family compromise entitled to the highest consideration in a court of equity and still higher in a court of law,—a compromise acquiesced in for more than 13 years and still acquiesced in and ratified by the petitioners themselves at this very moment while they are holding the money which the compromise gave them.

Was I not, your Honor, right at the outset of my argument, when I said that Hazen J. Burton, Jr., his counsellors, aiders and abettors are upon trial here, and that they are the real defendants in this case? Do they not deserve to be despised by all honest men for making such monstrous charges as were contained in the first petition, upon such a flimsy case as they had, and for prosecuting those charges with the malignity which they have shown? Their present counsel saw the error, in a legal point of view, of the old petition and repaired it by presenting a mild petition which, if it had left out the words "force," "fraud" and "collusion" in the 8th allegation and omitted the 9th altogether and left out "fraudulently," "*mala fide*," "false suggestions," and "surreptitious and clandestine conduct" in the 10th, would have been just as strong in a legal point of view and would not have been offensive. But even this petition, as it stands in its present form, is a surrender and would have been a more complete surrender if it had stated his case just as strongly without at the same time being offensive in any part. In a legal point of view the amended petition is stronger than the old, but in a sensational and blackmailing point of view it was weaker, and sensation and blackmail were what they wanted, and the present counsel yielded in a fatal moment, and went back to that old petition for his ammunition, and brought out in his opening argument all that the old petition contained and a great deal more and worse, and has prosecuted the case in a more aggravating and sensational manner, in the newspapers and in court, than even his illustrious predecessor could have done.

Mr. Chandler:—Do you intend that as a left-handed compliment? *Mr. Drury*:—I do,—a compliment if you take it so. I don't think that General Butler would have had the courage to do it, and I will give you the credit, sir, of having more courage than any lawyer whom I ever saw before, to bring such a case as this into a court of justice and face it through as we have seen here.

What escape is there for the petitioners? Why, your Honor, 134 authorities cited by the petitioners! Perfectly appalling! I think, your Honor, before you would read these cases through, would decide in his favor. I think any Judge would. Why didn't he abbreviate and refer your Honor to the first series of the United States Digest, 14 volumes, and the second series of I don't know how many volumes, and the Newgate Calendar at large, and in fact the whole Law Library? That would have made it short. In this list of authorities cited by the counsel and kindly furnished us I find,—" Formalities cannot be waived, confessions, accomplices, Heard's Mass., Criminal Law, *Commonwealth* v. *Billings*, *Commonwealth* v. *Wood*, Roscoe's Criminal Evidence, Ram on Facts, *Commonwealth* v. *Smith*," and a lot of criminal cases, " frauds, forgery, concealment, conspiracy, undue influence," blood, homicide, murder, and a great deal more. Your Honor will read of these as applicable to this case, if you read those authorities through. They remind one of the cry "stop thief" made by a thief when he is running away from justice. But that citation of authorities, if it were ten times as long, cannot save his clients from disgrace.

As I said before, I say now, and I will repeat; I will give the counsel for the petitioners this credit, this compliment, that he is the most hopeful man and the most courageous man I ever saw. He never will be deterred by any case that is offered him. If anybody hereafter wishes a leader to lead a forlorn hope to certain destruction, he will know to whom to go. He has clutched at every hope and found consolation in every trifle. And here I will mention some shifts to which he has resorted to get out of the position which he is forced into.

But I will pass on to that ear-trumpet part of the case, — that is the 9th allegation, — which says that the proof heretofore offered in this court was not sufficient to establish that will as the valid will of Ebenezer Smith. Now three witnesses were asked whether they spoke to Judge Ames through an ear-trumpet. I have heard that the sounding of a shepherd's horn among the Alps would set a vast avalanche in motion, but I never heard an ear-trumpet put in such a romantic position as it has been put in this case,—making a vast estate, amounting now perhaps to a million of dollars, and I don't know how many other estates, depend upon the ear-trumpet of a Judge before whom the case was heard. And they attack, your Honor, justice herself, — not only claim that she is blind, but that she was in this case deaf and needed an ear-trumpet and didn't use one, that 14 years afterwards — and I state it to your Honor to show upon what things they rely, — 14 years after a will has been admitted to probate, they bring forward the infirmities of the Judge who heard the case as a reason why that will which has stood so long should be overthrown.

Another thing which was clutched at very eagerly by the counsel for the petitioners was that the codicil of October 1st was not put into the probate court, but was concealed. But it was proved by the evidence of Mr. Welch who was of counsel for the executors that he knew of the codicil. He and Dr. Thorndike explain the matter plainly, and their impression as to the reason why it was left out is very reasonable and is undoubtedly the true one as we can see. Nobody could have reasonably offered that will of August 1864 for probate, except Mr. Bangs. He could not have done it with the codicil in, because it revoked his appointment. And then a hint was thrown out, I believe it was to Mr. Isaac T. Smith, by the counsel, asking him if he knew that the property could not have been distributed under that codicil; and now whether he is going to claim such an absurd thing as that, I don't know. It is true, your Honor, I have demonstrated it, that Ebenezer Smith by the will and two codicils does dispose of 19-18 of his estate as the counsel said, — 19-18 *plus* $581.25. That is true. But suppose that a man makes a will and gives to 20 men each $\frac{1}{18}$ of his estate, does anybody mean to say that the estate cannot be distributed under that will, because he has given away more property than he had? This will of August 13, 1864, was followed by a codicil dated September 2, 1864, the effect of which was to take out of the way the reversion mentioned in the will and to leave Isaac and Eliza W. and Sarah the same as in the will except as to that reversión. The codicil of October 1st giving Sarah $\frac{1}{3}$ of $\frac{2}{3}$ of the property, instead of what the prior will did, made the disposition stand in this way: — to his wife $\frac{1}{3}$ of his property, to Sarah $\frac{1}{3}$ of $\frac{2}{3}$, then came the legacies, and the balance was divided between Isaac and Eliza W. in the same proportions which they were to receive under the will. Nothing can be clearer, and if your Honor regards that as needing any demonstration I have demonstrated it in this paper which I hand to you.

Then another thing that has been clutched at is the fact that there were two compromises instead of one. What if there were two compromises? There was one compromise, which all the heirs had signed, which related to the Burtons, signed, sealed and delivered, and that was the compromise which Dwight Foster signed, that is the one which he entered into for his clients and which Andrew N. Burton signed, and the other compromise had nothing more to do with it than anything in this world, nothing at all. It was not necessary to get the Burtons to that, the other heirs-at-law were the only necessary parties to the second compromise which related mainly to Eliza W. Smith and her debts to her father.

And another thing has been that cell in the house. Now I will say one thing to the credit of Hazen J. Burton, Sr. He never heard of that cell until he heard it here. Young Ebenezer was the only person that called it a cell. On that slight word,—catch word,—the community has been made to believe that Ebenezer Smith was an old hermit running into a hole to hide himself away from his family, and keeping hid there all the time, when in fact he built in the lower part of his house a safe room, safe from burglars and safe from everything, a very comfortable room about 14 feet square, and nobody ever heard that Ebenezer Smith lived in a cell until the 4th of December last. And that was built to overcome a physical weakness, because he had the complaint which Dr. Thorndike testified to.

Whiskey! The life has been taken out of that charge, "dosed with whiskey." Primogeniture, what a shadowy hope! And guardianship, absurd!

Now if your Honor please, I will take a hasty glance over the case. They have called a great many witnesses, some of them very good men, but some of these men have known nothing of the case, and those who have known anything about it have, as a general thing, testified in our favor. Dr. Storer for instance. I consider Mr. Clapp in our favor, and Mr. Rollins and Margaret Patterson. Every respectable witness whom they have called, I think, has testified in our favor,—even Phippen and Sawyer the experts. A man had a case, I think it was in New Bedford, before some Magistrate there, and brought in his witnesses, and the lawyer who was acting for him saw them; they were a pretty hard looking lot of people, and he said "You cannot get your case with such witnesses as those, it is no use talking." Just then the Mayor of the City came in. "Call him," said the client. "Does he know anything about your case?" said the lawyer. "No," said the client, "but he will throw a kind of air around the rest of those fellows." So it is in this case.

Mr. Chandler: Judge Hoar I suppose. *Mr. Loring:* Yes, he threw an air. *Mr. Drury:* I thought he did throw an air,—a shot into their camp. Now I come to Mrs. Giles. I will consider her very briefly. I am not going to say very much about her. But I could not help laughing, my brother Smith could not help laughing, when counsel stood up here and said that we, on the cross-examination before those Magistrates, had not shaken her one particle; but we both knew that when we had got as far as we had in that examination when she played sick, we had riddled her to pieces. We went down, we searched into the depths of that memory of hers in every way in which we could and we brought out material, although it was disconnected, yet we brought out material which gave abundant proof that Ebenezer Smith—better proof than we got anywhere else—was of sound and disposing mind and memory on the 5th day of October. His talk of his going through life, his troubles, his soliloquies, and his reasoning with his physicians, and his family :—we got that all out of the mind of Mrs. Giles. And we knew that that testimony which she had given adverse to us could be shown to be utterly worthless from the internal evidence of the deposition which we had taken. And afterwards, after she came into court here, we there got very good material in support of our case. We knew it was impossible, she had ruined her credibility by saying, that she could remember accurately this and that, but then there was something which had gone out of sight, there was something about old Ebenezer Smith there which showed that there had once been a great deal there about him. We could see that there was considerable which he had said, although she perhaps didn't state it truly. She has made an utter mistake in four particulars upon which her testimony would be of any value to the petitioners :— *First*, as to the time of the execution; *second*, as to the mental condition of Ebenezer Smith ; *third*, as to the proceedings which took place at the time of the execution ; and *fourth*, as to the proceedings in the Probate Court. She is contradicted by Mr. Sohier. I asked her those questions as to those matters which are contained in that memorandum of what she said 14 years ago. She disputed it completely, although it was taken down at that time out of her own mouth by that upright man, Edward D. Sohier. She is contradicted by Hazen J. Burton, Jr., himself as to what she said at the first interview which they had in 1876, because he says that she told him all those particulars which she says in her deposition that she didn't tell him at that time. He knew the facts, according to his own testimony, two years ago, and yet he delayed to bring this case forward until 1878. Well, now a woman may remember the fact of witnessing a will, but there is a woman who is a nurse, attending people in their dying hours and has probably, since Ebenezer Smith died, seen a hundred death-bed scenes ; and one death-bed scene is so much like another that she gets things confused. It is impossible to remember all such things. There might have been times when Dr· Winslow Lewis was at some other place, or when Dr. Storer and somebody else were at some other place, and she might have got those things confused in that way. She has lived in disease and in a physical Golgotha. I once heard a physician say that he would rather live in a physical than in a moral Golgotha. That is, he would rather be a physician than a lawyer. We certainly have lived in such a thing in the course of this trial, and have seen the bad character of witnesses, and the testimony upon which they have attempted to overturn a will founded upon a solid rock, as that is now, after 14 years have elapsed. She looks back through all that busy scene, through those hundred death-bed scenes, back upon that of Ebenezer Smith, and through that distorting medium through which she looks, and pretends to remember accurately everything that took place on the day on which the will was signed. We know it is perfectly impossible. But she testified to it with the utmost recklessness. And if her memory is no better than her understanding, as my brother Loring has suggested to me, then her memory indeed is very poor : and how could she remember so well, a woman with so little intelligence really, who thought a "codicy" will was one made by a man after he became unconscious? She understood that this was a " codicy" will, and that Isaac T. Smith told her it was made by a man whose wits were gone, and who had no power to make it. Now I say the opinion of such a woman as that, so ignorant, is not good for anything as to the mental condition. He might have been in a perfectly good mental condition in the opinion of a court, even upon her testimony, when her mere opinion would be good for nothing. And then she undertook to remember the actual words, and to repeat from memory the words of an affidavit which she had given in January last ! No human mind could have done it, and she utterly failed. She said that she had said in that affidavit that Isaac T. Smith prayed with his father upon the morning upon which he died. She said no such thing in the affidavit, although she remembered so surely that she did say it, and she was as sure of that as she was of any part of her testimony ! Her testimony is utterly unreliable. She pretends to remember what was not said in the Probate Court 14 years ago.

I spare all comment upon Eliza W. Smith, after my able associate in this case has gone over that ground. There is nothing left of her. The picture is complete. I will not mar it. I admire the skill of the artist. And I will say that for a sister, for a daughter, for a woman, she has shown herself in many respects a monstrosity. It is said that a woman is an angel or a devil. She herself says that she is not an angel like her sister Harriet.

I will say nothing, either, of Hazen J. Burton, Sr., except one thing to which I will call attention. He says that the old man once met him on the street in a doleful and shabby condition and said " I have no home." He was then playing the Rag Picker's part,—the Rag Picker of Paris. To his credit there were two things which he did not say. One was he would not say that he ever heard that Ebenezer Smith lived in a cell. And another thing he never had heard of was, that there was ever any talk of putting him under guardianship. That is to the credit of Hazen J. Burton, Sr.

Now as to Hazen J. Burton, Jr., and his brother : I will class them together. What motive, your Honor, had they for bringing this case? Money by compromise must have been their motive. In 1865 the case in regard to their grandfather's will was settled by a compromise. In 1876 the case in regard to their grandmother's will was settled and compromised by the obtain-

ing of their counsel fees. Every time thus far upon which they have undertaken to break a will they have got money in some way. They have come to
think that "where there is a will there is a way"—to break it or get money
out of it, that any time they undertake to attack the will of their grandfather or
their grandmother, they can get money by it. They depended upon the dread
of family exposure, and the fear of the exposure of their own infamy which
would show these people against whom they were acting what infamous relatives they had. As I said before, I believe it to be a case of blackmail, because
it is founded upon nothing. It has been pursued in the most aggravating manner in the public prints, and made sensational by them. Now the publication
of those affidavits shows it in the first place, and publishing two which were
not filed,—showing that the newspapers could not have got at them except
through them or their counsel. People do not carry their cases into the newspapers, unless they mean blackmail. They were the instigators of that picture
in the *Police Gazette*, probably.

Mr. Chandler: There is no evidence of that here. I think, your Honor,
there ought to be a limit to this. There is no evidence of any such thing of
that kind. *Mr. Drury:* Now he talks about the wrong done him at the making of his grandfather's will. When he says it he knows it is false. He knows
when he says it that there was a will right behind it which nobody doubts that
his grandfather made. And the idea of his standing here and cherishing a hate
against these people, when he knows there is a will right behind it of August
13th, and saying that a great wrong was done him, and that he was talking
with his grandmother of the wrong done him about his grandfather's will!
Nobody did any wrong to him about his grandfather's will. Look at that list of
wills which is contained in that statement showing that "wonderful unanimity"
of which Hazen J. Burton, Sr., speaks. And I say he is a sneak to say here
that he thinks he was wronged by anybody but by his own father and his own
grandfather. The idea that these people, Mrs. Ebenezer Smith and his uncle
and aunt, had anything to do with his having only that $500, is perfectly absurd,
they had nothing to do with it. He got up here and undertook to say something in regard to Isaac T. Smith which was contradicted by Judge Hoar immediately afterwards; also something in regard to what Arthur G. Smith of
New York said, after Arthur had testified, and then to show how false he was
said that he had taken it down on a memorandum afterwards. He has shown
himself a liar upon the stand here. And here furthermore, sir, he said that
when he got his counsel fees paid in the case concerning his grandmother's will,
he told Mr. Ranney and Mr. Dillaway not to settle it in such a way but what it
could be brought up again. Now I say, that in getting that money in that way,
he has confessed himself dishonest. That is as bad as a thief, for a man to get
money in that way under a false pretence of settling a case, and then not settling
it, intending at that time to go on with the knowledge which he had and bring
that case of his grandmother up again. Then, too, if your Honor please, to
show his disposition, he went to Judge Hoar and wanted this charge of murder
investigated, which had been brought against Mrs. Thorndike, wanted it invest-

igated before anything was done in regard to that case concerning his grandmother's will. If your Honor please, what had the murder of his grandmother to do with her will, with the validity of her will, which had been made three years before? Why did he go there to Judge Hoar with that story? It had no bearing upon the question. And I don't wonder that Judge Hoar, a man who has been a Judge of the Supreme Court and learned how to abhor the idea of such a crime, became excited and indignant. If there ever was a man the sight of whom would bring feeling to the very toes of a man's boots, and make them wish to fly at him, that man is Hazen J. Burton, Jr. And I don't wonder that Judge Hoar boiled with indignation when he brought that accusation. Why, here is an old lady worth a hundred thousand dollars; she has made a will giving a large share of her property to her favorite daughter. If that old lady dies, that daughter will have money. Now that old lady dies an apparently natural death in the arms of that daughter at the age of eighty-eight years. That, to the mind of Hazen J. Burton, Jr., is conclusive proof that that daughter murdered that mother! God pity a man who has so much murder in his heart that he can conceive murder so easily. They have been trying to injure their uncle. Now what has the position of Isaac T. Smith in New York to do with the settlement of this case? Why should they have any desire to injure him in New York? It does not affect this case. Why should they have a desire to injure their uncle Isaac T. Smith. Why shouldn't they let him alone? Injure him through this case, and why? Not to have their case settled except by a compromise. It is blackmail and they are blackmailers. He has shown himself a suborner of perjury, or rather an attempted suborner of perjury, this Hazen J. Burton, Jr., has and I could tell more about this case, about the way in which he has conducted this case, but I will not at the present time.

Mr. Chandler:—Are you referring to me, Mr. Drury? *Mr. Drury:*—No. But like the assassin they have the satisfaction, probably, of having succeeded in creating a great deal of trouble and distress, and we know that it must have been great distress and great agony to Isaac T. Smith, and to Mrs. Thorndike before she died, to see such horrible things said of them as were said, because this case was prosecuted in such an infamous manner. Why, if they had stabbed Isaac T. Smith to the heart, they could not have done him an injury which he would more keenly have felt,—in his own feelings, an injury to his own feelings and distress to his own mind—to see his name brought in question because of this case.

Now I believe that is all I wish to say of their witnesses. I believe I have touched upon all their witnesses; and I ask your Honor to compare in one scale the witnesses upon whom they intend to rely for their case, and then put into another scale our witnesses upon whom we rely for the support of our case, and determine between them.

I shall not say anything of the characters of my clients and their witnesses, or of any of the defendants, because that matter has already been ably and sufficiently touched upon by the counsel who has preceded me.

Before I close, your Honor, I would like to say this. When I started out in this case I was alone and without the aid of Mr. Isaac T. Smith's able counsel, whose sympathy and support will be among my most pleasant recollections in connection with this case, and who has shared with me in the feeling that this attack upon our clients has been also an attack upon us, upon you and upon humanity itself. I started out with hardly any facts, with only perhaps three facts which I was then knowing to, but the farther I have proceeded, and the more research I have made, the more firmly I have become convinced of the truth of our cause. The scattered fragments of this case have fitted together perfectly. It has been like a sheet of parchment which had been torn into a hundred parts and scattered to the four winds of heaven, and then those pieces gathered 14 years afterwards and brought together again. It has been a great deal of labor to do this. I started out here with simply the memory of Dr. Thorndike as to that conversation between Andrix A. Foster and Ebenezer Smith, and as to what occurred at the execution of the codicil of October 1, and as to the contents of that codicil, which annulled the idea that Mrs. Thorndike had anything to do with the getting of a will by such means as were alleged. Those were the facts which I started out on. I proceeded to investigate that signature. I found out that you could not tell from its appearance who wrote it or how it was made. That is the way I started in this case, and I have had to beg men, as I did Mr. Sohier, as I was reluctant to do, almost to bore him to make a hunt through his papers to see if there was not something bearing upon this case. And your Honor can imagine my rejoicing when I found among those old papers of Edward D. Sohier the perfect corroboration of what Dr. Thorndike had said ; and also the perfect contradiction of Mrs. Giles. I also found papers preserved by the executrix of Paul Willard which corroborated what Dr. Thorndike had told me about the execution of the codicil of October 1st,—he told me the particulars about that in almost the exact words of the statement of James Wight, which I afterwards found. So the further research we have made the more we have found. These parts of the case fit together, and have established our case beyond any reasonable doubt. And I will close now, your Honor, thanking you for the attention which you have given me, by saying that I hope that this case may receive such a judgment and in such terms as it deserves.

www.ingramcontent.com/pod-product-compliance
Lightning Source LLC
Chambersburg PA
CBHW032001010726

47493CB00007B/2277